PROTECTING
THE
AMERICAN DREAM

A novel by
—Michael Sammaritano

PROTECTING
THE
AMERICAN DREAM

—*Michael Sammaritano*

Adesso Publishing Inc

3010 SW 14th Place, Suite 10
Boynton Beach, FL 33426-9032 U.S.A.

admin@adessopublishing.com

Library of Congress Control Number: 2010911689

ISBN 0-9779023-6-6   US $16.95

Printed in the UNITED STATES OF AMERICA

MS-120810-- 10 9 8 7 6 000-K5

I am proud of my ancestors for they spoke
the truth, thus creating their own destiny.

—*Michael Sammaritano*

Book One

Book One

1

The ride from Scarsdale into Manhattan was a breeze, even the parking was easy. Of course, it was Sunday morning. Eager for news, Ray took the short walk to Grand Central Station. At the newsstand, the headline read:

CAN MAFIA SURVIVE?

WITH NO APPARENT HEIRS, THE AGING AND ONCE POWERFUL MAFIA CONFRONTS A DOUBTFUL FUTURE.

In the elevator on the way up to his office, Ray thought about the headline. Sensing the stare of the other passenger, he folded the paper, glanced at the man, and said to himself:

Who is he? . . . I've seen those little quivers around the lips ready to smile. . . . I think . . . Is it him? . . . Can it be? The hell with him!

The elevator hummed to a bouncing stop. Ray pursed his lips and stepped onto the forty-second floor. The doors slid shut behind him. He headed for his office with a stop at the break room.

Balancing the paper folded under his arm, a bagel in one hand, and a steaming cup of coffee in the other, he pushed the door to his office open with his shoulder.

Glancing at an almost vacant space, he felt the door's edge behind him with his foot and kicked it shut.

Making his way past empty boxes and a few metal wastebaskets, he reached his desk and sat down. A few drops of coffee splashed on the blotter as he peeled off the lid to his coffee. He smeared them dry and thought:

What the hell . . . we're moving out!

Routinely, as he had done every working day for more than thirty years, he licked his thumb and reached for the daily calendar. Today, he ripped two pages instead of one. It was Sunday, November, 2 1997. He leaned back in his chair, gulped down some coffee, and opened the paper:

> New York—In the windows of the Sicilian Social Club, two faded yellow ribbons dangle as a reminder of a godfather gone for good. The dull fabric recalls a time when . . .

Appalled, he dropped the paper to his lap. He thought:

They don't get it. The more they write about Mafia on its deathbed the further they move away from the truth. They're blind. . . . They're not getting it!

The longer he read the article the more it brought to mind long past memories.

Every August 31 in Alcamo, as elsewhere in Sicily, the day marked the end of property leases as well as a time to settle uneven scores. No one is exempted.

Those seeking a new lease on life had to start with a clean slate and Don Saverio Cremona's blessings.

On this day some forty years ago, the phonograph split the stillness of the night; it played the latest American hits. On the dance floor, young couples swung their bodies to the beat of rock 'n' roll.

"In our days, you were not even allowed to talk to a girl, much less dance," the elders mourned. Then lifting their noses up, much as goats do to watch ahead, they said, "It's pitiful . . . rude . . . what has the world come to . . . and where are we going?"

To slow the pace, the guy manning the phonograph played Frankie Laine's "Jezebel." At the sound of two gunshots, the record screeched to a stop.

The party, the villa, the entire marina went quiet; the only motions were people swapping glances. From the crowded patio, you could hear the waves breaking on shore. It was a moment of terror lingering in slow motion ready to burst.

Carlo Cremona had shot his pregnant girlfriend first and then his brother, Stefano.

Carlo strolled across the patio to confront his mates, each step echoing on the terrazzo floor. "Tonight," he said with a smirk on his face, "I've settled the score with my brother."

Studying their faces, he noted their approval. To further his alibi, he walked to the guests at the other side of the patio. When Carlo drew near, mostly out of fear, they smiled. Satisfied, he nodded to the man near the phonograph, and the music began to play again.

Ray saw all of this from his usual position: sitting on the patio's ledge listening to the music. He enjoyed watching the sea, the breeze whipping his face, more than partying.

Tonight it was hard to see where the sea ended and the sky started. The never-ending lamps from the fishing boats merged with a parade of stars into a cosmic show. Alcamo Marina is nature's stage for people to party until dawn. Tonight was the season's last gasp.

Ray Greco was twenty years old and determined to avenge his father. His suspicions had driven him to join Don Saverio's family. Painful as it was, he had put his writing career on hold while he hunted for those responsible for his father's slaying.

Now as he sat at the party's edge and listened to music, Ray heard a girl howling. The mournful sound came from near the garden shack, the direction from which the two gunshots had echoed earlier in the evening.

A few days before his father was killed, young Ray was roaming about the house. He peeked into his mother's studio. In front of a sunlit window, there was the monster. On many nights, he heard the monster's voice—those rapid tic-tic-tics. He approached the monster daringly.

Tall enough so that he was about eye level with the monster, he saw an arena of black seats with white letters engraved. He stepped closer and touched the one to the far left. Nothing happened.

When he pressed harder, a hammerhead sped to the center gate smashing through the ribbon, leaving the letter A behind. Little Ray was mystified. It was fun. Then he pressed the Z, and the C, and the V, and the M, and the M again, and then the Q.

When he pressed the Tab, havoc struck. The carriage rushed to the left, striking a bell that reverberated through his entire body leaving him in shock. He stepped back in fear. He waited. When he thought it was safe, he moved closer again.

The ring got his mother's attention. Coming to his aid, his mother reached from behind him and slid the paper up a notch. Then, she took his little forefinger and helped him pound eight more letters:

R a y G r e c o

"What's that, Mama, what's that?"

"It's your name."

He giggled, then looked up at his mother and said, "My name, Mommy . . . my name?"

That was the beginning of Ray's enchantment with writing. His mother taught him how to read and type. Although he was bored in school, the teen-age Ray was a whiz kid. He became an avid reader and then a writer who published essays that attracted attention.

Twelve years later, one Sunday after Mass, Father Francesco and Ray were talking in front of the church. A tall man with a cane steered by a young girl joined them. On that sunny day the girl's radiant smile and her yellow polka-dot dress fit the encounter.

"Don Saverio," Father Francesco nodded to the man, "I want you to meet Ray Greco."

"Pleased to meet you, Ray."

Don Saverio shook Ray's hand while glancing at the girl by his side. She smiled. "Papa, Ray writes those essays you like so much in the *Gazette*."

"I enjoy your writing indeed, young man. Come visit me sometime. I would like to share some thoughts with you."

"How's Tuesday?" Ray promptly asked.

Staring at Ray for a moment, he said, "That's fine." He then leaned on his cane and turned away with a smile.

When Don Saverio looked at you, his smile either sent chills down your spine or uplifted your spirit. He loved to limp around; leaning on his cane, claiming it helped him carry his six-foot frame. The truth was that in his hands the cane was a deadly weapon.

Later, Silvana Cremona would tell Ray that on that day the thought of Ray coming to the house excited her; they might get to talk alone. Regardless, she knew this was the start of something good and so did Ray—this was his chance to get closer to Don Saverio.

Oblivious to what he had set in motion, Father Francesco's nose twitched. He glanced from Don Saverio to Ray and smiled.

Despite painful memories, Ray took pleasure in revisiting his native land, even if only in thought. After all, Sicily was where he grew up and where his mother and friends still lived.

As Ray's thoughts returned to the present and the newspaper in front of him, someone knocked on his office door. It was Silvana.

"Silvana, what are you doing here?" Ray said, rising in surprise.

"Who did you expect?" she laughed.

"Oh, stop! I thought you were in London."

"We landed two hours ago."

Ray came around the desk to greet her, wrapping her in his arms, and thought that his wife was more vibrant than ever. "I didn't expect you till Tuesday," he said.

Rubbing his back, she said, "I called home, and then here."

"I heard the phone but didn't answer."

"I thought I'd surprise you . . . and here I am!"

"You're not playing detective, are you?"

"Of course not, we've been married too long for that," she smiled. "I might get a little jealous now and then, that's all."

"Smile all you want, see if I care."

Ray wasn't worried, and, in an odd kind of way, he loved her possessiveness. The lovemaking that followed those jealousy-inspired encounters always gave him the feeling of discovering sex for the first time.

"What're you reading?"

Pointing to the headline, he said, "Same old stories, Mafia on its deathbed."

"Yeah right," she said.

"So how did we do in London?"

Silvana's face shone with a pleased expression. "The showing was a smash. The runway lineups attracted the world's best buyers. You should've been there. How did you do?"

Ray was proud of his wife. "Be patient a bit longer, Silvana, you owe it to yourself. We'll get there. Your resolve has made Giglio into one of the leading fashion designers in the world."

Tightening her hug, she said, "You big bull, if it wasn't for you, I'd still be in Sicily daydreaming. . . ." She dabbed the corner of her eye with her finger. "Ray, please answer my question."

Puzzled, he asked, "What question?"

"How did you do while I was away?"

"Oh, that," he grinned. "Look around. Besides the break room, I had the movers move everything else last week. From now on, we can walk to work."

Ray had moved Giglio's headquarters to White Plains, closer to their home in Scarsdale.

"So what are you doing here? Why don't you have this stuff moved also and go through it at home?" his wife asked.

"I don't want it home," he said. "Except for some books, I am trashing most of it."

"Ray, don't rush; it's early yet." Silvana hid a slight yawn. "Besides, from now on I'll have plenty of time for you and the family." Tired from the trip, she kicked off her high heels and eased onto the sofa.

As she fell asleep, he turned back to the newspaper. While the media reports on the "deathbed" of the Mafia, he thought, it fails to notice how a New Mafia has grown more zealous than the old one.

Watch those CEOs and congressmen, those world leaders and warlords, in action.

Ray's office included two conference rooms, a living room, and a bedroom with a shower. The living room had a large window facing east.

Until a new building had blocked the view, on a clear day, he could see Long Island Sound stretching all the way to his summer home in Montauk Point. To the left, if he stretched his neck a little, he could almost see his Scarsdale's home or so he thought.

Ray admired Silvana sleeping on the sofa. She was sixty-four and fascinating. The trip to London, the grind of the show, and the overnight flight had taken their toll.

Spreading a blanket over her, he caught a glimpse of himself in the mirror above the sofa. He looked back at his wife. They both had developed a few age lines around their eyes, lines that took nothing away but lent character to their faces. Her hair was black and shiny, his almost gray. Her skin tone was dark, his pale for lack of sunlight.

Back at his desk he swiveled the chair around. On the credenza behind him, he found more reminders of aging. The frame to the left held a picture of Silvana and himself in their twenties. To the right, there was a photo of Grandpa. The one in the middle was a large portrait of his parents, taken a month before his father was killed.

In the corner of the office stood the old Olivetti; the carriage held a yellowed sheet of paper with two faded lines. The typewriter served as a reminder for Ray to get his life back on track.

Breaking away from the past and looking across the desk at his napping wife, Ray realized he was a happy man. She was his business partner. She was also the mother of his three children.

Glancing at her sensual body, suddenly he got the urge to pack. He wanted to make it home before Sunday dinner with the kids.

With an empty box on the desk and a wastebasket by his side, he began tossing mementos. The tinkle of a master key attached to a silver dollar striking the metal trashcan brought to mind the kid from Brooklyn.

"That's him! . . . The man in the elevator," Ray cried out, startling Silvana out of sleep.

Son of a bitch—that's him, all grown up now, do you imagine? Maybe he didn't recognize me either. I swear I will . . .

Looking at Silvana barely awake, blinking at him sleepily, he said softly, "I'm sorry. I didn't mean to wake you. I'm through packing. I want to get home before the kids do."

"Me, too," she stretched with a passionate smile.

He pushed the wastebasket aside, approached the sofa, reached out for her. Smiling, he said, "Why wait?"

After a passionate lovemaking session, they headed home, very much satisfied.

2

Alcamo Marina lies on Sicily's northern shore on the Tyrrhenian Sea a few miles north of Alcamo and east of Castellammare Del Golfo.

It stretches from the sea halfway up a six-hundred-foot hill. Its four miles of coastline are crowded with bungalows and villas. Nothing in the chaotic landscape takes away from the beauty of the sandy white beach. It only adds color to the scene.

If you swim a short distance out and then look back, you will see over the hill, in the background, a square rustic tower on top of a mountain—Torre Saracena. This is Alcamo's most prominent landmark; it sits atop of the 2,600-foot Monte Bonifato.

Every year, from school closing to mid-September, Alcamo Marina becomes a nonstop playground for the young and a vacation bonanza for their mothers—it is a tradition.

It is also a tradition during that time, except weekends and nights, for the husbands and the fathers to stay back in town and work to support their families' time of leisure.

Going to school beyond the fifth grade was not the norm in Sicily until the fifties. It was not for lack of schools but for lack of purpose.

Celebrities such as Frank Sinatra, Elvis Presley, Errol Flynn, Humphrey Bogart, Fred Astaire, and many others helped turn things around.

Except for Ray and a few other well-to-do youths who were set in their ways, young Sicilians were dreaming of becoming singers, dancers, movie stars, even tough guys, or at least regular guys able to raise and support a family under one roof. Dreams that could easily come true in America, they thought, and so they yearned for that missing something. Responding to that mind-set, the school board promoted education as the *in* thing.

With diplomas in hand, Sicilians sought visas to enter the United States permanently. Those unable to get visas migrated to other countries to later enter the United States as residents of that country.

To give these young men a head start, the school board set up vocational schools in many cities, in addition to conventional schools. In these vocational schools, students learned a trade, as well as how to compete for better jobs in America or other foreign markets.

The program had three objectives: Give the students a greater global acceptance, pave the road for those who followed, and cut down unemployment at home.

Unbeknown to the promoters, it took Don Saverio more than a decade to persuade the board to plan and implement the vocational program.

Because of his ties with business tycoons and heads of state, nationally and internationally, Don Saverio stood in the background aggressively reforming Mafia to its original ideology—that is, men of honor who spoke the truth so they could, in turn, protect the dream the young longed for. He conquered that feat by waging war on mob families wherever they were.

In his fifty years, Don Saverio never made headlines. According to the locals, he never traveled beyond Sicily.

Ray was one of the young Sicilian men heading for the United States. Sad to be parting from his native land and leaving his writing career, Ray was at home getting ready for his move to New York City.

From his room, he could hear the sizzling of a frying pan. When the smell of fresh tomato sauce became mouth-watering, he followed it to its source.

There was a frying pan and two steaming pots and his mother standing in front the stove like an orchestra leader holding a wooden spoon in one hand and a fork in the other.

The larger pot, full of rapidly boiling water, was waiting for the spaghetti to plunge end first. The sauce was ready to complement the perfect gourmet dinner. Ray approached his mother from behind, wrapped his arms around her, and hugged her. He whispered in her ear, "I'll miss you, Ma."

Flipping a cutlet, the mother said, "Sure . . . sure!"

"For real, I'll miss you!"

Worried, his mother asked, "Good talk, son, and who's going to do your laundry? Tell me . . . who?"

"I'll send it back here or do it myself," he teased. Then he grabbed a loaf of bread, snapped the toe, soaked it in the sauce, and popped it into his mouth. "Better yet, I'll marry the cleaning lady."

His mother looked at him and screwed up her face.

"For God's sake, Ma, stop worrying." He licked his lips clean from corner to corner. "I'll be all right! You'll see. . . . Besides, you'll be there before you know it."

According to Francesca Greco, no one could care for Ray like his mother. She even barred the house cleaner from doing his laundry.

Ray was an educated young man with strong beliefs and a winning smile. He didn't need to go to faraway lands to fulfill his dream because his dream was home. For his father's sake, however, he decided to tactically endure all that life would dish out, including Don Saverio's Cause. Despite his imposing built, over six feet with wrists as big as other men's arms, Ray only used his smile and good sense to make a point or to fit the moment.

What fascinated people most about Ray was his narrow streak of white hair. Those who knew him claimed the streak was a sign of rare intellect, the root of his genius.

Others, especially old women, placed the blame squarely on the father for failing to satisfy his wife's desires when she was pregnant.

Ray's mother was convinced it was a sign that the gods had selected her son for a purpose not yet known. Nevertheless, she nurtured feelings that concerned her greatly.

Since the loss of her husband, Ray was Francesca's only family. As most children do, he did not think of his mother as a young woman. Nor did he think of her as beautiful. He assumed that her slender body, light brown hair, and blue eyes were ordinary. To his credit, he conceded that her suffering had worn down her smile.

Francesca had been a teacher from northern Italy. The traditional Greco family had never accepted her marriage to Luciano, which occurred while he was serving in the military away from home.

The Grecos had had no chance to approve her as family. They'd not been able to attend the wedding or view the bloodstained bed sheets the morning after, to prove her virginity.

"Who the hell is she?" they whispered among themselves. "She's a whore."

For her son's sake, Francesca adopted most Sicilian customs but all in vain. She never lost her northern dialect nor did the Grecos appreciate her efforts. This strained relationship had also built a barrier between Ray and Grandpa Greco.

On this day, she pulled her son away from the stove and closer to her, then staring in his eyes, said sternly, "If your father were alive, you'd be going nowhere, young man."

Ray stood at attention like a soldier facing his drill sergeant. After mustering enough courage, he relaxed, placed his right hand over his heart, and said, "Ma! . . . I swear, I'll send for you as soon as I settle down and my papers are in order."

To further soothe his mother, Ray added, "Besides, Don Saverio is behind me rock solid."

At the mention of Don Saverio, Francesca bit her lower lip, nodded twice, looked down, and murmured, "Sure."

He knew then that his mother had locked herself into secrecy.

Ray held her in his arms warmly. Finally, his mother looked up teary-eyed and whispered, "Trust no one . . . not even your mother!"

"I trust him . . . I have to . . ."

Tears rolled down her cheeks, cutting his sentence short and forever changing his life.

From that moment, Ray knew his father's death had more implications than he had first thought. Especially when his mother said: trust no one, not even your mother.

Unwillingly, in an odd kind of way, Francesca confirmed everything her son had suspected since his teen years.

Suddenly, Ray's conviction to avenge his father became an obsession. Driving blindly into the future was no longer an option for him. Don Saverio's family became Ray's port of entry into a world of intrigues and deceptions he couldn't ever fathom.

This was Ray Greco's last dinner at home.

3

In his late twenties, Luciano Greco was a handsome and energetic man of average frame with black shining eyes, a full head of hair, and small ears. He was a road contractor with associates and friends in the right places. Aware of his son's traits, he wanted to reinforce his character with firsthand experiences.

One day, father and son hopped in the car and the father asked, "Where would you rather go to the beach or to visit jobs?"

Little Ray gazed into the side-view mirror and said nothing.

It was not until he glimpsed the beach twenty minutes into the ride that he looked up at his father. His shining eyes said it all. He was disappointed; he would have rather visited Uncle Sal.

Luciano pulled off the road and nosed the car toward a roadside bench. He parked, shut the engine off, and stretched out a hand to straighten his son's short trousers and suspenders.

With the sun at about noon, they got out, walked to the bench, and sat facing the sea.

Little Ray made a pass at a fly buzzing to his right. It droned away. There was silence until a tingling on his lap drew his attention. There was the fly again, brushing its head over and over seemingly on borrowed time. He looked at the fly for a while as if it were an airplane refueling. Then, sensing his father's stare, he waved it away once more.

He watched Luciano kick a lump of weeds from under his feet. "Son," he said, "in life, you've got to make up your mind."

His father looked to his left and to his right and then kicked another lump. "When the choice is yours to make . . . you must choose. If you don't, someone else will choose for you. Like today, chances are you'll wind up where you don't want to be."

Luciano kicked one more lump, "Don't forget, son, never let others decide for you. Right or wrong, you must make your own decisions."

Luciano rose to his feet and walked behind the bench.

Little Ray looked down swinging his dangling feet. Then stretching the shadow of his legs longer and shorter he thought about what his father had said.

Looking at the sea, he rubbed his streak of white hair twice. He had made a decision. Jumping to his feet and holding hands with his father, they walked to the beach to watch the waves lapping on the shore.

Ray got his feet wet. "Look, Papa, from here I can see the other side of the sea."

"No, son. . . . The other side of the sea is a long way out," his father said, pointing outward.

"Then what is it . . . what is it?"

"That's the horizon."

"What's horizon, Papa?"

"The horizon is where the sky seems to touch the earth. Here it's about thirteen miles out. That's the furthest point a man can see from here on a clear day," his smiling father said.

Ray squinted at his father, "Oh, I see, I see now . . . the way you showed me once with the big balloon, remember?"

"That's right!"

"Because the world is round," Ray said, forming a circle over his head with his arms, "the only way you can see further is getting up higher as birds do. Right, Papa?"

"That's right, Ray. I'm proud of you for remembering that."

Little Ray was rubbing his streak of white hair once more. Often, his parents questioned whether this action was a habit or a natural reaction to stimulate his memory. Regardless, they thought he was developing a good attitude about doing things others would not, or could not do.

Later that week, little Ray went jobs hopping with his father. On both sides of the road, there were endless mounds of stones. A liquid heat wave enveloped the mounds and the pieceworkers atop them. They seemed like vultures on a kill tearing at remains others had left behind.

The two-inch gravel for roadbeds was hand-crushed by the roadside. Each pieceworker, with a double-headed hammer in hand and a straw pillow to sit on, relentlessly cracked stones from sunup to sundown.

The hammering, at first faint, sounded like thousands crickets out of sync, and grew louder as they drew near. Luciano and Ray stopped at the first mound.

Facing away, the worker stopped hammering but did not rise or look back. Little Ray climbed the mound quietly, sprang onto the worker's back, and blindfolded him with his hands.

"Peek-a-boo . . . guess who?"

"I don't know, who?"

"Ray, Uncle Sal. It's me . . . Ray!"

He giggled his way onto Uncle Sal's laps.

"Oh no," Sal said. "It's you again!"

Sal Rocca was the lead man for the pieceworkers. Sal was not Ray's uncle per se, but he acted like one. At twenty-nine, he was a year older than Luciano.

Little Ray's trick panned out every time. He always found another wooden soldier in Sal's shirt pocket. Thus far, he had collected a forty-piece squad complete with a captain on horseback and five vanguards aiming on one knee ready to shoot. The set was the envy of his friends.

Little Ray always cherished these moments with his father and Sal. He loved them dearly.

4

In 1951, as part of the educational program, the Sicilian School Board opened a vocational school in Alcamo. The first year's enrollment fell just short of one hundred students. By 1956, it was a wonder that out of a bunch of young men who hated school, most of them graduated.

What kept them focused was their common dream to break into the world in style, a trait Don Saverio considered the core of his plan.

For his master plan, Don Saverio handpicked two students from the vocational school and eight from the high school. He groomed each of them personally for the roles they were to play. His son Carlo and Ray Greco were special additions to the group.

As the students' skills developed, Don Saverio breathed easier. He was confident that, at the right time, he could pass the torch to his next in line, risk-free, for these students would support his heir unconditionally—they were the Class of '56.

There was no doubt that Don Saverio Cremona was the head of Mafia. There was also no doubt that he averted the end of Mafia. And, there was also no doubt that no one was privy to his ultimate plan.

This was the Class of '56's last summer in Alcamo. Because they had a common cause, its members developed an unbreakable bond.

Led by Ray Greco, the Class of '56 worked on counseling corrupted Mafia families willing to reform. Don Saverio's plan was to dismantle unwilling families by planting destructive moles in their midst. He called these moles Street Warriors.

The Street Warriors, by design, had no links with the Class of '56, but they were Don Saverio's power base and his most trusted men. Every day they put their lives on the line for the Cause.

5

The party had dwindled into the wee hours of the morning. Two police officers were looking into the shootings of Gloria and Stefano, but everyone they interviewed claimed to know nothing. No one heard or saw a thing.

Rumor had it that Stefano, shamed for having an affair with Carlo's girlfriend, Gloria, had shot her and then himself.

Ray was sitting on the patio's ledge, as usual, when he saw the police officers approach Carlo and group of men on the far side of the patio. Carlo was waiting to start a meeting with the Class of '56.

The elder officer drew closer and said, "I'm sorry about your brother, Carlo. The evidence is still there. If you care to see it before we move the bodies. . . . Your brother is still holding the shotgun. . . . It's only up the hill."

Looking the other way, Carlo said, "No, I don't think I can bear the sight. At daybreak, I'll drive home. I'd rather tell my parents myself."

The officer looked at his partner who nodded in consent, "We'll keep it quiet until noon. Please, give your father our condolences."

Angelo Sutera and Victor Como were the first to arrive for the meeting of the Class of '56. They walked casually toward Ray. To his dismay, neither said a word. They stood by quietly. As the others arrived, they also sat along the ledge in silence.

Perched like roosters waiting for the first rays of daybreak, they waited.

Identifying with their ordeal, Ray wondered:

Are these people still in shock or unmoved by it all? If the shooting tonight was the test Don Saverio always talked about, they all passed with flying colors. No one blinked.

To break the silence, smiling Ray looked at Victor and asked, "How was Gina?"

"It's none of your business!" Victor lashed out at the men staring at him. "What are you laughing at?"

"Victor, how was Gina?" Ray asked again, "and this time don't give me any hogwash . . . we're all ears."

Victor bent over to shake the beach sand out of his curly hair. He conceded, "She was nervous at first, but then wild and crazy like all the others. Why even ask? . . . I'm sure you all heard her loud and clear."

"How could she do that?" Angelo asked, surprised. "I thought for sure the gunshots would scare the living daylights out of her."

"She was shaken up at first, but when I got there, she came down running. You heard the rest." Victor grinned.

At nineteen, Victor Como barely stood five-six. When he talked, his thin lips parted just enough to let the words slip out. He feared nothing, and while most men feared him, the girls loved him. He blamed his sex appeal.

To play it safe, he didn't wait for girls to seek him out; he chased the ones he liked and the ones who played hard to get.

Nothing escaped Victor's detective mind. He held on to his convictions until he reconciled the facts. He understood Don Saverio the man and his ultimate Cause. When compelled to act, he acted swiftly and unconditionally.

Smiling, Angelo shook his head, "Victor, I thought you knew Ray by now. I'll bet he heard nothing. He's like Don Saverio. Once on your case, he'll leave you no place to hide." Angelo Sutera, also nineteen, had the same physique as Victor. His eyes sparkled with fervor. He was the peace maker of the group.

"Look, Angelo, you're not that shabby yourself," Ray said grinning. "For you to know, I heard Gina from start to end."

Another classmate asked, "Ray, how did you know it was Victor? . . . We know how she sounded, but how did he sound?"

Ray said, "No. I never heard him. He was the only one missing."

The classmate said, "I'm surprised you guessed it. It can be dangerous."

With daybreak approaching, Carlo, four to five years older than the rest, herded the classmates to the center of the patio and said, "Okay, listen up. In the future, our mission will prevent us from gathering together in one place. We've known each other most of our lives.

"Thanks to my father's teachings, we're better than brothers. Our bond will always go beyond Christmas dinners, birthday celebrations, and any future family ties we might develop."

The twelve men formed a circle.

"This bond," Carlo added, "will stand forever above any other obligation we undertake.

"Although we'll part, we must remain loyal to one another always, for we're one. When one hurts, we all hurt."

Bonded as spokes at the hub of a wheel, they held hands as a falling star streaked across the Sicilian sky decreeing its approval.

6

In Alcamo, the rules were clear. If you killed yourself, no wake was allowed nor would the church offer a funeral service. The coroner would take the body directly to the mortuary. If the family so chose, a brief ceremony was allowed at the burial site.

The Cremona family laid Stefano for viewing on a makeshift bed in their large guest room. They propped him up and dressed him in a dark gray suit, white shirt, and tie. A new pair of black shoes with mirror-like soles faced all comers squarely. To disguise the damaged skull, his head was halfway sunk in a thick pillow. The face was repaired with skin-colored wax giving him a peaceful look sufficient to comfort his grief-stricken mother.

Donna Maria, touching her lips with the tips of her bony fingers, looked on and leaned toward Silvana and whispered, "Your father doesn't believe your brother killed himself. He promised me he will get to the bottom of it . . . he promised."

"He will, Mama. . . . Believe me, he will."

Two massive candelabras stood at the foot of the bed as guardians of the dead. Each spewing black smoke branding the white ceiling as sins brand the soul.

About the room, there were eight freestanding wreaths, each with a golden ribbon and the donor's name.

There were many other bouquets at the base of the candelabras, around the bed, and outdoors.

The smell of burning candle wax mixing with the fragrance of the flowers choked the air with that unique smell of funerals that lingers in one's mind for a long time.

Stefano's immediate family and friends sat teary-eyed around the bed. They were dressed in black from head to toe.

Donna Maria, Silvana, and Don Saverio's two sisters sat to the left. Don Saverio's sisters-in-law sat directly behind them.

Except for Silvana, these women seemed experienced at weeping to a beat. They moaned in harmony and often cried aloud as if riling the onlookers.

Squeezing her mother's hand, Silvana looked for familiar faces nodding in appreciation. Eyeing her mother's agonizing face, she thought:

How can I tell her Gloria was pregnant with Stefano's baby when Carlo was due to marry her in December? Carlo did what any man of honor would've done. The family could not endure such a shame.

To the right side of the bed, there were two rows of chairs reserved for latecomers and acquaintances who only wished to make a brief appearance.

Any other seat, except Don Saverio's chair and the chairs designated for his two brothers at the head of the bed, was fair game for those wishing to prolong their visit.

Don Saverio spent most of the morning in his studio with his brothers, Gaspare and Carmelo, accepting condolences from friends. His plain mahogany desk stood foursquare and sturdy on the two-toned marble floor. It plainly said: If you've nothing to do, don't do it here.

The morning paper rested on its polished surface. The lead article read:

STEFANO CREMONA DIES OF BRAIN TUMOR

> Don Saverio Cremona's elder son died last night despite emergency brain surgery . . .

Father Francesco not only spun the media, but arranged a first class funeral in church. To Father Francesco, the Cremonas were not common people. Their donations always topped those of any other churchgoer.

Don Saverio heard Carlo running up the stairs. He entered his father's studio breathless, "The hearse is . . . here!"

Uncle Carmelo stared at him, "What's the hurry, Carlo? Stefano's dead. You can't hurry dead people."

Carlo stared back at his five-foot-four, husky, squared-faced uncle and said nothing.

Sensing hostility, Don Saverio drew his brother's attention to an unframed photograph. It showed Stefano holding four-month-old Silvana in her bath. Carmelo passed the photo to Gaspare, who handed it back to Don Saverio. He slipped it back in the drawer. Gaspare was taller than his two brothers. He had a deceptive smile that led you to believe he was confused.

Don Saverio asked, "Are Ray and Victor here?"

"Yes," Carlo said hurriedly. "So are the others. The room is packed with people."

With a disturbing smile, Don Saverio followed his brothers and his son out of the study. They descended the marble stairs under the gaze of a room full of people.

Carmelo and Gaspare headed for their seats. Holding on to Carlo's arm with one hand and to the cane with the other, Don Saverio led him to an empty chair next to Ray.

Like an appraiser, Don Saverio circled his son's body once and sat between his two brothers. Ray looked at Don Saverio and thought:

The king of the jungle has circled the kill.

Don Saverio sat quietly presiding over his dead son. Leaning on the cane with both hands and staring at his feet, he looked up occasionally to greet people with a nod and a washed-out smile. Ray wondered:

Is he using Stefano to show how far he goes to defend his honor?

Maybe he's sending a message to the old Mafia with his brothers as witnesses to proclaim the game's over.

The morticians began to move the body into a shiny mahogany casket. Recalling his mother's words to trust no one, Ray looked around for unfamiliar faces. Feeling secure, he thought once more:

A man of his caliber, in the business he's in, has to put that kind of stuff behind him quickly. He couldn't have blessed Carlo unless he had written Stefano off first.

Why had he turned on Stefano? . . . Maybe he did not?

As for the showing of his son, cruel as it seems, it is politics at its best—making the most out of a crisis.

When the body had been transferred into the casket, Ray rose quietly and left for the restroom.

Still staring at his son in the half-open casket, Don Saverio gave two long nods, rose to his feet, looked around once, and then announced, "Before they close the casket, I must ask you to leave the room. I would like to be alone with my son one last time. . . . Thanks."

Carlo was the last to leave.

The father approached the half-open casket, placed one hand on the lid's edge, looked down at his son, and roared, "Bastard!" He spat on Stefano's face, slammed the casket shut, and wailed, "Go to hell!"

Unaware of Don Saverio's request for privacy, Ray had returned to the room. Having witnessed the outburst, he stood out of sight until Don Saverio restrained his emotions.

Aware of each other's presence, both men left the room in silence.

They knew that only in the throes of such an ordeal is one forgiven for breaking the most sacred rule men of honor live by—what's in your heart should never reach your lips.

7

In the early evening, three days after Stefano's wake, Don Saverio and his two brothers sat around the dining room table. They met on the first Wednesday of every month, a tradition started after their father's death.

A traitor had shot the old man during a scuffle. Before he died, the old man found enough strength to push a knife through his attacker's throat, tear it out, and watch him bleed to death.

With Don Saverio at the helm and Carmelo and Gaspare as counselors, the brothers vowed to defend the Cremona family.

Carmelo was sixty-five and Gaspare sixty. In their own ways, they were men of honor with common sense and good business skills. Neither was motivated to lead the family, nor could they offer the kind of leadership the job demanded.

Although Don Saverio was the youngest, Gaspare and Carmelo always respected him. Their talks were candid and held in secrecy. No matter how intense, all feuds were over at the end of the meeting.

Leaving behind a box of cigars, a bottle of Sambuca, and a pot of espresso coffee, the wives cleared the table and retreated to do dishes. In contrast to the men, these women had a lot of gossiping to do.

Gaspare filled three demitasses to the rim and pushed one to each brother, "How come those two kids were alone?"

"You mean Stefano and Gloria?" Carmelo asked.

"Who the hell do you think I'm talking about, Romeo and Juliet, for God's sake?" said an annoyed Gaspare.

Then turning to his brother, Gaspare asked. "Saverio, wasn't she a Campo?"

"She was," he said, shaking his head looking at his brothers. "As for being alone, that's the way most people fool around—alone. Wouldn't you agree, Gaspare?"

"I guess so. . . . What pisses me off is Carmelo with his stupid questions."

"You know, Stefano used to unload his thoughts on me," Carmelo said, looking at his brothers. "Maybe he didn't care much about traditions, but he sure wasn't that kind of a fellow. He loved Carlo. If what did him in was a rumor, that's a bad rap."

"I agree," said Gaspare, troubled. "That's a shame."

Don Saverio fiddled his cane but remained silent.

"How in hell did it happen?" Carmelo puzzled. "Not even a hint?"

"Look guys. . . . I'm the one who lost a son. Let me remind you that I'm the head of this family. I'll take your advice when I ask for it . . . I'll advise you when I think I need to."

Don Saverio never eased off on his brothers for pulling him out of college. Back then, they claimed that it was for the best, for the stability of the family, if they carried on as counselors. Don Saverio knew better. Neither brother wanted to give up his business. Don

Saverio had taken the job with a solemn promise to reform Mafia and to pursue his dream.

Before college, Don Saverio accepted the way Mafia did business. In college, though, freed of constraints, he realized how far off course Mafia had strayed.

Families were feuding over territories, instead of working for the same cause their ancestors had worked for—for centuries.

The ideology of Mafia was no longer the credo of men of honor. He also realized that corrupted Mafia was unacceptable to educated men and dangerous to freedom.

Those years of college changed him from a would-be mobster into a man of honor with deep convictions about his heritage and the rights of man.

Locked in a prison of his own making, he promised to reform Mafia. On the surface he conducted business as usual and at times more aggressively than his father had.

In the background, he planned a cause he considered higher than himself and his family—reform Mafia to his ancestors' ideology and spread that ideology worldwide by recruiting and training principled men of honor to wipe out corruption in government and big business wherever it flourished.

Don Saverio stared at his brothers and said, "To get off Stefano's ordeal, let me say that he wanted nothing to do with family business nor did he honor our traditions.

"That's unacceptable, especially when the rumor of him cheating on his brother was growing louder."

"Who started the rumor anyway?" Gaspare asked.

"What difference does it make?" Carmelo said. "Even if you whack the person who started it, the rumor lives on. It grows faster and louder."

Irritated, Don Saverio said, "I could've accepted him having nothing to do with family affairs, but to fight it? On the other hand, I've had to hold Carlo back. Sadly, he doesn't have what it takes."

"You see, Saverio?" worried Gaspare. "That's what concerns me. Carlo is too ambitious. Don't you agree, Carmelo? He might have given you some cockamamie story. Started the rumor and you bought it. Tell me I'm wrong."

"Forget Carlo for now. I'll deal with that later," Don Saverio said, discounting the issue with a wave of his hand. "Unfortunately, in our business you have to dismiss those rumors before they start. Once they get legs, there's no telling.

"If you let a rumor grow, it could choke you to death. When the end is near and the ride to that end is harder than the end itself, why suffer?"

Gaspare and Carmelo nodded supporting the proposition.

"I know," Gaspare said. "Rumors are no good anywhere, but I think either Carlo or you got duped and will never admit it."

"Now, stop! Don't even go there. I believed Carlo," Don Saverio said, angrily. "Stefano and Gloria did meet alone all summer long. To that extent, the rumor was correct. I agree Carlo acted too quickly. But, for the sake of the Cause and the family, I can't go out there and put up a banner explaining the whole deal. As I said, if Stefano was cheating, Carlo is right."

"That was your bungalow, right?" Carmelo asked.

"It is. When Stefano graduated, he wanted a place of his own. He spent most of his time there."

"Water under the bridge, Carmelo," Gaspare said, grabbing a cigar. "What's the use of talking? The man made up his mind and that's that." He turned to Don Saverio, "But Saverio, in the future, let us in beforehand on this kind of stuff. We want do more than just talk."

Don Saverio fixed himself another coffee and dismissed his brothers with another wave of the hand.

"What about Carlo? . . . Is Gaspare right?" Carmelo asked.

"At times, doubt can be harsher than rumor," Don Saverio said, putting down the demitasse on the table. "Something tells me to watch him. Until I'm comfortable with him, he stays right here with me. For now, we must be careful not to start another rumor."

"You better keep an eye on him." Gaspare was suspicious.

"I wish my two boys were like Silvana."

"By the way how is she?" asked Carmelo.

"I'm meeting with her on Friday and with Carlo tomorrow. She thinks I don't know, but she wants to talk business. On Saturday I'm meeting Ray Greco."

"There goes your week," grinned Carmelo.

"Well, that's my job. Teach them, set them in the right direction, and hope for the best."

"Are you talking about Silvana and Ray or all of them?" Carmelo asked.

"There he goes again!" Gaspare shook his head. "Carmelo, who the hell do you think Saverio is talking about, you and me?"

Don Saverio stared down his two bickering brothers and said, "Calm down. I'm talking about the Class of '56. The time has come for them to learn what the real deal is. There can be no illusions about their role."

"Is there any news on the credit card deal?" Carmelo rubbed his fingers together, much as greedy people do when thinking of money. "The more I think about it, the more I like it."

"With that we must be patient," Don Saverio said. "It's going to take lots of work. For now, it's right on target. The promoters know what they have.

"Believe me; they're on it worse than leeches. Give it fifteen years tops, and like the airplane, they'll make this one fly, also. Trust me; it'll fly even higher. It'll spread worldwide like wildfire."

Gaspare puffed smoke to the tip of his burning cigar, blowing ashes everywhere. "Jesus . . . fifteen years?"

"What's wrong with that?" Carmelo asked. "Are you going anywhere soon? . . . and watch those ashes."

"You mean to tell me that people won't have to use real money to buy things?" Gaspare said in surprise. "You must be kidding me. In my book, money talks."

Don Saverio glanced at his brothers. "I don't have to prove a thing. Fifteen years suits me just fine."

"That's right," contented Carmelo said. "What's the matter with you, Gaspare? Most people are emotional and impatient, the same as you.

"When they find something, they want it now. With money in their pockets to spend, if you show them what they want, they'll buy it on impulse.

"Without cash, the impulse fades quickly. That's bad for the economy. . . . Isn't that true, Saverio?"

Don Saverio nodded. "That's the idea. Likely customers always have the right emotions to make big business work.

"Since ancient times, merchants have sought ways to tap that market, through one form of credit or another. The twentieth century has all the right ingredients. Finance companies are developing that idea as we speak, and we want part of the action.

"They've been experimenting with it for some time. Six years ago, Diners Club and American Express launched the first charge card in America. They called it plastic money.

"The following year, Diners Club issued a few hundred credit cards for use in selected restaurants. . . . Wake up, Gaspare. In less than five years, the credit card is already a success."

To celebrate good things to come, Carmelo reached for a cigar, and Don Saverio poured the last of the espresso.

"What about Ray Greco?" Carmelo asked. "Does he know about his father and his roads diversion deals or for that matter, about Sal's crush on his mother?"

"I don't know. The rumors are out there," Don Saverio said, making a pass at his mustache with his forefinger. "But I can't distort his thoughts about his father or I'll lose him. For that matter, no stranger can. Most people are in denial regarding their parents' moral values.

"His mother, being a northerner, should know better about our moral principles. Her family didn't live a lavish lifestyle on road contracts alone. She should be truthful with her son, not as much as to her private life, but about his father's fate at least. Before I turn him loose, I'll try to read him as to what he knows and where he stands.

"What worries me, though, is him dropping his writing career. He was very passionate about it, and he could have fulfilled his dream right here.

"Let me also say, he's the brightest and the most capable when it comes to handling business—either our deals or any other. He's a born leader.

"But to offset the downfalls . . . I think Silvana likes him a lot."

"Saverio," Carmelo was taken aback, "you're taking a big chance on both fronts."

"Not in the long run. . . . For the good of the Cause, at times you have to take some chances. People risk their lives every day for smaller causes. For now, I'll keep an eye on him."

Carmelo drained his demitasse, pulled out his pocket watch, and scheduled the next dinner for Gaspare's home.

8

To keep up with the latest political and economic events, Don Saverio spent most of his time in his library, reading. This did not upset Donna Maria. If anyone had a reason to complain about his reading, it was the mailman. He had to lug the extra mail, newspapers, magazines, and books arriving from other parts of the world halfway up Monte Bonifato. It was a large load for anyone to bear every day.

Don Saverio's second floor study was mission control. The large conference room next door was his battlefield. One look at his library attested that he was well read. The library was stacked with biographies of the world's most prominent political leaders. There were also books and essays on history, human events, and geographical and economic growth. Don Saverio and his library were an inspiration to Ray Greco.

The rustic credenza and the red maple bookcases were in harmony with the decor of the cypress-paneled studio. The chairs were handsome, and all, except for Don Saverio's, were stiff and did not invite loitering. Behind the mahogany desk stood a grandfather clock and a three-foot-high wooden stand, which held a huge globe.

Every other day Don Saverio had to move the clock and the globe back to their original places. The house cleaner never set them back after she dusted.

While he thought it was a vengeful act, he took the slight with a smile, to keep peace with Donna Maria.

To the right of the door there was a coat hanger. Directly below, his black and silver cane and an umbrella stood next to each other, stiff and ready.

Holding the drapes to one side, Don Saverio stood at the north window looking over the city. Amid the chaotic display of thousands of red-tiled roofs, he most admired the prominent churches with their centuries-old steeples, the old castle, and the middle and high schools.

From here, he could also see Alcamo Marina and Castellammare Del Golfo. It intrigued him to think how the city and its surroundings had survived centuries of conflicts, including the World War II bombings.

It was through this landscape that Don Saverio let his mind wander through the hills and the valleys of the past as he imagined the future.

As the clock struck ten, Silvana came in with a pillow under her arm. She placed it on a chair across from her father's desk. The father waved his little girl to his side. She walked briskly and clasped his hand gently. "How are you, Papa?"

Don Saverio hugged his daughter and kissed her forehead. When his daughter showed up with a pillow, he knew she needed special attention.

Although she was still grieving her brother, Silvana was full of life. At twenty-three, she was the youngest of his children. Her radiant face spoke of her willingness to endure life. Her black and shining eyes missed no trick.

Locked in a man's world with her every move dependent on her father's approval, she was restless. In the past, the closer she tried to get to her father, the more it set them apart.

From an early age, Silvana had been instructed in housekeeping, cooking, and needlepoint—the skills Donna Maria considered vital for building a dowry that would attract a husband. That was traditional in Sicily. Yet, so many teen-age hours spent in her aunt's embroidery shop also had inspired an independency in Silvana.

"Papa, it's been five years since I graduated from high school."

"And with honors, I must say," Don Saverio said. Walking to their seats, father and daughter exchanged smiles and sat down.

"Those are moments parents don't forget."

"Papa . . . I . . . I want to go to college."

Don Saverio glanced out the window and back at his daughter, "College is out of town. You know how people talk around here when a single girl leaves home. You've a reputation to protect."

Leaping to her feet, Silvana pleaded, "Papa, these are the fifties. . . . I always thought you were open-minded enough to trust me."

"Silvana . . . sit down . . . listen," her father said patiently. "It's not a matter of trust. It's a matter of tradition. I know you don't want to hear that, but, with us, it's a way of life. Our traditions may take several generations to catch up with the rest of the world. For now, that's what we live by."

"But this is my generation," she said. "I simply refuse to stand by idle watching my dreams die. . . . It's unfair. . . . Tradition or not, I won't do it."

Don Saverio never doubted that his daughter knew what she wanted or why. Being the visionary he was, he knew that unless he treated his daughter as an adult with rights of her own, he would lose her. Therefore, he was careful, for in a peculiar way, she was destined to play a great role in his Cause.

He sat back, drumming his finger-tips on the desk, and nodded. Silvana, who had returned to her seat, shifted restlessly as she watched her father.

Don Saverio paused then spoke, "Silvana, we all have the need to fulfill our dreams regardless of how big or small they are. They are the driving force behind human achievements."

For the first time in their relationship, the father was biding time with what he thought was small talk and so he ventured on.

"To fulfill our dreams doesn't mean we have to destroy what we already have. At times, unless we're in the right environment, we're better off leaving dreams as dreams. They often help us cope with the realities of the present."

Fascinated, his daughter kicked her shoes off, folded her legs under her, and listened.

"If dreams, however, are justifiable," Don Saverio paused and allowed a small smile to twitch his lips, "we not only have to fulfill them but protect them as well."

"What do you mean . . . justifiable?"

"I don't know . . . it's the way it came out. I guess when you talk from the heart things come out that way, without warning. . . . Let me ask you, do you have a justifiable dream?"

"Do I have a justifiable dream? Are you kidding me?" Silvana said in surprise. With a glint in her eyes, she shook her ponytail loose, stood up, and walked across the room. Then leaning against the window sill facing her father, she detailed her plan.

"For the past four years, I've been noticing a bizarre trend in town that gave me an idea."

"And that is?" the father asked.

"Papa, take Uncle Gaspare's wine business, for example. He used to sell wine in large containers marked with gross, tare, and net weight with no names or labels.

"Now, he pours wine into dark glass bottles with fancy labels. He packs twelve to a box with the buyer's name on it.

"Almost every other farm in the region is doing the same thing. The buyer makes money by shuffling papers and shipping them worldwide.

"Take Uncle Carmelo's macaroni shop. He only makes a few packages with his label for the locals. Again, the rest are packaged for outsiders."

"Obviously," Don Saverio said, "it's good for the economy. The locals make more money."

"I don't mind people selling their products to outsiders for more money," she said. "I agree. It's good for the local economy.

"What I mind are outsiders making windfall profits by draining our resources. We're getting a fraction of what we could be making if we got more involved," his daughter said with firm conviction.

Don Saverio nodded and smiled contentedly.

Silvana continued her sales pitch, "There are at least a dozen other similar cases, and the number is growing across the region.

"Anyway, what concerns me most is Aunt Laura's embroidery business. She's placing American labels on my creations, and the buyers are selling them worldwide.

"Papa, Aunt Laura says I should be proud, but I think it stinks. For starters, no one will ever know my name."

His daughter's perspective on the worldwide market intrigued Don Saverio. He listened keenly.

"Papa, day in and day out since I was seven, I've been chasing threaded needles through all sorts of fabrics. All for the sake of building a dowry for when Prince Charming shows up.

"Well, I've grown out of that dream. If my creations are good enough for others, then I'd be a fool to let them suck my blood. No. . . . I won't allow it!" she said angrily.

"I understand, calm down," the father said. "What's your plan?"

"Papa, I want to go to college and earn my master's in business administration," Silvana eagerly replied. "I'll work day and night if I have to."

For the next two hours, Don Saverio listened without dampening his daughter's enthusiasm. What amazed him was how independent her thoughts were. Her plan did not consider his wealth, nor did she express any desire for marriage, although she had spent most of her life getting ready for it.

She was focusing on a viable goal. She was a creator, a doer, and a leader who knew how to get things done. Unbeknownst to her, deep inside, she longed for the American Dream.

After a final thought, the father said, "I like it! . . . I like it a lot. . . . Let's do it!"

"Do you mean it?"

"Yes! I'll back you up," he said decisively. "Before we put any wheels in motion, though, we must lay out a plan that protects you and your dream. Then we'll start at once."

"How?" Silvana asked, concerned. "College comes first."

"You don't have to go to college," her father said with confidence. "You'll do fine. Here's the plan. We'll set up the business in America. I have someone in mind to get it started. He'll hire the brains to run it and the best ad agencies in the world to market and promote your lines worldwide. Plus, we'll use our connections.

"For now, let your imagination run free and keep on thinking beautiful things. Besides embroidering, look into jewelry, dresses, men's suits, and leather products. Anything fashionable people buy and wear."

Don Saverio could tell that his daughter was not sure yet about putting her college ambitions on hold. With her father's backing, Silvana could live in New York City or anywhere else. Also, she could enter college without breaking traditions. In time, the world will be her stage.

Quivering, her lips burst into a smile. "Papa, what will my job be?"

Smiling, Don Saverio rose, came around the desk, and looked at his daughter squarely. "Fashion designer, young lady . . . fashion designer."

Silvana burst from her chair and hugged her father. "I like that! . . . I like it a lot . . . especially the young lady part."

She turned to leave, her spirits high with a brighter outlook and a sure shot at her dream. As she reached the door, Don Saverio said, "Don't forget your pillow, young lady. . . . By the way, how are things with Ray?"

Silvana paused at the door, her hand on the doorknob. "Same old story . . . I think he likes me."

"Is it because you're older?"

"No. It's tradition again. For now, I believe he wants lots of children, and I want a career. At times, I think he's acting strange." Silvana paused and frowned. "Papa, have you talked with Carlo lately? He seems depressed."

"We met yesterday. I've had better meetings with strangers."

Father and daughter exchanged a look then Silvana nodded and left, shutting the door quietly behind her.

9

In Alcamo, a two o'clock dinner is a tradition. After each dinner, Don Saverio would reset his biological clock with a nap followed by a shower. This pattern allowed him to squeeze two working days into one.

Refreshed, he was ready for the afternoon session. On this afternoon he had a meeting with Ray Greco.

At five o'clock, Ray pulled up outside the Cremona home and then rushed into the house and up the stairs.

Since Ray Greco had joined Don Saverio's family, anyone who knew or talked about his father's fate was a suspect. Mafia, however, has an inescapable rule.

To avenge someone with honor, the killing had to be unjustifiable. If the killing was justifiable, then the man who carried out or ordered the killing is not only excused but respected.

Based on that rule, Ray had his work cut out. First, he had to find the hit man and then the man who ordered the hit and the motive for the killing.

Ray was suspicious of Don Saverio. Schooled by him three years longer than the Class of '56, he had grown to care for Don Saverio's Cause, although, he often wished it wasn't so. But, every time he thought of this, a curtain of shame obscured his thoughts. For the thought was not a wish but a dilemma.

Cordially, Don Saverio said, "Come in, Ray . . . Have a seat."

"Good afternoon, Don Saverio," Ray said, smiling.

Leaning back on his pivot chair Don Saverio stared at Ray for a moment, then twitched his eyebrow once and said, "Ray, I asked you here to go over a few points before next week's general meeting."

Nodding with a subtle smile, Ray said, "Don Saverio, my thoughts are yours."

Don Saverio was hesitant to talk about an off-limit subject but he had to, so he ventured on, "Let me ask you, Ray, what do you think of Mafia?"

Ray readjusted his chair, cleared his throat once, and said plainly, "I don't think Mafia is going about it the right way. The tactics the so-called Mafia employs these days are not in keeping with our heritage.

"These people should learn from the past and apply those experiences to the future. In a democratic society, people will give in more readily to what they perceive as right than from threats of broken legs.

"Even if *right* will cost their financial freedom and impose new kinds of oppression."

Ray's deliberate response did not surprise Don Saverio. What most people did not know about Ray was that he had a hidden talent for observation and reporting.

And that talent had been honed by Don Saverio's teaching: First, in the art of rational reasoning by analyzing the facts followed by the logic of events. Second, in the art of intuition by controlling speech and emotion so one can conclude. Third in the art of decision making with due respect to consequences.

When asked about his talent, Ray would promptly credit his father and grandfather's genes.

Don Saverio made a pass at his mustache with his forefinger and asked, "Do you think I'm a Mafia man?"

"Who am I to say?" Ray answered with a smile. "I believe you're a man dedicated to a righteous cause. In my opinion, if you succeed, generations to come will succeed as well.

"I look at you as the leader of a new enterprise. A leader who needs all the help he can get from the powers of your past and the strength of our future while keeping them apart. A feat only you can carry out."

It was that kind of reasoning Don Saverio sought in his successor. Aware of Ray's suspicions, however, he was also in a dilemma: replace Ray or bend the rule for the good of the Cause. Don Saverio bent the rule.

The two men sat in silence. Ray leaned forward a bit staring at the floor in thought with an occasional nod. Don Saverio, also in thought, watched white clouds in the blue fast drifting by the window. Both were biding time for what seemed an eternity.

Finally, Don Saverio smoothed his mustache, then staring at Ray, said casually, "I hear you're looking into your father's accident."

Sounding indifferent, Ray said, "Not really."

"What does your mother say?"

Ray looked away as if to shield his mother. Then he said, "She's hesitant. I don't think she's sure it was an accident. For her sake, I thought I could bring it to a closure."

"If you feel you must get to the bottom of it, go ahead," supportive Don Saverio said. "In the process, try not to mess up your life. For what it's worth, back then some people looked into it. Besides rumors of wrongdoing, they concluded it was a freak accident in the making."

"Please don't mistake her doubts for mine," Ray said in earnest. "She also doubts my career change. You know how mothers are."

Ray had committed himself to trust Don Saverio, work for his Cause, and put his writing career on hold. Ray's true commitment, however, was to investigate and avenge his father's killing at any cost. As a starter, Ray thought:

If the killing was an accident, why did the hunter fade away soon after?

Don Saverio looked at Ray as if in doubt and said, "My own father was killed when I was twenty-two. I know how it feels. Trust me, at times life can dish out ugly deals. Often, we have no choice but to learn how to accept them, or they can wreck our dreams and, ultimately, our lives.

"My deal was cut and dry," he recalled. "Quit college, come home, and run the family. Yes, life can dish out many deals if you know what I mean."

"I know exactly what you mean," Ray said. "If you can accept the deal, that's fine; and if you can't?"

"Then you're screwed!"

"And if it's family?"

"Especially when it's family. If you don't accept it and stay iffy, you could waste it all for everybody."

Ray knew they were really discussing Carlo now. The two men were playing Ping-Pong using Carlo as the bouncing ball. Watching the game keenly, he could see Don Saverio smashing Carlo out of the game entirely.

"I don't blame you to act the way you do," Ray said. "You worked hard for this new deal. Or shall I call it New Enterprise?"

"For now, you may, but not to change the subject, let me ask, do you think the others know about our mission?"

"Except for Victor and Angelo, I don't think so," Ray said doubtfully. "I'm sure they're not thinking of going abroad to convert a bunch of dysfunctional Mafia families—make them attend Mass on Sunday mornings, kiss and make up for the rest of the week."

"No, I don't think so either," Don Saverio said, smiling. "You know . . . I get good vibes from Victor. The way I'm reading him, he's very committed to the Cause and confident in my teachings. He's a surprising fellow; he asks lots of good questions; I like him a lot."

"Don Saverio, you know them better than I do," Ray said. "They're a bunch of smart fellows. They are well educated and eager to start a new life abroad."

"That they are," Don Saverio agreed. "But, they have quite a ways to go in their education."

"I think they have figured that much already," Ray said. "They might dream of fancy lifestyles, but they're aware that they have been prepped for something much more rewarding than being gangsters.

"They are not thugs. In their own right, each is a highly principled man with a dream of his own."

Curious, Don Saverio asked, "How did you figure that out?"

"To me it's obvious. Although the thrust of your mission is to reform Mafia and dismantle opposing families, I'm sure you have other people in mind for that kind of work."

"You're somewhat right. . . . As a starter, besides dismantling families, we have to stop corruption in government. You think the others have figured it out?"

"I don't know."

"Although the others might have put the pieces together," Don Saverio lowered his voice, "I think we should keep it to ourselves for a while longer, wouldn't you say, Ray?

"Mind you, this is a big deal. By early 2000, give or take a few years, we'll be running most political clubs and big businesses in America and, if we want, in every other corner of the world—all legal."

Ray listened keenly. Don Saverio continued. "After we set up our people, we'll branch out. We'll allow other ethnic groups to enroll.

"The power this New Enterprise will exert over the masses and the money it will generate for politicians and business leaders alike will influence the best of the best to join our Cause. That's how big this New Enterprise will be."

Not knowing if—influence the best of the best—meant buy and corrupt, deep inside, Ray was fascinated by the plan. Although he knew that Don Saverio was nurturing something different for him than buying and corrupting the world, he didn't know what.

Puzzled, Ray asked, "I understand your sentiment about Mafia families' blind eye to self-destruction. . . . But how and when did all this come about? . . . I mean, what caused you to act?"

The light posts along the driveway were glowing. In the western sky, the setting sun was turning thin layers of clouds red. Looking up at the blue, Don

Saverio said, "Red evening sky brings good weather ahead."

Ray smiled and nodded.

Standing by the window now, Don Saverio was also admiring nature's contrasting colors: earth, sky, the autumn leaves.

On the eve of a new era, Don Saverio waved Ray to his side. Resting his hand on Ray's shoulder, pointing at the fallen autumn leaves in awe, he said, "Watercolors, son, that's all it takes: a good base and a few colors."

"Not everyone sees it that way."

"Precisely. What's important is that you do. That's all that matters."

Don Saverio led Ray to the wet bar to celebrate their unity of thought. He mixed a Cinzano, Ray an Orzata without liquor. With drinks in hand, they toasted and returned to their chairs.

Committed to confiding in Ray, Don Saverio went on, "About eleven years ago, right in that conference room, we had a grueling three-day meeting on reform with ten of the toughest Mafia families, eight from the United States and two from Canada. It was their blindness that made up my mind. Their cowardice solidified my convictions."

As if foreseeing the future, Don Saverio paused and then continued, "I knew then that that kind of Mafia couldn't sustain itself without an aggressive reform. Within a couple of years from that meeting, three of those families wiped themselves out.

"A month ago, aware of their predicament, one of the Canadian families came back to join our mission. They asked me to approve and groom one of their protégés. They claimed he had grown with all the makings of a world stage ambassador. Their only concern—he is not Italian. I said, if he is the right man, that's better.

"Ray, I'll evaluate him next month after your people leave. If he doesn't fit the bill, we'll find someone else."

Wanting to hear more, Ray looked on.

"Ray, I am not privy to comment further. You take care of our mission in the United States—that is, lead our people through graduation and into getting jobs at Capitol Hill. The Canadian deal is part two of our mission. On their own, both missions will culminate into one. Trust me, someday you'll see.

"As to their protégé, frankly, I was looking for someone to fit that job, maybe this is that someone."

Ray smiled and tactically said, "I understand . . . I trust you."

Don Saverio pulled out a yellow newspaper clipping from his desk drawer. There were three men sitting and smiling. A closer look revealed that the man to the right sported a large, black, bushy mustache and a sinister smile. The man in the middle, with puffy cheeks and drooping lips, held a large cigar. He stared into the camera through a pair of solid black conservative eyes. They were hard to read.

The man to the left was wrapped in what seemed a military blanket. He sported a half-moon smile accented by a cigarette holder pointing up as if to say: Don't worry. Daddy is here.

The clipping was dated February 11, 1945. The headline: "Yalta Conference." The caption identified the trio as Joseph Stalin, Sir Winston Churchill, and Franklin D. Roosevelt. The caption referred to their feats and defeats and their effects on the world and the ending of all future wars.

Waving the clipping, Don Saverio said, "This photo changed my outlook . . . Back then, I saw the past, the future, and where I stood.

"As Mafia, communism changed from a revolution for the people to a suppressor of the people and, therefore, was doomed to die. Presently, any communist regime raised to power is doomed to die. The people it suppresses, riled by outsiders showing freer lifestyles, ultimately will revolt. In a democracy, liberal and conservative alike will survive as long as everybody is happy and they all have a clear shot at their dreams.

"I could hear Roosevelt saying: Have I got a deal for you. . . . He offered two deals—the old deal and the new deal. As the old one failed and the new one wasn't doing well, people paid their dues with a smile and followed him blindly."

Concurring Ray said, "As long as the masses get the so-called free services and big business can skim the fat from the top, politicians will be elected and reelected under the same democratic flag to keep the action going."

"Exactly," said Don Saverio, smiling. "That's a predictable equation. For as long as the masses seek protection and have the money to pay for it, big business will help elect sophisticated thugs. With the majority of them controlled as puppets on strings.

"For God's sakes," an excited Don Saverio added, "look at the record. Most of the so-called democrats in America are nothing more than reformed socialists and communists, or whatever other political school they come from.

"They will stay on until they milk the masses dry. At that point, if they want to keep going, they will have to figure out a way to replenish the masses with gullible investors and fresh taxpayers.

"What better way than a global regime recruiting third world countries. And there are plenty of them on standby outside the borders of the United States.

"But in fairness to the American people, it truly doesn't work that way. When their basic way of life is attacked, they will revolt and expel any suppressive regime more readily than our ancestors did. That's why that lunacy has to be stopped. And we have to help as much as we can."

As Don Saverio discussed his plan, Ray thought of his own mission—investigating his father' death. There weren't many people he could trust. He also accepted that these people, including Don Saverio, often offered viable information. Hence, he mixed another Orzata, stroked his streak of white hair twice, and listened.

"Don Saverio," Ray said, "my take is that when we convert that equation into business terms, one can say that for now the most valuable market to infiltrate is the United States."

"For now, yes," Don Saverio said. "Thanks to the Americans' inexhaustible resources, their democratic system will have the run of things for a while longer.

"Any governing system man devises will run aground when it has squeezed every dollar from the masses. At which time," Don Saverio said with a smile, "our New Enterprise will take hold and survive under any form of government the masses choose, for we'll be that government."

"In other words, your vision is to run a political Mafia?"

"No, it's to run a fair and lawful regime supported by New Mafia," Don Saverio said. "After all, for the last four hundred years, Mafia has been a political force that most governments, in one way or another, have contended with.

"To flourish in America and elsewhere, Mafia needs to reform and change its identity and what better disguise than a new government." Don Saverio shrugged.

"Let me tell you, Ray. Give the American people carefree times; relief from personal responsibility; public services such as medical care, welfare, and childcare; and toys such as automobiles, low-cost housing, and modern gadgets.

"And don't forget prepared foods and disposable wares—and they'll elect and reelect anyone who promises all that good stuff. Even if that good stuff slowly kills them through financial stress or debilitating diseases."

With confidence, Don Saverio added, "Believe me, Ray. It's later than you think. The race is well underway. What's comforting is that the real attack is at least thirty to forty years away, plenty of time for us to settle in and stop that lunacy, which is to radically transform a free nation into a land of suppressed."

Wanting to hear more, Ray leaned toward Don Saverio, encouraging him to go on.

Pointing at the bookcase, Don Saverio said, "Look what Roosevelt and his gang started with these New Deals. Thanks to their progressive ideas, many are still making millions if not billions and counting.

"Down the road, under the disguise of serving humanity, corrupted politicians and big business will concoct many other similar deals."

"In your own words," Ray grinned, "life can dish out some hell of deals."

Don Saverio stroked his mustache and said, "Talking about deals, yesterday Silvana proposed a deal I think we can turn into a super-deal."

Dumbfounded, Ray asked, "Did you say Silvana?"

Smiling to himself at Ray's surprise, Don Saverio explained Silvana's ideas about fashion design and her desire for a career. He also explained his ideas on how to get things moving by hiring contractors, subcontractors, distributors, shippers, and retailers and how to market and advertise new lines through worldwide contacts.

Resolute, Don Saverio said, "Look, Ray, these are new times, and we can't let tradition stand in our way as the world's moving forward.

"Silvana's an aggressive woman on a mission of her own. No tradition will hold her back. With or without our help, she'll move ahead, at least until she gets it out of her system. And I don't want to lose my daughter, nor does Donna Maria."

"I didn't know she felt that way," said a still surprised Ray. "For all I knew, she was the typical girl who longed to get married some day and raise a family. You know I'm very fond of her. She never said a word about this to me."

"I know, Ray. . . . Now listen carefully. For obvious reasons I decided not to have the family name linked with any new deals.

"As my liaison, you'll be at the helm of all new deals. Carlo will handle old business, and, with your help, Silvana will start the fashion business.

"As I told you, we don't want to lose my daughter. Promise you'll see to it."

Concerned, Ray said, "I'll do my best."

"No, 'I'll do my best', does not do," Don Saverio spoke plainly. "You have to do better."

"I didn't mean to be evasive, Don Saverio," Ray said. "I promise on my fathers' grave."

Smiling, Don Saverio said, "That's better."

On second thought, Ray asked, "But if you want your name out of it, what about Silvana? . . . She's a Cremona."

"Don't worry," Don Saverio said. "The whole deal can take as long as seven years to get off the ground, and as much as ten before it's fully implemented.

"By then, the boys will have settled down and learned how to run things and you'll be back here. For now, let's worry about the work at hand."

Ray was not concerned about Don Saverio's plans for new deals. He would let Don Saverio worry about that. More often than not, Don Saverio mulled ideas over for some time before landing the right person for the job, as was the case of the Canadians' protégé.

What concerned Ray was not the New Enterprise, nor for a brief moment his father, but Silvana Cremona becoming Silvana Greco.

10

September 21, 1956; 5:00 p.m.

After five years of extra curriculum in Don Saverio's school of honor, it was the day of the much-discussed meeting. In anticipation, most classmates were speculating about their assignments.

The setting resembled The Last Supper except the Master, Don Saverio, faced his disciples. Across and to his right were Angelo Sutera and four others. To his left were Victor Como and four others. Facing each other at the ends of the table were Carlo and Ray.

The vaulted ceiling, trimmed with a Florentine border, matched the delicate gold, green, and blue shades of the walls. By design, there were no windows. Three crystal chandeliers hanging over the long table illuminated the large conference room. A Persian rug covered the marble floor.

To create a friendly atmosphere, there was a bottle of red wine, a basket of fresh fruit, and a pitcher of water and glasses positioned under each chandelier.

Don Saverio's most trusted men stood guard indoors and out. They kept the door closed; in fact, the entire second floor was off limits to outsiders. These men were proficient at what they did. Secret meetings were regular occurrences at the villa.

Don Saverio sat down, hooked his cane on the edge of the table, glanced at each student once, and promptly started, "Gentlemen, I'll get right to the point. Our mission is to infiltrate the United States' political system and big business from within. A feat I estimate will take the better part of the next ten years . . . just to get it up and running.

"When I say from within, I mean from the grass roots of the American political system, starting in the colleges and universities where Americans first form and nurture their political clubs."

They all looked in dismay but listened.

"In these clubs, you will mingle with the rich and powerful and the upcoming candidates for political stardom. From there, you will enter the political arena and corporations, paving the road for those who will follow in your footsteps. That includes people from other ethnic groups and American generations to come.

"The number of groups making up our people will be large enough to fill both houses of Congress to the brim. This move will reform the largest political club of them all."

"The man is insane," whispered one classmate to another at the far end of the table, while others reached for water to help disguise their astonishment.

Their apparent concern did not perturb Don Saverio. He went on, "To break from within, we must first set up bases in some of America's most populous and richest states: New York, New Jersey, Connecticut, Massachusetts Illinois, California, and Texas. Then we will target the most prestigious universities in the northeastern region.

"Your residences and your designated campus grounds will give you a dual base from which to work. To get accepted by your new communities, you'll spend two years at the most prominent prep schools before you apply to any universities.

"There you will strive for the highest academic grades and learn how to speak American English. In so doing, you will also build good fellowship credentials and gain popularity by joining social, athletic, and community events."

From their alarmed expressions, Don Saverio could guess what they were thinking:

God knows, how much more he wants us to slave on books.

For a short moment, the men looked away from their master. Then respecting the man they had come to admire over the years, they paid attention to the speech.

In appreciation, he nodded and smiled, "For those of you entering college later on, I see no reason not to become the most sought-after students by fraternity houses and other prominent groups on and off campus. When that happens, you'll know you have arrived. Can anyone disagree?"

Don Saverio swept his gaze to the right, and then to the left. Sensing tension, he toned down his speech, "In time, your hard work coupled with your good looks, like Victor here, will give you the run of the town."

Except for Victor, no one smiled. Don Saverio sighed inside. They were young and too serious about themselves and their futures. They were worried about the two years of prep school, not to mention college. He could read their minds. They could easily accept college, but prep school:

Give me a break . . . please.

Staring at Carlo at the other end of the table, in concealed sign-Sicilian language Ray told him:

If they thought that your father would be arranging for their college admission, they missed the boat entirely . . . nothing illegal.

Carlo nodded and smiled back at Ray.

Coming to the rescue and to ease their minds, Don Saverio said, "Look, guys, nothing will please me more than to see you finished with college four years from now. That would get you out of college fast, and you can drop out of sight faster. But there is too much at stake to rush things.

"The world you're about to enter is the big league, where stakes are high and mediocrity is unacceptable. When you get good at what you do, don't stop there. Get better.

"And when you get bright and smart, everyone will pull you to their side ready to do whatever you ask of them."

Don Saverio scanned each face once more and said, "To be effective, you must earn each and every credit on your own, fair and square. Prep school will help you achieve that goal with ease. Besides, where else can you mingle with most of your future college classmates?

"For the success of our mission, I can't stress how important this is. Be yourselves, relax a little, and apply all you have learned. Above all, have fun doing it. I'll guarantee that before you know it, you'll be out of school and living as one of them—rich and powerful. And because you are rich already, we might call the job half done.

"Remember—planning, perseverance, and hard work will always produce large dividends. It only takes one match to start a big fire."

Raising his hand, Ray said, "Don Saverio, they would like to know their final roles."

They all seconded Ray with a nod and a smile.

"Let me put you at ease," Don Saverio said. "None of you will have to run for elected office. To help mold the newly elected, we need you at your jobs for more than a term or two. Your job is to influence and guide others in what they should be: men of honor who speak the truth with untainted loyalty to the American flag. When you achieve that feat, you have served every American citizen, dead or alive, and their ancestors. Future generations will also benefit from your work. And when your work comes to fruition, you will take great pride, and you will be immensely rewarded."

Puzzled, Angelo raised his hand and asked, "I truly appreciate your effort and I am eager to start working. . . . But how do we influence those politicians?"

"Always remember," Don Saverio said, "the people in the background carry the heaviest load. In other words, behind every successful leader, there is a staffer or two and speechwriters, strategists, and consultants.

"The more you stay in the background, trading punches with friends and foes, the better you get at what you do and the more indispensable you'll be.

"The rest is easy. On its own, our ideology will spread like wildfire, infiltrating politics and big business from within. Right from here, every year we'll have a flow of people following in your footsteps."

"Don Saverio," Marco said, "we want you to know that we're committed to your Cause. We appreciate your trust. You can count on us."

"Thank you all," Don Saverio nodded, acknowledging their trust and commitment. Then to inspire them further, he added, "At one time, I was young and in college also. Like Ray here, I gave up my dream for a better dream—our Cause. You'll do fine. Remember, by the time you get out of college, your input will help Ray lay out a road map to the most vulnerable posts for you to attack."

Across the table there were smiles of admiration and acceptance. Most members of the Class of '56 would enter the United States permanently. For the rest, it was student visas. To get student status, each member had to set up a trust account in America and use that money to pay tuition; they must find room and board with people not linked to Mafia.

Don Saverio had waited ten years for this moment. During that time, he had laid out every detail summed up in three never-to-be-broken rules:

Never break American laws.

Never associate with members of the old Mafia.

Never take on money or women problems.

"In America, Ray will be my liaison. . . . He will be the only link between you and me," Don Saverio said. "When you communicate among yourselves, be discreet. Always assume that someone is listening. Remember the old cliché: walls have eyes and ears.

"Technology is getting better by the day. Be cautious when writing documents or notes. They tend to show up when it is least convenient. They can destroy grand careers.

"Keep all your fiscal and private records in order and be ready for magnifying-glass scrutiny. One false step and you will be out of the game and no one will come to your aid."

To stress his next point, Don Saverio looked at Ray. "In New York, sometime next year, sixty heads of Mafia families will attend the largest meeting of its kind ever assembled. They are attempting to reorganize. I declined the invitation for it is no good for our Cause.

"Make a mental note of that event. Stay clear of the area and be aware of anything you say, especially when you recognize some of the people involved. The media will have a field day. It only takes a single unwary answer to make worldwide headlines.

"This event will probably be your first experience with prejudice. America is full of it. If you're not alert, you'll fall for its fallacies and regress instead of progress with your mission.

"Because we're Sicilians, people will always associate us with Mafia. This can be detrimental or beneficial to you. It'll depend on how you handle the situation. Ironically, if you take the obvious action and distance yourself from Mafia, you'll have the most advantage.

"No matter what you say or do, the doubt will always linger in most people's minds—so will their respect for your words and actions. For example, next time such an event grabs the headlines, you'll find the same people, in a subtle way, asking the same questions to test your integrity.

"As a precaution, you'll find that a few derogatory comments about old Mafia will bring you a step closer to your objective—which is being accepted as one of them."

The Class of '56, having accepted Don Saverio's conditions, was puzzled at the mention of prejudice. It was nonexistent in Sicily. Wisely, Don Saverio called for a break.

Carlo called the meeting back to order.

"With my father's permission," he said, "I want to propose a vote of confidence for Ray."

Don Saverio waved him on.

"With Ray at the helm of the New Enterprises," Carlo said, "I think it's vital that we take a vote showing our support for the difficult job he's undertaking."

Raising his hand, Victor seconded the motion, as did Angelo, and the rest. To reinforce their solidarity, Don Saverio raised his glass and proposed a toast that concluded with a round of applause.

Standing up and sporting his contagious smile, Ray accepted the vote with gratitude.

"Until things get on track," Carlo continued, "you will not be alone. Our good friends in America will be watching, ready to assist you. Those are our people reporting to me.

"They will not interfere. You probably will not recognize any of them. If you do, make no contact. Talk to no one but Ray. He'll know what to do. For the future, I'll show you the draft of an insignia I'm working on so you can recognize worthy associates."

The artist's rendition showed a diamond-shaped object with a blue surface on which a small shiny star streaked through a classically scripted letter A. The date, 1956, was written in a font similar to stones. The insignia looked like a coin without a border.

"Powerful," said Angelo. "The letter 'A' not only stands for Alcamo but for August as well. Maybe if I keep pushing, it'll stand for Angelo or maybe America."

With drinks in hand, they joined Angelo in much-needed laughter. Carlo called the meeting back to order.

"In the future, you might see this insignia on rings, lapel pins, paper stickers, and any other form that will help identify our people.

"Don't forget, though, the insignia will only identify the bearer as a friend or mark a transaction worth looking into. Beyond that you must always get clearance from Ray before engaging in any dealings with others."

The Class of '56 liked the insignia. It reassured and anchored them better to the Cause.

Ray sipped some water and pulled on his red suspenders. He said, "Harvard, Princeton, Cornell, Yale, Georgetown, Stanford, these are the some of the universities we are targeting. As much as I'd love to, I will not attend college. While you're in school, Silvana and I will start a fashion business."

As skeptical about Silvana as he had been earlier in the week, the men at the table glanced at each other then gave Ray their attention. Ray told them how the post-war period had infected the new generation with an insatiable desire to imitate Hollywood fashion.

He explained how it all related to marketing fashionable products worldwide. He also explained the inner workings of the new business and Don Saverio's relations with a network of contractors and marketing people.

Above all, he explained how talented and committed Silvana was to the development of the business.

"With the help of good friends," Ray continued, "I'm sure that, by the time you're out of school, it will turn into a big business.

"Now, I wish you luck. I'll see you on the other side. I want you to know that I have wanted to see the other side of the sea since I was a little boy," Ray said, with a kid's smile on his face.

Taking the floor once more, Don Saverio said, "Before we adjourn, I want to talk about the reason we must set up shop in America. All legally, mind you. In a free society, the amount of money one controls equals the amount of power one can exert."

They all agreed, smiling.

"To attract the young and educated people to our Cause, we must dismantle old Mafia. This has to be done at the same time as we infiltrate politics and big business so corruption can be wiped out."

He paused. Then with a dramatic tone he said, "Today, Mafia violates every rule of decency laid down centuries ago by our ancestors. While living under totalitarian governments, they adopted a code of secrecy for the survival of their cause, later known as *Omertà*.

"The code, coupled with fair and swift justice, gave the victim's family instant gratification and respect. It instilled pride and confidence in every member.

"As an independent revolutionary body, Mafia sheltered its people from oppression and allowed them to follow their dreams. Their strategy, as it's ours now, was effective.

"They spread across the countryside in as many independent groups as possible then infiltrated the ruling government. The aim was to expand, unify, and strengthen their cause.

"Contrary to historians' accounts, our ancestors were no criminals. Taking into account the ruthless suppression they endured, we should never forget their relentless drive for self-rule and freedom. For the sake of humanity, we must prevent it from ever happening in America.

"Many societies became extinct by yielding to the will of their oppressors. Our ancestors got their resources from their oppressors any way they could. To defend their own, Mafia leaders were no less daring than any man of political principles today.

"As late as 1948, they rendered Sicily independent from the Italian government. Today, regardless of geopolitical maps and understanding, Sicily is autonomous with its own council. The assembly consists of popularly elected counselors and a president. Sicilians, not outsiders, thanks to Mafia, elect their own government."

Don Saverio stood more erect and said, "I'm proud of my heritage.

"The Mafia I know, not gangsters, has been instrumental in scores of government reforms over the years. Mafia enhanced our way of life and increased our people's acceptance worldwide.

"Your level of education and of those who will emigrate after you is the living proof of those reforms. Your talent is the same as that of our ancestors. I will not allow any of our future generations to waste their talents on the present Mafia—a decaying institution on its way to self-destruction.

"Our Cause, as that of our ancestors, is a cause filled with honor, pride, and self-respect. We have to protect our heritage at any cost.

"The current Mafia, in and out of Sicily, with no concern for its heritage, is congregating in small tribes. They are distrustful and ready to kill each other at the turn of a coin.

"Their passion for killing each other is an act of greed and suppression that lacks logic and purpose.

Some of these families have strayed off course beyond recovery. They are stigmatizing an entire population, corrupting the American political system and big business alike.

"When faced with family feuds over rank or territory, they kill each other rather than trying to reconcile and unify. They defeat the very principle of *Omertà* they claim to live by.

"They seek media coverage to advance their power within their limited tribes. The survivors declare themselves self-made leaders. At no time has Mafia been faced with such a spectacle."

Don Saverio held everyone's attention, smoothed his mustache with his forefinger, and continued, "In an open society, today's Mafia is a stigma. It stands out as a sore thumb. They deal in prostitution, drugs, gambling, loan sharking, and any other illegal activity they can mastermind.

"Some might even get to be glamorous enough to attract attention, but with no good values. Contrary to our morals, they are criminals with a vision obscured by greed.

"Because the power of this self-proclaimed Mafia stems from terrorizing and suppressing similar thugs, we shall do all we can to put them out of business or at least distance ourselves and our people as far as possible.

"In fairness to the men of honor out there who will join those already serving our Cause, I ask you to respect them when they cross your path. They are an intrinsic part of our mission. Whenever necessary, they will identify themselves with the Class of '56 insignia Carlo showed you.

"As you know, next week there will be a dinner honoring all the 1956 graduates in Alcamo. There you'll meet the men committed to our Cause. While others called them moles, I call them the Street Warriors. They'll keep on working with Carlo and me. They will also migrate to the United States before year's end. Their mission, unlike yours, is to infiltrate old Mafia from within."

After the meeting adjourned, ten young men's dreams of reforming a bunch of Mafia families as they set themselves up in lives of luxury, became one unified dream with the sole purpose of advancing their ancestors' ideology in America.

For that, they committed themselves to follow Ray's lead. For without a leader with a set of principles and strict rules, their dream would die.

11

After World War II, nothing molded people more into modern lifestyle than movie theaters and ballrooms. Alcamo was blessed with the Cinema Esperia at the east end and the Sala Arlecchino, a modern ballroom, at the west end.

In the ballrooms, people sported fashions and espoused the liberal ideas they had learned from the movies. Changes were certainly taking hold, but because it was all new, not swiftly.

Cinema Esperia's spacious ground floor and horseshoe mezzanine was in keeping with the wide screen, the stereo sound, and the new films it featured. The comfortable chairs made movie going a special experience.

Thanks to a mirrored wall and high ceiling, the lobby seemed twice as deep. It was not until word of this illusion spread around town that moviegoers stopped slamming their body onto the mirror attempting to walk the full length of the lobby.

After all, mirrored walls, as new fashion designs, were yet to become part of their imagination much less their reality.

Celebrations in the modern ballroom marked the start of an era in which the young defied the old. Prior to these changing times, the locals used ballrooms mostly for wedding receptions.

In the old ballrooms, there was a *bastoniere*—chief chaperon—and a young man needed to ask permission from the *bastoniere* to dance with the girl of his liking. That was no longer the case. At Sala Arlecchino, there was no *bastoniere*. If he could survive the hostile gaze of most parents, a young man could invite a girl to dance from afar with a single bow. Even more shocking was the girl's newfound right to refuse.

Raising their hands to the air, the elders moaned, "The *bastoniere* is a thing of the past. The *bastoniere* knows who's who, and who but the *bastoniere* can split a grinding couple on the dance floor? Times have changed indeed."

Unlike the older ballrooms that held a few rows of chairs around the dance floor, Sala Arlecchino was large enough to accommodate thirty tables seating ten at each. Each table held a flower arrangement and refreshments. If patrons were dining, the table held a complete serving including dishes, silverware, glasses, napkins, and even toothpicks.

Once when ballrooms were used only for weddings and the *bastoniere* kept the young in check, the most one could get at these gatherings was a sliver of the wedding cake and a glass of wine. Occasionally, there was champagne, but few had acquired a taste for it. Although considered an elegant touch, it often was pushed aside to bubble itself away.

Thanks to the macho characters of the movies, scotch, once a taboo, was replacing ice cream and soda. Also showing at the movies was the serving of dinners in public. Regardless of cost, up to now, dining out was thought to be sinful.

Tonight's gathering was in keeping with this new lifestyle. Perhaps it was Don Saverio's vision that allowed these changes to take place. Perhaps it was the times. Perhaps it was a little of both. In any case, the mixture was right.

The celebration belonged not only to the Class of '56 but also to all students graduating in Alcamo that year.

Sala Arlecchino was the place where men of honor had come to celebrate their Cause—Mafia reform.

On the right side of the ballroom, away from the loudspeakers, a table had been reserved for Don Saverio's family. There, waiting for his parents to arrive, Carlo was discovering scotch and soda.

On the opposite side of the ballroom, there was a two-seat table reserved for Ray. Out of respect for her dead husband, his mother, Francesca, did not attend the party.

The Class of '56 and Don Saverio's other protégés and their families were seated at tables throughout the ballroom.

Two nationally acclaimed bands had come from Rome to entertain the young. To soothe the older crowd, there was a piano player and a female singer.

Contrary to local tradition, Victor was the first ever to date a girl alone without ruining her reputation. To the astonishment of his family and all the guests, Victor walked through the main door, arm-in-arm with Brigitte. They headed straight for a table next to Ray's. Other novelties were Brigitte's soft, ash-blonde hair and the fact that she was one inch taller than Victor.

No chaperon from the girl's family was there to look over their shoulders. Victor had broken the local rules—with the blessing of Brigitte's mother. She had asked Victor to take Brigitte to the party. Brigitte and her mother were visiting from Tunisia, and her mother was determined to find a date to remember for her daughter before they returned home, where dating without a chaperon was forbidden.

Escorting Silvana, Ray followed Victor. Their entrance was not so shocking because Silvana's parents were to be present in the ballroom.

Ray was dressed in a black suit with cuff-less trousers—another first— and sported a million-dollar smile and a Superman physique.

Silvana led the way like a fashion model. She walked in perfect cadence, wearing the simplest and most elegant black-sequin dress ever seen on a young woman in Alcamo. She wore a white *giglio*—lily—on her left shoulder and a French-twist hairdo.

The short-sleeved dress reached just below her knee—also another first. She clutched a small golden hand-purse, which matched the gold necklace that accented the dress' scoop neckline.

A pair of black high-heeled shoes and shadow-black seamless nylon stockings complemented the flattering dress. Each step she took revealed her sensuous bodyline.

A closer look revealed the details of her creation. Each of the hundreds of sequins placed precisely in the center of small diamond-like satin embroidery made the dress sparkle even more, complementing her dark glinting eyes and her rounded glowing lips. The dress was the first of Giglio Enterprises' fashion line.

Consumed by the experience and the gaze of the onlookers, Ray and Silvana felt their body temperatures rise as they crossed the room and sat at their table. Once at their table, they stared at each other in silence trying to figure out what to do next.

After a moment, they glanced at Victor and Brigitte but got no help. They looked around for any cue. On the other side of the ballroom, they saw Don Saverio nod at the band. As though in answer to a prayer, without delay, the band played "Love Is a Many Splendored Thing." Ray and Silvana, accompanied by Victor and Brigitte, were the first to hit the dance floor. By the second refrain, they danced almost unnoticed on the crowded floor.

While the couples danced, Carlo was getting drunk on scotch. Carlo saw his mother's subtle smile when she looked at Ray and Silvana dancing. He realized that changes had hit home also and that his mother wasn't powerless after all. In a peculiar way, she had exerted her will on Don Saverio to let Silvana and Ray date by themselves.

It wasn't until well into the night that Silvana and Ray walked over to her parents' table. No sooner did she hear her daughter say powder room, than Donna Maria was on her way with Silvana in tow leaving the three men to themselves.

"Well done, Carlo," grinned Ray. "I saw a dozen people wearing the insignia already."

"With plenty of overtime, the jeweler got them ready. How do you think they look?"

"They're sharp." Ray turned to Don Saverio and asked, "Do you think they'll do the job?"

"Yes," he said, pushing the flower arrangement to one side. He lowered his tone, and the two men leaned forward. "In our business, to know is always better than to be known. In your own words, Ray: Our mission is to strengthen through the powers of our past and yet keep the past from overshadowing the future."

Ray nodded.

"Ray, take a good look at them." He motioned toward the ballroom. "Study their faces. They're the grunts of our mission. The moles if you will—the Street Warriors. With the support of our people abroad, they'll be working the front lines. In time, they'll place themselves in Mafia families of our choosing and dismantle them one by one.

"Before you leave, Carlo will give you their identities and whereabouts."

Ray and Silvana returned to their table with a brighter outlook. They looked at each other in wonder. In their hearts, each knew what the future held but neither spoke about it.

She wanted freedom from old traditions. He wanted to discover the motive behind his father's slaying, then move on with life and get back to writing.

This night was changing them and their relationship.

She said, "I hear you're going by sea."

"That's right."

"Why?"

"After my friend's tale of his trip from New York last month, I simply refuse to fly for now," Ray said.

"What happened?"

"He told me that the only things he could see that night were flames shooting out of the engines and four propellers spinning almost red. No thanks . . . I'll wait for the jet before I think of flying. It'll be in service soon."

"You're not choosing the ocean liner for its nightclubs, are you?" she teased, but feeling a sudden pang of jealousy. She smoothed things over with a passionate smile.

Overlooking her remark, Ray asked, "Silvana, what do you really want out of life ... do you have a dream?"

Blushing, she said, "I do. I want to be an independent human being, valued for who I am and what I do. Only then will I be ready to set up house and raise a family. That's my ultimate dream."

Ray said nothing, but rubbed his streak of white hair twice.

Her passion for business made her sound more like an entrepreneur than the romantic person she really was. Because he sensed her fervent passion, he knew he must work her carefully as if taming a wild mare. Not for the prize but for the love she could offer.

She asked, "What do you want?"

Hesitant, faced with the dilemma of choosing between the consequences of his disclosure and the need to know if she was ready to part from her father, he chose the possible consequences.

He cradled a glass of scotch in both hands and said, "With one exception, the same things you do. Before I settle down, I must comfort my mother and myself. I've got to find the motive behind my father's slaying. I must put that behind me before I can move on with my writing career."

Puzzled, she asked, "But why do you need a motive?"

"Silvana, I think I know who ordered the killing, and I don't think the motive was justifiable."

"And if it was?"

He whirled the ice cubes around with his forefinger, "If the killing was justifiable, no matter how close to the killer or to the victim you are, as a man of honor you must accept the event without prejudice.

"Throughout history, many men of honor sentenced their own when they found them guilty—do you subscribe to that rule?" Before she could answer, he pointed at Victor at the next table. "If you ask Victor that is the only credo he lives by—no exception."

She took his hand in hers and said, "It's the only rule of justice I know. If I might add, no matter how much it hurts, you must always accept its outcome."

"You mean like Stefano and Gloria?"

"Truthfully, Ray. . . . I'm having second thoughts about that whole deal, but it's too late to do anything. As much as I feel for her, Gloria wasn't family."

"I knew her well. Gloria came from a proud family. For the life of me, I can't imagine her cheating, especially with your brother Stefano. Again, life gets complicated at times."

"I'm too remote to feel their pain or, for that matter, yours," she said. "I'm sure that if there was foul play in either case, the truth will come out. When it does, I must accept it, even if it involves my family."

With that, Ray and Silvana joined Victor and Brigitte on the dance floor. Starting their relationship with respect for each other's convictions, they danced the night away.

12

Ray had yet to visit his father's grave, and it was the day before he left for America. In the last fourteen years, he had only visited the grave twice. It was not for lack of love or respect, but because of the cold relationship between the Grecos and his mother.

Driving down Main Street that afternoon, he found himself turning north then down a dirt road until he reached the old water fountain. He drove a short way past the fountain and stopped at the cemetery.

Strolling through an array of headstones, he headed for the mausoleum, his father's resting place. As he passed the tombstones, he read the epitaphs, saluting the deceased as if they were old friends. The lifelike photos on the headstones made them seem alive.

At the end of the stroll under the autumn foliage, Ray climbed six steps. A few feet down the veranda to the right was his father's tablet.

Since his last visit, Ray had grown taller. He no longer had to tiptoe for a glimpse of the photo. At eye level now, he found his father much younger than he remembered. The engraving read:

Luciano Greco
June 18, 1914 – October 12, 1942
Luciano Lives Through His Son, Ray

Now the writing meant something more than a scribble. With tears blurring his vision, Ray vowed:

I'll get them . . . Dad; I promise . . . I will!

Pressing both palms against the tablet, Ray read the script over and over again, each time pressing harder and harder.

To his left, a footstep echoed off the marble floor. From the corner of his eye, he saw the shadow of a man. Frozen in thought, he stood still.

When the man touched his shoulder, he turned, only to find himself wrapped in Grandpa Greco's arms. "Grandpa . . . I'll get them . . . I'll get them."

"I know you will," the deep-voiced man said. "I know you will, son."

Grandpa and Ray were strolling along the arched veranda, which stretched alongside the mausoleum overlooking the cemetery.

The trees had ceased to cast long shadows. In the red twilight, each step echoed off the marble floor in sync with their words and the hooting of the owls.

"It feels good," his grandfather said, resting a hand on Ray's shoulder. "I've waited a long time for this moment."

At seventy-five, Grandpa Greco was as tall as Ray. He wore a large brown hat with a small pheasant's feather tucked in the band on the right. He had small pointing eyes. His black cape reached below his knees. His well-polished knee-high boots served him well for he was a well-to-do farmer.

"Grandpa, I don't know what to say. Sometimes life can be unfair. Tomorrow I'm leaving for . . ."

"You don't have to explain, young man. I know all about it. Lately, I've been talking with your mother. I should have done it sooner. Sometimes life is unfair. For being stubborn, we often pay a price."

Pleased, Ray said, "I'm glad you have."

Grandpa Greco faced his grandson squarely, and then looking in his eyes said, "She's a good woman. She has raised a fine man. Tradition or not, before you get to America, I'll have the entire family talking. . . . She'll have a family to count on."

"As to my father, before I make a move, I must know who pulled the trigger and why," Ray said.

"I've followed your every move since you joined the Cremonas. As much as I've promised not to interfere and as much as it kills me, deep inside I know that only by staying closer to them will you learn the facts and stay true to your calling."

Ray said, "Perhaps my way of doing things is different. No one has told me my father did something wrong. I want to avenge him with honor."

"Son, you said it right. That's *omertà*. When you get to America, look for a man named Santo Pellegrino. He's not from Alcamo. He's slick, moves around a lot, and rumor has it that in America he's protected by some mob families. Some say he's their best hit man. They say he's afraid of nothing, but I don't buy that. I think he's a coward.

"He left shortly after your father was killed. He's missing his left forefinger. The last I heard, he was in Brooklyn. You should ask Sal Rocca."

"Since my father's accident, Sal comes over to assist mother and me, often staying over for dinner. As to asking him about my father, I've asked him, but he wouldn't ever give a straight answer . . . he says he is not too sure."

"Sal appreciates the opportunity you gave him," said Grandpa, smiling. "He's very loyal to the family. He says he is ready to help you with whatever it takes. He tells me he wants to avenge my son more than I'll ever know."

"I know that. My father trusted Uncle Sal implicitly. So does my mother now. Do you know what I remember most about Sal when I was a kid?"

Grandpa shook his head.

"Whenever Dad and I visited him at the job sites, he always gave me a wooden soldier."

Grandpa grinned again but said nothing.

"Guess what?" Excited as a child, Ray said, "I got one every Christmas until last."

Grandpa reached in his pocket, "You mean the same as this one?" He handed the wooden soldier to his grandson.

Ray paused and stared at the old man. They exchanged smiles. Instantly, he knew that Grandpa had carved all the others in his collection as well.

As they parted, Ray hugged his grandfather and waved. He stood there for a long time, long after he watched the darkness of the night envelop his grandpa.

13

In Brooklyn, in the winter of 1956, Ray experienced the most snow he had ever seen. Except for a single light snowfall one morning in Alcamo, this was Ray's first experience with snowstorms.

With legs still wobbly from eleven days at sea, he rented a split-level apartment in a three-family house. The house had dark brown shingles and a waist-high black iron fence; it resembled a brownstone of some sort.

The fence enclosed the front yard but not the stoop. Through a gate to the right of the stoop, clear of two trashcans, a walkway led to the ground floor entrance. On this floor there was the kitchen, the laundry rooms, and a dining room with a spiral staircase leading up to the living room on the first floor. The set-up gave the living room a theatrical atmosphere.

The upper quarters were also accessible from the first floor entrance. Except for putting out the trash, Ray hardly used the ground floor entrance. He would climb up the stoop, check the mail, then take three steps down the hall and disappear into his apartment. Once inside, the spiral staircase almost forced him downstairs.

If he had skipped the door to his apartment and kept on walking down the hall and up a flight of stairs, he would face a fire escape ladder leading up to the roof through a hatchway. There was no lock there. People could come down from the roof at will.

In Brooklyn, Ray learned all about snow removal, tire chains, alternate street parking, city buses, elevated trains, and subway routes.

What captivated Ray most were the never-ending lines of parked cars on both sides of the street. With few parking spaces up for grabs, he tried to avoid the city's tow trucks by parking on the lawful side of the street the night before. Short of a legal spot, he would get up early the next morning and hopefully find one.

This morning, after an overnight snowstorm, Ray came out the vestibule and onto the stoop. With cars half covered with snow, he stretched his neck in disbelief to get a better view. Taking a step forward, he tumbled down into a snow bank; he was engulfed in snow up to his ears. He laughed his heart out for forgetting about the seven steps.

It seemed that all the snow that had fallen overnight in Brooklyn piled up on his street. Cars, stoops, railings, garbage cans, basement windows, front yards, everything on the street was covered in snow.

A few days later, Ray dug his car out. It was a losing proposition, however, for every day after the storm, the city plows piled up more snow on the parked cars. The locals thought it was a conspiracy to keep them off the roads.

Since Ray did not mind public transportation, the conspiracy was fine by him. A short walk to the bus stop and fifteen cents took him anywhere in the city and kept him warm to boot.

Ray was eager to start working on Don Saverio's New Enterprise. A task that would allow him to seek out Santo Pellegrino before the Class of '56 would graduate from college; he would marry Silvana and join Giglio full time.

To find Pellegrino, Ray began mingling with the locals of Bushwick. He had chosen this neighborhood for its rich mix of Italian descendants. It also had another plus—not a single Mafia family dominated the neighborhood. Here, they seemed to live in harmony.

Poolrooms and social clubs in Bushwick were Ray's starting point for tracking down Pellegrino. Each Sicilian club-goer belonged to his own social club with a hierarchy that tied him to his town back in Sicily.

It was a scheme that helped Ray in his hunt. His immediate concern, however, was not how to find Pellegrino—he sensed he was in the right neighborhood for that—but how to nab and dispose of his father's killer.

Unlike social clubs, poolrooms were the places for criminals and hustlers to mingle with churchgoers, non-churchgoers, and other people. Here, a newcomer could learn the makeup of the neighborhood, the news the media reported, and the events it did not report. In short, poolrooms were open to people from all walks of life. No membership fee was required, only enough cash to pay for games and lost bets.

The poolroom tables captivated Ray. Each had a hooded fluorescent fixture hanging over the green felt, illuminating the players and the game. Two cue racks, six wooden benches, and two vending machines, one for cigarettes and one for sodas decorated the walls.

The owner, a thin, middle-aged Italian man, received and dispatched messages better than an answering machine. In that same fashion, he tracked down monies due him plus interest. The one-and-one-half percent weekly interest was a bargain compared to the going three percent others charged.

Amazingly, the thin man subdued scuffles that could have erupted into violent fights. He was a bundle of nerves with lots of contacts. He could have anyone's legs broken without lifting a finger. No fighting was allowed in his poolroom, although, there were plenty of memories of bloodshed among the patrons.

Here, Ray met many faceless people, quickly improving his perception about the good, the bad, the in-between fellows, and the hustlers. He learned where they came from and where they were going. He had never experienced such a diversity of races. He could have written countless pages on that subject alone.

This Friday night, folks were late in arriving. Ray was playing with a cue ball at an unlit table. Looking at the empty table next to him, he imagined the break; he could hear the blast followed by the thump of a ball dropping into a pocket.

Looking up, he noticed a short, skinny, nondescript man step down onto the poolroom floor. "How're you doing?" the man said, grabbing a cue stick from the rack.

"Fine," Ray said, bouncing the cue ball off the side cushion and watching the stranger.

"Did you get paid? Want to shoot pool?" the man asked, rolling the cue stick on Ray's table to check it for bents.

"Get paid for what?"

"You got no job . . . do you?"

Staring at the man, Ray asked, "What's it to you?"

The man returned his stare.

Ray shifted. "I'm going to ask you once to take that stick off my table . . . if you don't, I'll shove it up your ass and . . . ."

Before Ray could finish the sentence, the man grabbed the cue stick off the table and sighted it from butt to tip. Unhappy, he tried another stick, this time on the adjacent table.

"Let me tell you," the man smirked, "as long you got cash, whether you got a job or not means shit to me."

"I got cash . . . but no thanks."

"I don't care much about a job myself."

Ray stared at him for a long moment.

The man looked Ray up and down, sizing up Ray's massive wrists. Cautiously, he said, "I take it you just got off the boat . . . didn't you? I tell you this for your own good. Get a job. Any job, at least until the word spreads, or people will stop talking to you and soon label you . . . loser."

Ray kept staring.

"There's no action here," the man said, looking up at Ray as he bounced the cue stick back onto the rack. "Lots of luck, I've got to go. By the way, I like your red suspenders but do something about that bit of white hair . . . I know better."

Ray's stare followed him up the steps and out.

How are you? . . . When did you get here? . . . What do you do for a living? . . . Are you working? . . . How is your mother? . . . Is she coming soon?

This litany of questions from friends, relatives, and new and old acquaintances followed by subtle frowns prompted Ray to look for a job, any job, quickly.

His idle presence in the neighborhood during working hours was noticeable and suspicious. He found that empty greetings and chats about the weather did not do the trick.

The stranger was right.

Ray got himself a job, but he did nothing about his hair.

In Brooklyn, Ray also learned why Don Saverio and Carlo sent their most-trusted men into large tenements in quieter neighborhoods.

South Brooklyn and parts of Queens offered the largest selection of those kinds of buildings. There, the neighbors asked no questions of you as long as you asked none of them. Manhattan, Staten Island, and the Bronx were out of reach, giving him more room to work.

Ray got a job in the garment industry. He was learning things that would be useful in establishing Giglio, but more importantly, the job gave him much-needed social status in Bushwick. The locals were vital to Ray's pursuit of Pellegrino. To that end, he dined with many different people.

No sooner had the word of Ray's job spread, than a friend of a friend invited him to dinner.

Mr. Catania lived a block away from the poolroom. Alerted by a matchmaker, Mr. Catania had set his eyes on Ray for his daughter, Concetta.

The dinner invitation pleased Ray. The spaghetti, meatballs, and veal cutlets tasted almost as good as that of his mother. After dinner, to show off Concetta, Mrs. Catania asked her daughter to clear the table and serve coffee.

With coffee served, the hollow-eyed and ready-to-smile Concetta sat across from Ray. Mrs. Catania complemented the coffee with a basket of walnuts and a tray of cookies.

Mr. Catania made a mess while waiting for the coffee to cool. He pounded three walnuts with his bare hand on the table, flinging bits of nuts and shells onto his lap and the floor. Picking nut crumbs from the tablecloth and munching like a rabbit, he said, "My friend tells me you work in the city."

Ray was used to stretching the truth to fit the occasion. "Yes, I'm a bookkeeper . . . but for now, I am working as a labor recruiter for a dressmaker in Manhattan."

"That's good." Mr. Catania rubbed his full belly. "Per our tradition, a man over eighteen has to have a trade and carry on as a mature man. For that matter, a girl has to have a steady job, also. Concetta is a beautician with a steady income. A good one too, I should say."

Concetta said nothing; she blushed and smiled.

"Yes, you got it right. In Sicily, those are the rules," Ray said, covering the nutcracker with his hand to crack a walnut for Concetta and one for himself.

"Isn't your boss . . . what's his name?" Mr. Catania quizzed Ray, snapping his fingers while winking at his wife. "You know, the gentleman that makes the headlines all the time . . . what's his name?"

"Mr. Catania, believe it or not, I've never met the man. Nor do I know his name. The only thing I care about is my paycheck on Friday."

Concetta mirrored Ray's smile, served more coffee, and said nothing. Her father was steadily chatting, and she had no chance to talk. Nor did Ray ask her questions.

Mr. Catania, stirring his second cup of coffee, looked at Ray and said, "Because you're new in

America . . . between the two of us, if I were you, I'd be looking for a safer job." Then he held his nostrils shut with his fingers as if smelling a skunk. "He stinks, your boss; his father is worse."

"Well, what do you know? I left Sicily to get away from that sort of thing and here I am."

"Don't worry, Ray. My father told me about you Grecos. You're good people. I'm glad to have met you. Call on me for anything you need."

What unsettled Ray most about people was not physical strength but lack of strength in personality—weak-minded people. Although Concetta held a tough job dealing with the public, to him, she seemed vulnerable, a walking tragedy.

He never visited the Catania family again. He always felt for Concetta's weakness. He wished he could have helped her. As for his own job, Ray was a recruiter for dressmakers. He worked a five-day week from morning to noon, a schedule that fit with the New Enterprise's activities.

His boss, as Mr. Catania pointed out, was none other than a declining mobster's son who spent most of his days defending his business' legitimacy.

In his position, Ray provided jobs for many people in Bushwick. That gave him plenty of influence, especially among those who did not speak English.

He soon became the most sought-after person in the neighborhood and respectable indeed. Because he played it straight, the locals trusted him. Just the kind of trust he needed for his underground work.

By the end of his second year in the States, Ray had gone to work for another company—one of the largest fashion houses of the day. The company was legitimate and fell within Don Saverio's rule—no Mafia links.

He worked for this company for five years, spending the last three as a production manager while he and a limited staff got Giglio off the ground and running.

With the Class of '56 coming out of college and Silvana coming to Manhattan to head Giglio, Ray had no choice but start expanding Giglio to the fullest from behind the scenes.

14

Nineteen sixty-three was a year of revelation for Mafia and politics as well. The general mood among Mafia members was somewhat somber for those accused and defiant for those still seeking recognition.

In the early evening at a social club in Brooklyn, two senior Mafia members were debating the latest of the televised organized-crime hearings from the comfort of their recliners with coffee in hand.

Gino, a retired barber of fragile frame with prune cheeks and green eyes, glanced past Dominick's shoulder at a stranger mingling with members.

Dominick, a retired baker with reddish puffy cheeks and black olive eyes, cocked his head to one side to look at the stranger as well. It was instinctive for these cautious men to notice things and people not usually in their world. The men exchanged glances then Dominick dismissed the stranger with a wave of his hand. He asked Gino, "Did you see Joe Vallaci last night on television?"

"You mean the squealer?" Gino smirked. "Can you imagine that? He revealed *Cosa Nostra* on primetime for the world to hear."

"He's got some nerve," Dominick said. "Before the hearings are over, he's going to get a bullet between the eyes."

"I agree," said Gino angrily. "After what he did to *Cosa Nostra*—if I could get closer to him, I'd shoot him myself."

Rocking his recliner, Dominick said, "It's no use. I can see him spilling the beans. After all, the boys didn't do much right by him either. After thirty years, they dropped him like a hot potato, but *Cosa Nostra*?"

Gino's face paled at just the thought of such a betrayal. He bit his lower lip and said, "He shouldn't have touched that. That's like talking about your mother's sex life in public. . . . That's not right."

"Look, Joe Vallaci was in a bad fix with no way out." Dominick gulped down a mouthful of coffee. "He had no choice but to turn informant."

"Wait! Hold your thoughts for a moment, Dominick. I heard John DeMaria's name mentioned a few times in the hearings the other day. Do you know this man?"

"Can't say I do," Dominick said, "but I think he's with the FBI. Anyhow, how do you think those Mafia bosses feel about Joe spilling his guts?"

"I tell you, Dominick, every time Joe opens his mouth I bet they wet their pants. They never know what's coming next."

"That's nothing, Gino. I'll bet they squirmed when the committee showed all those organizational charts. The guys on the committee play the game better than any Mafia boss I've seen. They act as if they were trained in Sicily."

Gino nodded. "I think their bosses deserve what's coming to them, and I don't think Joe Vallaci should walk away scot-free into the FBI program and start all over. He should get a dose of his own medicine.

"Once the committee's done," Gino went on, "they should send him down the tube with the rest of them. That's what I think is going to happen anyhow."

"To hell with them all," said an angry voice.

The two old friends turned toward the voice. It was the stranger they had notice earlier. The stranger said, "This is America. Those guys have put all Italians through hell, painted us all with shame."

Wrinkling his forehead as if to get a better read on the man, Dominick asked, "What's your name?"

"Vito Catania. I'm not a member yet. Sorry for the outburst. But I can't stand that kind of trash."

"Mr. Catania, you seem to know your stuff," Dominick said, staring at him for a moment. "Tell me, what do you think is going on with Bobby Kennedy and Jimmy Hoffa?"

Vito exchanged glances with both of them. "For my money, I think Kennedy's zeal got his brother killed. Again, that's my opinion."

"I think so, too," Gino nodded. "You know what's funny. The head of the FBI . . ." He snapped his fingers a few times for help. "What's his name?"

"J. Edgar Hoover," Dominick answered.

"Oh yeah, him . . . that son of a bitch finally admitted that organized crime exists in America."

Sweeping a glance across the room, Vito said, "That's a laugh."

"I know, and guess what?" eagerly Gino went on. "He's going to wage war against organized crime. I thought only the president could declare war."

"You know what's amazing?" Dominick said, smiling. "In the end, neither Fidel Castro nor the Kennedys will have any use for mobsters. With big business' help, politicians are organizing themselves better than Mafia."

"Who's going to touch those politicians now? God? I don't think so." Swinging his armchair upright, Gino said, "As you said, Dominick, I think they are Mafia now."

Such speculative discussions about the hearings could be heard in most Sicilian clubs. Revealing *Cosa Nostra* to the public drove most debaters in taking pride in their fight against organized crime.

Don Saverio, who was chiefly responsible for the demise of old Mafia, keenly followed the debates from abroad and smiled.

The poker game was well underway. From the front room, one could hear the prelude to the next round.

"I take two."

"I take one."

"I'm out."

"Dealer takes none."

A thick cloud of cigarette smoke engulfed the players. A Tiffany lamp overhead cast a shadow over the players' faces, emphasizing the deep wrinkles around their mouths. They wore their weariness with pride.

The first round of bets raised the pot to five hundred dollars. The amount was too much to bear for the mostly jobless level-three players.

Most social clubs in the area had four levels of play. The first level consisted of members seeking to meet local politicians. In the front room, during daylight hours and early evening, they engaged in a casual game or two of penny-ante rummy, pinochle, or *briscola* for the old-timers.

The second level, the working members, played from six to ten at night, stretching the game to eleven o'clock if they were on a winning streak or if they thought they could get even. They played rummy for a couple of dollars and seven-card poker with a twenty-five-cent ante.

Anything above that went to level three, the ten to one crowd. Their aspirations were to one day play with the high rollers and fix all their problems at once.

Of the last two levels, most players could not afford to lose more than a round without affecting their families' welfare. Yet most of them went on gambling, either to try to win enough to feed their families or to win back their losses.

At about one-thirty, the high rollers began strolling in for the two o'clock game, as most of the level-three gamblers, dissolute and empty-handed, filed out for home. Others, hoping to win the respect of the high rollers, stayed as spectators.

Thanks to Nino Maltese, Ray Greco became a spectator in these social clubs. The short and husky twenty-nine-year-old Nino was not a gambler per se. everyone recognized Nino coming down the street by his slow gait; he waddled like a duck.

He was the son of a couple whom Ray had helped find steady jobs along with fringe benefits and a good shot at a pension—a dream come true. Nino, a devoted son and an avid club-goer, kept himself up-to-date on Mafia gossip. He went to social clubs more often than he visited church.

Nino led Ray out of the smoke-filled room saying, "Tonight is going to be some hell of a night here."

"Why?"

"Let's sit down first." Ray and Nino found two recliners by the picture window facing the street.

Ray eyed Nino suspiciously. "Nino, let me ask you, what's wrong with these clubs?"

"What do you mean?"

"They make me feel like a Martian."

"Ray, it's a cultural thing here, especially with Sicilians. Unless you come from the same town and neighborhood, you might as well be from a different planet. . . . Get used to it, Ray."

"Uh-huh."

"Brooklyn is a large city with people from all over the world." Then gazing into the approaching darkness, Nino said, "You'll get used to it, you'll see. Besides, not everyone can be from your town."

"You really know your way around," Ray said, in an admiring tone. "If it wasn't for you, I don't think I'd have set foot in any club."

The bald club keeper approached and asked, "Mr. Nino, what can I get you?"

"Don Mario, is it too early for a rum and coke?"

"If you don't tell, I won't tell," he said with a smile.

"Okay, two rum and cokes on the rocks with a twist of lemon."

"Isn't liquor a good business for these guys?"

"It sure is, Ray. These club keepers can't live on tips alone. You know how it is, don't you?"

"No. I don't. What's his real job?"

"Don Mario collects the house cuts and keeps the games going with fresh cards and refreshments. If the take is good, he serves free pizza. What do you expect from an eighty-year-old man?"

As Nino continued rambling about club keepers, Ray was debating whether to leave. He decided to stay a while longer.

"Remember, Ray, like most other club keepers, Don Mario is trusted by people for his tight lips. Or at least that's the way it was until Joe Vallaci came along. Now, thanks to Joe, club keepers have lost a lot of income in the way of tips from the big guys. Mafia meetings in clubs are things of the past.

"Maybe because of Joe, more club keepers are loosening their lips now," Nino said with a shrug.

"What's there to say?" Ray asked. "Here they go again . . . that's the old Mafia syndrome."

Nino rose halfway up from his recliner staring at Ray incredulously. "What're you talking about? I tell you, you definitely know something I don't. Something is fishy, and I don't know what."

"Stop the nonsense," Ray said, dismissing Nino's question. "Where is Don Mario from . . . and where are our drinks?"

Nino stared back at Ray unconvinced, then hesitantly replied, "He . . . he's from Calatafimi."

For the first time Ray began to doubt his ability to find Santo Pellegrino, much less unearth the true story behind his father's fate. Seven years had passed since Ray's arrival in America, and he was settling nicely into his new lifestyle. But between his job and his entrepreneurial activities, there was not enough time in the day. And as the New Enterprise was taking hold, the time he could spend in Bushwick was reduced to occasional visits.

To carry out Don Saverio's agenda, Ray spent most afternoons in Manhattan meeting heads of Mafia and other people.

He had much on his mind: there was his mother to settle by his side, his marriage to Silvana, and the expansion of Giglio Enterprises. Not to mention the Class of '56 graduating from college. That left little time for hunting Pellegrino.

Grandpa was right. Santo is slick. He moves around leaving no traces. No man is an island though. I'll get that son of a bitch if it's the last thing I do.

Perseverance was Ray's best ally. For the sake of finding Santo, he even put up with Nino's Mafia stories as they club-hopped on late nights.

Don Mario placed two drinks and lemon wedges on the coffee table and hurried to the back room.

Ray twisted a lemon wedge in his drink and asked, "Nino, what's so special about tonight?"

"I don't know if I should trust you with this one."

"Why not?"

"Something's off," said a puzzled Nino. "You were born in Sicily. . . . At times, it sounds as if you're afraid of Mafia. Other times, it's as if you *are* a Mafia boss. I don't get it. Either you're pulling my leg or you're full of hot air. Something has to give. Deep inside, I got these funny vibes, you know what I mean?"

Ray tried to smooth Nino's nerves. "You've got the whole thing wrong. It's not that I don't care about Mafia stories. Lately, my mind is on my job, the remodeling of the house, and on getting married. You know life-altering stuff. That's all. It's not easy. Trust me . . . it's not."

Nino looked at him, still puzzled but calmer.

Ray cleared his throat, "Nino, I admit it. . . . As most people, I too like to peek into the world of Mafia. . . . By the way, being a Sicilian doesn't automatically make me a Mafia man, although at times I wish I were. I'm very much impressed with your Mafia connections. Someday I might come to you for help."

Regaining confidence in Ray, Nino said, "We'll see. Anyhow, tonight they're expecting Mickey the Cat."

Before Ray could ask: Who the hell is Mickey the Cat? Nino filled in the blanks. "Mickey Argento, to be exact; he's the most feared and highly paid hit man."

Ray shook his head in dismay at the awe in Nino's voice.

"Rumor has it, that until Marcello had that nut Oswald hit Kennedy, Mickey held that contract," Nino reported. "Some say that Mickey is now holding an open-ended contract on Joe Vallaci."

"I never heard of Argento or Mickey the Cat. Where's he from?"

"He's from Calatafimi, the same as Don Mario," Nino said. "They say, when he first arrived in America, he was nicknamed Argento for his shiny silver hair."

"Where does the name Mickey the Cat come from?"

"A nickname he earned for his trade," Nino said, laughing, "sort of a cat chasing a mouse. Why don't we ask him when he shows up?"

"What does he look like?"

Nino ordered another drink for himself and a coffee for Ray. Having reconciled their differences, Nino was gossiping like an old lady, "He has a tall, slim body. A full head of hair, like yours, polished silver though, with no streaks."

While listening to Nino chatter, Ray thought:

I know someone will reward me somehow for this torture.

"Two-thirds of his hair is perfectly styled over his forehead like a visor. The rest neatly parted to his right. I tell you, Ray, this man can model for a magazine. Anyone who knows him says the same thing. You've got to watch out for Mickey, though.

"His whole demeanor, with his blue eyes and soft smile, draws you into a certain kind of intimacy that makes you tell him all he wants to know and more.

"But, in that moment, if you look deep into his eyes, you see a man bragging about how many men he killed. No different from a hunter boasting about how many deer he shot. That's his trade, killing people for money."

Ray took another sip of coffee and forced a smile as Nino continued, "I tell you, Ray, he can lure anyone laying eyes on him. I kid you not. He's a powerful figure."

Ray stopped quizzing Nino. The hyper man was getting drunker by the moment and beginning to act brave and silly at the same time. Such men made Ray wary.

Nino's compulsive need to gossip about Mafia intrigues is dangerous to me. He must feel some kind of freedom by always being in the know. But, I fear, some day Nino will talk too much.

Shutting out the clamor of the back room, Ray closed his eyes and stretched back on the recliner thinking about Mickey.

Ray awoke at ten past one. He got up, rushed to the men's room, refreshed, and returned to the recliner. He pretended to sleep as Nino, long gone on rum, snoozed beside him.

At twenty past one, Mickey Argento entered the club in a sandy-colored suit with a light blue long-sleeved shirt, silver cufflinks, and a burgundy tie. He scanned the room, paused for a second to glance at the two sleeping men on the recliners, and walked toward the back room.

Peeking through his eyelashes, Ray recognized Mickey; he was just as Nino had described.

Stopping at the club keeper's post, Mickey bent down to collect a friendly hug and a thick envelope from Don Mario. His arrogant eyes roamed the crowd. He then walked toward a table where three players were setting up the game. The spectators began to circle the table.

No man of good judgment imagined that inside that well-presented body beat the heart of a cold assassin for hire. Mickey's speech was calm and deliberate. He left no illusion as to the meaning of each word he spoke. He planned his every move. He traveled alone and had only a few close friends. These were his links to the world of Mafia. Because these friends brought him business, he kept in touch with them regularly.

Otherwise, Mickey retreated into his own world as an average family man where no one believed he could hurt a fly.

Ray was impressed with Nino's description of Mickey. But, he was not impressed with Mickey the man. In the assassin business, hit men were traded as commodities, and they were not worthy of respect.

Finally, Ray woke up Nino and motioned to follow him to the back room table.

At two o'clock, Don Mario brought six new packs of cards to the table. The players were: the Butcher, who sat across from Mickey; the Bookie; the Tailor; and Mickey. The Bookie randomly picked up a pack and handed it to the Butcher, who ripped the cellophane off and took out all the twos, threes, fours, and jokers from the deck. Aces played high and low.

With spectators at a safe distance and four five-hundred-dollar antes in the pot, Mickey was about to deal the first round.

He went over the rules first, however, "A pair of jacks or better opens. The most you can open with is a thousand dollars, but you can raise twice on the first go-around. After discard, you can open with two thousand and raise three times. Check and raise, it's okay."

The Tailor cut the deck, and Mickey dealt the first hand. For the first two hours, the game went by without incident with the house winning.

As a spectator, Ray looked at Nino disappointed. Hoping to deliver on his promise, Nino insisted things will warm up.

They were dealing the last hand. Ray and Nino stood behind Mickey.

The Tailor, the first to bet, checked.

Mickey opened with a thousand dollars.

The Bookie saw the thousand, and the Butcher raised the ante to two thousand.

The Tailor pushed his two thousand in, and Mickey raised another thousand.

With all bets in at an even three thousand dollars each, the Tailor declared himself served and took no cards.

Mickey took one card, the Bookie one, and the Butcher three.

"Opener talks," the Butcher said.

"Opener bets two thousand," Mickey said without hesitation.

"I . . . I'm in," said the Bookie.

"He might as well fold," Nino whispered.

Ray shrugged his shoulders.

The Butcher rechecked his hand.

"I'll see your two thousand and raise another two."

The Tailor studied the table for a moment and then pushed his four thousand in.

At this point, no matter how closely the spectators watched, no one had an inkling of what was in any player's hand. These men were practiced gamblers, lifting barely a corner to view their cards.

Mickey looked at the Butcher, "I'll see your two thousand and raise you another two."

The Bookie, with a straight going in, folded.

The Butcher rebuffed Mickey's bet and raised another two thousand.

The Tailor, disgusted, folded with a served flush.

Mickey matched the Butcher's two-thousand-dollar raise. Then looking at the Butcher, he said, "Now that we're alone, what do you say we spice up the ante by another ten thousand?"

The Butcher paused for a brief second, stared into Mickey's sparkling eyes, and said, "Sure, why not? Let's see what you got."

The pot was fifty-six thousand dollars, including the antes. Mickey laid one king after another on the table then, with a smirk, reached out to rake in the pot.

"I culled a card for show. These four gentlemen," he nodded at the kings, "were in my hand right from the start."

"If you don't want your hand chopped off here and now, I suggest you leave that pot right there," the Butcher said, staring at Mickey as he was reaching for his six-inch blade. Mickey paused.

In that suspended moment, Ray noticed Mickey's left hand. No forefinger. He was standing only a few feet behind Santo Pellegrino. He wanted to act then, but he knew better. He must bide his time.

To the surprise of Mickey and all the spectators, the Butcher had assembled four aces.

Mickey raised his hands in the air, relinquishing the pot.

That night Ray learned that Santo Pellegrino, alias Mickey the Cat, was slick; he was not from Alcamo; he was indeed missing his left forefinger; and above all, he was a gambler.

On that night before Christmas, Ray walked home contented and already beginning to reshuffle his priorities.

15

In good company, New Year's Eve in Manhattan can be the most exciting night of the year. Ray had reserved a table at the Tavern on the Green.

At seven-thirty, dressed up like Eskimos ready to attack a blizzard, Ray and Silvana left her Thirty-third Street apartment. Walking to Central Park seemed Silvana's secret pilgrimage.

Holding his arm, she said, "Ray, there's nothing better than a brisk walk to the park."

Watching their breaths in the frozen air, he said with a smile, "I don't know what's so good about it."

"I feel invigorated. Fresh air going through my lungs, blood rushing . . ."

"Save it, Silvana! I only feel your body shivering and my nose about to freeze, and we're two dozen blocks away. If we ever make it alive, by then the party will be over. . . . Forget it. . . . This is nuts! . . . Let's get a cab."

"It *is* rather cold," she admitted.

They hailed the first cab in sight, but it did not slow down. The next fifteen minutes were miserable. Finally, a shiny yellow limousine beeped the horn and pulled over. It was not until they got in the backseat that they realized it was a rattling old cab, a lifesaver nevertheless.

Through the rear window, Ray spotted a blanket of scattered clouds. Leaning back, he saw never-ending rows of lights reflecting off tall buildings surrounding the park. The roundabout motion against the swirling view reminded him of the carnival rides with his father. Only this time he got dizzy. This ride was with Silvana on a larger merry-go-round—Central Park.

They arrived with a half-hour to spare, and the host led them to their table. As soon as they were seated, a well-tailored elderly waiter with a downcast face and a wan smile approached, told them his name was Dick, and took their drink orders.

Ray ordered two rum and cokes with a twist of lemon. Dick hovered for a moment after delivering the drinks then faded away when Ray frowned.

Twirling the straw in her drink, Silvana looked shyly at Ray. "When are you giving up the apartment in Brooklyn?" she asked.

"Give it up? I just bought the entire house, Silvana. I'm kicking the two tenants out, and I'll start remodeling in a few weeks. I'll double the rent. It's a good investment, you'll see."

"What about us?"

He frowned, puzzled. "What about us?"

"Aren't we getting married in April?"

"That's right, April 10," he said.

"We're moving into my apartment, right?"

"That's right! What's bothering you, Silvana?"

"Ray, I don't want to live in Brooklyn."

"Silvana . . . neither do I." He shifted his drink from one hand to the other. In a soothing tone of voice, he said, "Don't get all riled up for nothing. We'll be okay."

She looked at him, puzzled.

"Buying the house has nothing to do with our wedding plans. I bought it for business and sentimental reasons."

"What sentimental reasons?" she said, with a hint of jealousy. "Is there something I should know?"

"Sherlock, there's nothing you don't know already. I spent seven years in that apartment. Besides, it'll help me stay in touch with old friends in the neighborhood."

Pushing her hair behind an ear, she said, "I'm not Sherlock Holmes, but I understand now. When did you decide to buy it?"

"Christmas Eve," he said. The night he found Santo Pellegrino.

When Victor and his girlfriend arrived, Ray stood up to greet them. He saw Silvana, the fashion designer, sizing up the woman's low-cut double-breasted red outfit. He and Victor shook hands. "Victor, I'm glad you could make it. Silvana, this is Nora, Victor's girlfriend. Please sit down."

As the excitement at the restaurant began to build, Marco and Angelo joined the table. Unbeknownst to Nora, Marco sent a Sicilian sign-message to Silvana to take her away from the table for a while. Smiling, Silvana nodded and asked Nora to join her in the powder room.

When the women were out of earshot, Marco stared at Victor and asked, "Why the tail?"

"What's the difference? We couldn't have talked with Silvana present anyhow. Besides, Nora was invited, and I didn't know we were discussing any hot topics tonight."

To stop the bickering, Ray intervened, "Victor's right; I invited Nora. Before they come back, however, let me tell you, Victor, your ex-girlfriend Gina is making trouble for Carlo."

Victor protested, "She never was my girlfriend. I only dated her once. What is she up to now?"

"And what does she have to do with Carlo?" Marco asked.

Reaching for his drink, Ray said, "The only thing I know is that Benito Campo, Gloria's brother, all grown up now, is asking lots of questions."

Concerned, Victor asked, "What's Carlo saying?"

"I haven't heard from him yet."

"I sense trouble," Angelo said.

"May I bring another round of . . .?" the waiter was back, hovering again.

Ray glared the waiter, "Listen, Dick, if you show your stupid face here once more . . . better yet, have someone else serve this table."

When Dick left, everyone, except Victor, burst out laughing.

"Why did you call him dick?" a troubled Victor asked.

Smiling, Ray said, "That's his name. Probably short for Richard."

"Ray, don't presume that sort of thing. Someday, calling a guy a dick could get you in a lot of trouble."

Dismissing Victor's remarks, Ray said, "Don't worry."

Then getting back to business, he asked, "Angelo, how's your deal with the insurance company coming along?"

"The people at Hartford wouldn't take *no* for an answer. They're in love with my credentials. I took a job as a junior construction loan specialist. After a year of training, I'll head my own department. Then, I was promised to head the Northeast Branch."

"What about you, Marco?" Ray asked. "How are you doing on the Hill?"

"I'll tell you," Marco said, "with Lyndon Johnson and Lady Bird in the White House, the word is that Bobby Kennedy and company are out. LBJ hates his guts.

"With Bobby out and the administration in turmoil, we'll position our people in the right places. As for me, I've got a job in the House of Representatives, where I can do the most good."

"I hope so," confident, Ray said. "You sound like a politician already. From now on, we have a bunch of new people coming out of college every year looking for places to go."

He turned to Victor. "How are you doing in California?"

"I'm doing fine," Victor said. "The coast is a place on the go. I'm working on two hot deals. Soon, I'll know enough to decide. In the meantime, I'm doing consulting work for some start-up companies.

"I'll let you know as soon as I decide which deal is best. We'll work things out. I don't think either deal will take much to close."

Ray gave a report on the state of the Class of '56. "I didn't want to take a chance with us all meeting in one place. The others are doing fine. Luca and Paul are setting themselves up nicely in the credit card business.

"That industry is a much larger deal than anyone thought, and growing. I think Don Saverio hit the nail right on the head with that one. By the way, keep an eye on anything that has to do with credit cards. You'll never know what else is lurking out there.

"As for me, let me say that next month I'll start full time at Giglio. I've secured shelf space for the new season in over eight thousand fashion outlets. Through a line of subcontractors, we anticipate going into full production by the middle of next year.

"Since Silvana arrived in New York, she and her staff have worked on new creations and gradually have increased sales, an essential move for a good business foundation. The time has come to get it up to speed."

Watching Silvana making her way back with Nora, Ray said, "Look at her. . . . Everyone is looking at her outfit in awe. I tell you she's good. Can you believe she made that entire outfit at the last moment and almost out of nothing?"

Pressed for time, Ray got back to the business at hand, "Soon I'll hire more office help for back-room operations. Silvana and I will handle marketing with publicists and advertising agents from here. We have secured copyrights and company trademarks.

"Soon, I'm sure I'll need your help. But, for now, let's stop talking business and celebrate the New Year."

The house photographer, a voluptuous young woman, arrived at the table at the same time as Silvana and Nora. Everyone posed for photos.

The new waiter politely asked Silvana if she cared for a fresh drink. "No, thanks," she replied, "but, refill the others, please."

When she asked, "What happened to Dick?" the men laughed. Everyone then turned to the table. It was quite a sight. The table overflowed with platters and bowls filled with dressing, potatoes, gravy, cranberry sauce, vegetables, fruits, and hot rolls. And at the center of the table, a silver tray cradled a golden turkey.

Three buckets of ice held bottles of wine and champagne. Ray sat at one end of the table and Silvana at the other. He surveyed the spread, and then tapped his glass with a knife to signal his approval.

For Ray, the homey feeling did not come from the taste of the food but from the after-meal pleasure of being with his own people. It saddened Ray to see the waiters begin to clear the table at the end of the meal, for it signaled the end of good times. When people gather, a cluttered table is much cozier than an orderly or empty one, he thought. After this sort of dinner, free of table manners, it is a pleasure to reach for another piece of cheese, a stalk of celery, or some other leftover. And it is especially nice to savor that last cup of coffee with good conversation.

The evening galloped toward midnight. With glass in hand and Santo in mind, Ray proposed a toast for better things to come.

The talk turned to the wedding. In keeping with her father's plan, Silvana had moved to Manhattan and adopted Ray's last name. In the world of fashion, people knew her as Silvana Greco.

"Did you set a wedding date yet?" Nora asked.

With a wide smile, Silvana said, "Yes, it's April 10 here at City Hall."

"Why at City Hall?"

Grinning, Ray pierced an olive with a toothpick and said, "Convenience and legality. The marriage license will get the Immigration Department off Silvana's back and the low-key ceremony hopefully will keep things quiet."

"What about the church?" Nora asked, somewhat puzzled. "You're Catholics . . . are you not?"

"It has nothing to do with us being Catholics. As I said, the whole ceremony is at City Hall."

With wedding questions out of the way, Silvana walked around the table and faced Ray squarely. She teased, "Mister, when you hear our tune, you and I are dancing."

"Yes, ma'am!" Ray grinned.

Victor laughed, plucking Nora from her chair and heading for the dance floor. "You had that coming."

When the band played "Love Is a Many-Splendored Thing," a jubilant Silvana rushed Ray to the floor. He folded her into his arms. They danced to one tune after another.

A few hours into the New Year, with the party behind them and a new resolve, Ray walked Silvana back to her apartment for another celebration.

This time, although the temperature had dropped several degrees since their earlier walk, they felt no cold.

16

That infamous August 31 changed the exciting life of eighteen-year-old Gina Campo into one of seclusion, despair, and fear. Since the incident, she had refused to speak about her ordeal with anyone. Today, seven years after she witnessed the slaughter of Gloria and Stefano, she agreed to tell all to Benito Campo, Gloria's brother.

The sheer curtains in the living room window dimmed the afternoon sunlight. Benito, an energetic young man, resembling a soccer player, with a round face and bright eyes, sat at one end of the sofa waiting for Gina patiently.

Gina entered the room, a scarf wrapped around her head and framing her worn and ashy face. She sat at the other end of the sofa and pulled her skirt tight over her knees.

Benito looked at her and politely asked, "How're you doing?"

"I never thought I'd do this," she said. "It's not going to be easy. . . . Please, bear with me, Benito."

He nodded his approval.

She stared at the far wall. Then, teary-eyed, she told her story:

"My date with Victor wasn't for another hour. All day, I counted every minute, waiting. When I grew impatient, I walked to the bottom of the hill to wait for him. If I had waited a little longer, I would've missed the whole thing.

"I was standing by the shack's railing, and night had fallen, when I heard faint voices coming from a little way up the hill. I moved within earshot. From across the bungalow behind a knee-high wall, I watched the ordeal unfold.

"When Stefano pushed the window open, I guess to let some breeze in, I saw an unframed single bed and a wicker chair. Gloria was in the chair.

"Stefano, Don Saverio's older son, was only twenty-six. He was handsome. He had a strong-boned face with a head of black hair parted near the middle. Stefano was easy going but also smart. In fact, he had a brilliant mind. Like his sister, he was anti-tradition, and he didn't approve of his family's business.

"All summer, as a friend, he had counseled Gloria who had fallen out of love with his brother, Carlo.

"Stefano was leaning against the window facing Gloria. I saw Gloria get up and walk toward him. I heard her say, 'Stefano, I don't know how to thank you for listening.'

"'That's okay, I'm glad to help.' Stefano said."

"Gloria was distraught. She said, 'Carlo told me to get an abortion or else.'

"Stefano reassured her. He said, 'Don't even think of it. We'll find a solution.'

"Gloria nodded with tears in her eyes. 'That's well and good. . . . In this town, with a baby and no husband . . .'

"Gloria pulled a letter from her skirt pocket, waved it under Stefano's nose, and said, 'My cousin from Roma wrote me. She moved there with her husband to look for a job two years ago. She wants me to come there; she's very excited about it. She even found me a temporary job.'

"Stefano said, 'Well, that's a start.'

"Gloria said, 'My cousin talked it over with her husband. I know it will break my brother's heart, but he can join me after the baby is born. For now, the baby comes first. Benito will understand. Please don't tell Carlo about Roma. I want him to leave me alone.'

"'Don't worry; you go ahead,'" Stefano said in an effort to soothe her. 'If I have to, I'll speak with my father. He's a reasonable man.'

"Gloria doubted it. She said, 'I don't think so. Your father, like your brother, is more concerned about family honor than my problem."

"'You might be right,' Stefano admitted.

"'I know I'm right," Gloria said. 'Your brother is not the man he used to be. I don't understand him anymore.'

"Stefano said, 'My brother and I used to share secrets and help each other out. Now, every time I talk to him he looks at me cockeyed and walks away. My father is acting the same. Frankly, I don't know what to make of it.'

"Gloria looked at Stefano, concerned, and said, 'The other night I had this dream of Carlo telling your father that you and I were having an affair. Then, laughing like a wild joker, Carlo made you disappear so he could become the next in line to inherit the kingdom. Your father was dressed as a king with a crown on his head that read: Don Saverio, King of Mafia. The terrifying part was when Carlo managed to push me, your father, and his grandchild into an inferno-like crevasse spewing flames.'

"'Everything makes sense now,' Stefano said. 'Please, Gloria, say no more. Let's get out of here. Tonight is the perfect time. These people are capable of anything. They'll turn on their own mothers, much less a brother or a son.'

"Gloria was terrified. Stefano pushed himself off the window frame and told her, 'Gloria, I'm afraid your dream is an omen. Everything is coming together now. How can Carlo ever think that we're cheating on him? How can he?'

"'He can!' cried Gloria.

"Stefano looked out the window distressed, 'I've got to clear things up with my father before it's too late. Let's get out of here. I think that you, the baby, and I are all in danger. We're in Carlo's way. We must go now.'

"Stefano grabbed her arm and headed for the door but stopped short. There was a noise outside. From where I was hidden behind the wall, I could see two men, shotguns in hand, crouched under the window and two others by the door. Suddenly, Carlo appeared.

"Carlo and two men burst into the room as the others jumped in through the window. They grabbed Stefano. With a single blow, Carlo knocked out Gloria. She fell to the floor. Stefano was struggling and Carlo was shouting, 'You son of a bitch. You've been screwing her all summer long and now you want me to stop? By the time this is over,' pointing the shotgun toward her limp body, 'there will be nothing left for you to screw or take over. Trust me, idiot!'

"Stefano cried, 'Take over? . . . Does Dad know you're here?'

"Carlo said, 'Who in hell needs his permission?'

"Stefano was wrestling to free himself. "You bastard, you planned the whole thing! Why are you doing this? . . . You know how I feel about our family business! . . . You're a degenerate, you're insane . . ."

"Before Stefano could finish his sentence, the man behind him plunged the butt of his shotgun into Stefano's neck with such force that his head bounced back as if dangling from a rubber band.

"They stripped the unconscious Stefano from the waist down and sat him on the wicker chair with his head thrown back. Then they stripped Gloria naked and lay her on the bed.

"Nonchalantly, Carlo thanked the men, "You guys better go. Calatafimi is a long way out. I'll take care of the rest."

"As Carlo waved the men away, the breeze carried the tune of "Jezebel" from the party. I watched Carlo walk back inside the shack. He stared down at Gloria for a moment then spread her legs a little with the tip of the shotgun. He knelt on one knee at the foot of the bed and pushed the double barrel into her vagina. I heard him say, 'Didn't I tell you to get an abortion?' Then he pulled the trigger once. Her body jolted, but did not splatter.

"With shotgun in hand, he rose, walked toward his brother, placed the double barrel in his mouth, and pulled the trigger once more.

"By the second gunshot, the music had stopped playing. Carlo surveyed the scene, placed the shotgun in Stefano's hands, and wiped his own hands clean. He walked calmly back to the party. I collapsed to the ground and cried. I could not believe what I had seen."

With her story told, Gina glanced at Benito. His face was red with rage. He was trying to control himself. He nodded, blinked a few times, gritted his teeth, and looked away.

Tears rolled down Gina's cheeks. "Benito, now the only thing I see in my mind is Gloria and Stefano begging for help. Were they begging for my help? What could I have done? I ran to Victor, and I tried to explain but then I . . . I can't recall."

Gina had gone to Victor but instead of telling him what she had seen, her mind just wanted to forget, to get lost in Victor's lovemaking, to erase the murders of Gloria and Stefano. That was Gina's first and last sexual experience, and she had no recollection of it.

The sun was setting when Benito shut the door behind him, and Gina's anxieties were much relieved for having shared her ordeal with someone.

Sunday afternoons at Piazza Ciullo are what every town square should be, crowded yet peaceful at the same time. Men gather, talking at sidewalk cafés over a cup of coffee. Women rarely participated in this event, for they understood their men, or so they thought. In the early evening, they usually joined their men either to stroll down Main Street or to visit relatives. In short, Sunday afternoons are men's time-outs in Alcamo.

The larger of the two cafés in the *piazza* had eight tables with four chairs at each. The café, with a patio-like setting, was in full view of the crowd. Carlo Cremona and two of his men sat at one table facing the square.

Benito Campo had a plan, and his investment in informers had panned out. He was disappointed, though, that only two of the four men who had helped murder his sister were present. Still, he entered the café from the side door and came out the front walking behind a waiter. When he reached Carlo's table, he raised his gun, and before they could run for cover, shot one man and then the other. It all happened in the blink of an eye. Ignoring the terrified customers, the shocked crowd in the *piazza*, and the two men slumped in their chairs, he pointed the gun at Carlo's head.

Carlo begged, "Benito, no! It . . . it wasn't me. I loved Gloria. Your sister was . . ."

"You lying bastard!" he shouted. Then he pulled the trigger.

Benito walked calmly around the table, knocked Carlo to the floor, and kicked him, seeking signs of life. He stared at the crowd blindly, raised the gun to his temple, and pulled the trigger a final time.

Although his deed was justifiable, as a man of honor, Benito Campo knew he was doomed to die. And for that, people revere him still.

17

At New York City Hall, the chapel for the two o'clock ceremony was ready. The justice of the peace was Jewish, and the best man was Irish. When the clerk called in the Greco party, the only guests present were Sergio Bruno and his wife and Pat O'Brien and his girlfriend. Sergio was Giglio's controller, and Pat was the company's vice president of marketing.

At that moment, Silvana and Ray were stuck in a traffic jam on the Williamsburg Bridge. That morning, they had gone to Brooklyn to pick up Ray's mother and the other guests. The party rode in two limousines: The first carried Silvana, Ray, his mother, and her new husband, Sal. The other carried Victor, Nora, Angelo, and Marco.

The thing Ray hated most—being late—was happening on his own wedding day. Don Saverio and his wife, owing to Carlo's death, had excused themselves. Ray knew better—Don Saverio would never venture outside Sicily.

Since Carlo's death, Ray had taken over Mafia's activities in America—the good and the bad, the legal and the illegal, the dismantling of the old families and the organizing of the new.

The limousines were at a standstill in the westbound lane. Looking out over the city, Sal wondered aloud, "Who would think to create this chaos of skyscrapers, streets, elevated roads, and bridges? God must have been asleep when they did it."

He continued, "And the smog. You can barely see the Brooklyn Bridge."

Ray sat in the tight quarters of the limo facing his mother and Sal. Although he favored their marriage and respected Sal as family, for Ray had grown up with Sal at his side since his father's death, he wondered why his mother had traded a life in New York City near him for one in Alcamo with Sal. And then he thought:

Who am I to understand women? Much less my own mother?

Envisioning the man who once sat on a mound cracking stones, Ray couldn't accept Sal as his mother's lover and business partner. No matter how much he liked Sal, he found Sal's gestures of intimacy toward his mother repulsive.

The fifty-year-old Sal Rocca was not, nor had he ever been, a handsome man. On the contrary, he was a burly fellow of medium height with a square, sun-hardened face, kind eyes, and a flattened nose that seemed to hold no bone. His thick black hair was greased to keep it from springing up in all directions, and his bushy mustache went lopsided when he smiled. In spite of it all, because he was soft spoken and had an easy informal manner, Sal had sex appeal.

Through no fault of his, Sal had lost his business In the aftermath of World War II. Idle and out of work, he found an opportunity in the Greco Materials & Contracting company.

He started as a pieceworker, and because he was good at what he did, he quickly gained the confidence of the Greco family. After Luciano's death, Sal's loyalty to the family and his knowledge of business placed him at the head of the firm.

Francesca, a few years younger than Sal, was an educated and attractive woman. All things about her seemed strange to her son now. She had pushed away the self-inflicted layers of suffering that had crept upon her ever since Luciano's death. She no longer looked so weary. Now she revealed her deep beauty when she smiled.

Ray was trying to recollect when he last saw his mother smile that way, but the stop and go of the traffic broke his thoughts.

Looking at Sal, Ray held Silvana's hand.

"Ray, we've been here only a day," Sal smiled at him. "With the exception of the spiral staircase in your apartment, so far I like everything. But just because I like it doesn't mean I'd live here. For a small-town person, it's too much. I'm sure I'm speaking for your mother as well. If you were thinking of us moving here, who would run the gravel business back home?"

Cars and trucks packed the bridge. Silvana looked ahead and said, "If this traffic doesn't move soon, we'll have to walk off this bridge and get a cab."

"Don't worry, Silvana, Pat is a good talker," Ray grinned at her, unconcerned. "By now, I bet he made a deal with the judge to wait until midnight if he has to. . . . I know better, trust me."

Looking back for the other limo, Ray noticed it was only a bumper away. Then turning back to Sal, he asked, "How's the crusher working out?"

Before Sal could answer, Francesca intervened with a wide smile, "Sal is a genius. Right from the start, the crusher was a remarkable sight. Trucks back up to the ramp and dump large stones into a chute. A pair of hydraulic jaws splits them into smaller pieces allowing them to free-fall into another chamber where they're crushed into gravel. A conveyer collects and sorts it all into three different bins according to size."

Flabbergasted, Ray said, "Ma, you sound like an engineer. Since when have you even watched a hammer swing?"

She looked at Sal, smiled again, and with a sense of contentment, said, "Now, thanks to Sal, I do much more than watch. We spend a lot of time together at the site and other places."

Ray was taken aback by his mother's candid remarks.

Sal said, "Look, Ray, in Sicily the days of hand labor are gone. For my money, a mobile crusher is the way to go. We can set one up wherever gravel is used. What do you think?"

The traffic jam eased off and began to move. "It makes sense," Ray admitted. "You'd better start working on it as soon as you get back to Alcamo before someone else jumps on it.

"Also, start thinking about ready-mixed concrete. They're not going to mix concrete by hand much longer either."

Under Ray's watchful eye, Sal smiled and squeezed Francesca's hand. Ray shook his head and moved closer to Silvana.

At the foot of the bridge, the limousines pulled straight ahead onto Delancey Street then turned left toward City Hall.

It was three o'clock when they walked into the chapel. Twenty minutes later, Ray and Silvana were on their way home as Mr. and Mrs. Ray Greco.

It was two days after the wedding. To spend some time alone with his mother, Ray arranged for Sal to visit a ready-mixed concrete plant in Queens. He knew that it would take Sal the better part of the day, since Sal would likely check every nut and bolt there.

Mother and son sat on the sofa, enjoying the moment in silence. Impatient, Ray finally asked, "Ma, what do you think of this place?"

"Son, I want to stay on solid ground. The squeaking of wood as I walk through the apartment gives me the weird sensation of falling through the floor with every step I take.

"That stupid staircase of yours, if you climb it fast, it'll get you all bruised up. The other day, if it weren't for that card table by the window, I would've dropped a tray full of coffee cups and cookies.

"You'd better replace it with a wider marble staircase and take that one where it belongs, to some old theater's backstage."

Ray listened to every word she spoke in awe. He was satisfying seven years of hunger for motherly attention. No matter what she said or how she said it, he knew she meant no harm. They were words of wisdom that only he could understand and no other could deliver.

"Ma, the problem isn't the wooden floors or the spiral staircase. The problem is that marble is cheap in Sicily, depriving you of the warmth of carpeted floors and wooden walls.

"As for the spiral staircase, it came with the house. When I remodel the apartment, it will be the first to go," he reassured her. "Anyhow, how's Grandpa?"

"Your grandfather is a great man. I'll be indebted to him always. He made me realize that my self-inflicted sorrow didn't only hurt me, but those who loved me as well. . . . That's a lesson I'll never forget."

"How's Sal treating you?"

His mother patted his hand and said, "Calm down, son. I noticed how your face turned red when Sal held my hand. Although no one can fill your father's void, Sal is a caring, gentle man who fulfills me now. You also must let go of the past and pursue your dream as I did."

Ray rose and walked to the window. Looking up past the rooftops, he anxiously said, "It's not that easy, Ma. I don't know what it is, but something blinds me when I think of Dad's fate. I guess I loved Dad so much that I could kill if I have to."

Deep in thought, she looked at him from the sofa and wisely said nothing. His mother did not want to spoil her moment with her son, and he didn't want to spoil his time with her. He glanced back at her with a soft smile and said, "Ma, I'll try my best. . . . I promise. I love Sal. I've nothing but fond memories of him. Dad trusted him and so do I. . . . I guess it's the blood rebelling . . . I'll get used to it. . . . I will."

Ray returned to the sofa near his mother, but he was restless. After a little while he kissed her forehead, got up, and walked back to the window. Moments later, he felt his mother beside him. She rested her head against his arm and peered out the window, too. Then she squeezed his hand and said, "Now that you've asked about me, how are you doing? Or shall I ask, what are your plans as a married man?"

"After you leave, the first thing I'll do is take Silvana on a honeymoon. She wanted to be here during your stay."

Ray knew his mother still worried about Silvana being Don Saverio's daughter. She did not trust that family, but she was coming around on the subject of Silvana. Grinning, she said, "She's a good girl, isn't she? What about after the honeymoon?"

"Silvana's been working hard at building up Giglio, but she's agreed to slow down to build a family," he said proudly. "We want at least two children. We figured by the time she's needed back at work, the children will be in middle school. She can still design from home."

"What home are you talking about?" his mother asked, puzzled. Ray knew his mother wished he would settle back in Sicily and take up writing again.

"There's this place at the tip of Long Island that reminds us of Alcamo Marina. Visiting friends there last month, we found a nice house for sale. To make a long story short, Silvana fell in love with it and we bought it."

Before she could ask more about the new house, he said, "Not a word to Silvana, please. She wants to drive you there and show and tell you all about it before you leave."

"How far is this place?"

"Quite a way, almost a three-hour ride."

"You'll spend your entire life on the road."

"No, I won't; I'll be going mostly on weekends. During the week, I'll stay here or at the office. I'll be okay, really. It's only for the summer."

Concerned, his mother asked, "Does this house have a backyard?"

"Does it have a backyard? . . . Wait until you see it. The house sits on a large fenced lot with an enclosed swimming pool and a veranda facing the ocean. It's the perfect summer place, you'll see. The kids will love it!"

Francesca, somewhat satisfied regarding the welfare of her future grandchildren, looked at him and narrowed her eyes. Without warning she asked, "What about Santo Pellegrino?"

Astounded, Ray asked, "Who did you say?"

"You heard me!" sternly the mother said. "I know how you and your grandfather feel. But I say to both of you let bygones be bygones and get on with life.

"Son, if you want to enjoy your family, you have to let it go. We're not that kind of people. Besides, we don't know the whole truth, and I don't think we'll ever know. Time will take care of things."

Ray said nothing; he refused to hear his mother's words. He only saw the inscription on his father's headstone and heard the promise he made in his heart to revenge him:

Luciano Greco lives through his son Ray.

On a bright spring morning, Silvana drove Francesca to Long Island. The apparent objective was for Silvana to show Francesca the house and for Ray to visit with Sal. The true objective, however, was for the two women to strengthen their relationship and for Ray and Sal to sign off on ongoing business.

Driving through the streets of Brooklyn, Ray wondered how his mother knew about Santo:

She hasn't changed, I guess. Like all mothers, they always know somehow. It wasn't Grandpa. He wouldn't tell a woman.

Upon arriving at his destination, Ray automatically parked the car on what he thought was the lawful side, but it was Saturday and no parking rules applied.

Admiring the wax job the neighbor and his son were giving to their '57 Chevy, he approached them. Smiling, he looked at the kid, "How old are you?

"Nine."

"Do you know how to write?"

With little quivers around his lips ready to break into a smile the kid rolled his eyes, "Of course!"

"Don't do like I did. Give your father a rest, and don't forget those whitewall tires. Do a good job, and when I come down, I'll give you a buck."

Excited, the kid said, "Wow!"

The father reached for the pail and the kid for the scrubbing brush.

With a deal made, Ray went up the stoop and into the apartment. Smelling coffee, he went downstairs making a rare appearance in the kitchen. Sal was brewing espresso with a percolator. He looked at Sal and said, "Why didn't you ask? For God's sakes, I've got an espresso machine. That's not coffee. That's tinted water."

"It'll satisfy the intent," Sal said with a smile. "If it weren't for that stupid staircase forcing you down here, you would've said: Gee, it tastes good. When it comes to taste, I know you well, my friend."

With coffees in hand, they made their way up the stairs to the card table and sat opposite from each other.

In his late twenties, Ray was no longer the little boy who used to tap Sal's shoulder for a toy; he was the head of Don Saverio's enterprises in America. Sal was no longer a laborer chopping stone; he was the head of the Greco family's enterprises in Sicily. Both men stared at each other, waiting. Finally, Ray confided in the only man he trusted. "The night before Christmas . . . I saw Santo."

"Did he see you?"

"He might have and if he did, so what . . . it makes no difference."

"Your grandfather will be delighted to hear that," Sal said, pleased. "Since Santo left Sicily, no matter how we tried, we couldn't get a lead on him."

"How could you? Santo entered the United States with an illegal passport under the alias Mickey Argento, and later picked up the nickname Mickey the Cat."

Sal looked at Ray puzzled.

"I had Marco at the FBI check his passport. It was issued a month before my father was killed. We can surmise that Don Saverio set him up here.

"Back then, only a few heads of families knew about him, the more unknown the hit man the better."

Sal nodded. "It all makes sense. Now it's time for you to step aside and let me handle this guy."

Ray looked out the window, shook his head slightly searching for words. Then seeing the sparkling whitewall tires and watching the kid playing stickball with his father, for a moment, he imagined himself as a little boy playing with his own father.

Ray turned to Sal and emphatically said, "No! It cannot be. This is my deal."

"Ray! You must be joking. There's too much at stake here. You never did this sort of thing."

"Never did, but I promised I would. There will be no other way. It's final," a resolute Ray said.

"Okay, I won't argue with you. When?"

"Not yet. Before I do anything, I've got to link Santo to the man who hired him."

Puzzled, Sal asked, "Good, how do we do it?"

With a smirk on his face, Ray said, "Trust me, I know how. Before we make a move, we must do a few things."

"Ray, what do you want me to do?"

"For some strange reason, as recently as last December, I was hoping to find my father's murder justifiable," Ray said with regret. "I wanted to believe that the man who ordered the killing was following some rule of *omertà*.

"Not so much so that I could quit, but to liberate the man who I think hired Santo, Don Saverio himself, perhaps as a way of paying my dues for something . . . I don't really know.

"Perhaps it's because I'm beginning to believe in the New Enterprise. . . . I don't know.

"Or maybe it's because there's something I don't know," Ray shook his head, baffled. "Still, I have to do it."

Concerned, Sal said, "That's what your grandfather feared most when you were growing up. But he never lost confidence in you. He always said: He's a Greco . . . leave him alone and he'll come through."

With pride, Ray said, "My grandpa's right. When I first spotted Santo, sitting only a couple of feet away from me, blood rushed to my head. At that moment the only justifiable thing I could think of was to slaughter the son of a bitch right then and there with my bare hands."

Sal stared at him.

"Sal, acting on impulse is a mistake," Ray said, wisely. "I want to hear it all from Santo himself."

"How are you going to do that?" asked Sal, still puzzled.

Ray looked out the window once more, paused for a second, and said, "We'll hire Santo to kill me."

Almost laughing, Sal said, "Get out of here! You're crazy!"

"No. I'm not!" Ray said. "I am dead serious."

"We're dealing with a pro, Ray. It's too dangerous. Can't you think of another way?"

"No, there is no other way. I told you already. This is my deal. Everything will work out fine."

Ray could see Sal clenching his teeth.

"If Don Saverio was the man who put the contract on my father, then Santo believing he's getting another contract from him will take this one also. Only this time, it will be his last contract as well as the end for Don Saverio.

"When you go back next week, drive out to Calatafimi and see Don Nardo," Ray said in a commanding voice. "Ask him for an introduction to Don Mario at the social club here in Bushwick. Tell him you want Don Mario to put a contract on a man from Brooklyn and you want him to use someone that's not connected with us."

"What if he tells Don Saverio?"

"Sal, he won't," patiently Ray explained. "He knows I run the operations here. Besides, he thinks Santo is working out of the West Coast. Don Nardo will only be concerned with his cut.

"Put the money on the table first. He needs lots of cash these days, and he's indebted to Don Saverio. Once he takes the money, although he shouldn't, he'll never make mention of it to anyone, much less Don Saverio."

"Who do I say I am?" Sal asked.

"I'll make sure he'll be expecting you. By then, he won't care who you are as long as you give him the cash and say: Ray sent me.

"You see, Don Mario will not call Santo unless Don Nardo approves the contract first. And don't worry," in an effort to soothe Sal, he added. "I can't afford my mother widowed again."

When Ray left the apartment, the kid was sitting on the bottom step. He looked up at Ray. Ray reached into his pocket and gave the kid a dollar. "A deal is a deal," Ray said with a smile. "From now on, if you want to make more bucks, the only thing you have to do is watch out for strangers looking at my place.

"If they drive a car, write down their license plate number and give it to me the next time you see me. Above all, say nothing and don't take orders from anyone else."

"It's a deal!" the kid said, running across street.

18

In 1964, Lyndon Johnson was pushing the Civil Rights Bill through Congress. He also declared war on poverty, and the Vietnam War was on the horizon. During that time, thanks to Bobby Kennedy leaving the post of attorney general, investigations into the mob dropped dramatically.

A month after his wedding, Ray laid out a business plan for Giglio and offered it for review to his two top executives, Pat and Sergio, with a copy to Silvana.

In the conference room, Pat O'Brien, was doodling on a pad and occasionally glancing at Ray. Pat was undecided as to whether to reject Ray's plan flat-out or tactfully. Somewhat resolute, he stopped doodling, looked up at Sergio then at Ray, and said, "Ray, I'm afraid your marketing plan might be too bold for the times."

Pat was thirty-two and a handsome man of medium height. He had blond hair, blue eyes, and a short jaw line. Thanks to his boyish smile he did not look a day over twenty-two. His upbeat speech and candid charm made him a great negotiator and a smooth part-time lover. A Harvard graduate, he was most confident at his job when dressed casually.

Ray discounted Pat's statement and looked at Sergio Bruno.

Sergio, general manager, was pushing thirty. He was the kind of executive corporate America relished: a Yale graduate dressed in a perfectly tailored dark blue suit. He wore a crisp white shirt and a dark striped tie that matched his black hair. His tall, slim body said, "I'm here for the long run, no matter what." Contrary to his body language, his granite face, brown eyes, and slanted smile revealed nothing he did not want you to know.

"Ray, why are you looking at me?" Sergio asked. "I told you about Pat already. . . . Frankly, I agree with him. America, for that matter the world, is not ready for a fashion explosion. I say let's take a more prudent course at a slower pace . . . what do you say?"

Pat turned his pad around, grinned, and said, "Look, Ray, what concerns me most is that we might lose it all and for what?

"Maybe, if we get lucky, sales will increase. That'll hasten overgrowth, which leads to chaotic production. Again, for the life of me I can't see the hurry."

Ray twirled a stub-pencil between his thumb and forefinger, pursing his lips. Then looking at the two of them he contained a smile.

Pat was doodling again, with a light smirk on his face.

Sergio looked ready to debate the next speaker.

Two more twirls of the stub-pencil and Ray broke the silence, "I suggest that we start looking at Giglio as a fast-growing company. The sooner we get in that mind-set the sooner we'll be able to handle its ups and downs."

Pat and Sergio exchanged glances but said nothing.

Ray said, "Face it, guys, no one's saying it's going to be easy. There comes a time when we must decide. For Giglio, this is that time. I believe in this plan and so does Silvana."

"Frankly, the numbers are too optimistic for me to accept," Sergio shook his head.

"Guys," Ray said. "It's a balancing act, cause and effect, if you will. In a business plan, positive numbers are always interconnected to equal positive efforts by executioners or the plan collapses."

"Then, why not lay it all out for us?" Sergio asked.

"Sergio, that's why we're here," Ray said patiently. "It would have taken me a couple of hundred more pages just to make a dent on the philosophy and the strategy behind each number you two are questioning." Ray paused. "Had I done that, I'm sure . . . I would've lost you somewhere in boredom hall."

If there was a belief that Don Saverio had instilled in Ray, it was in creation and acceptance. He did that while admiring nature's colors with Ray on an autumn afternoon: Watercolors, son, that's all it takes—a good base and a few colors.

Ray's plan had that and more. It had a good company, Silvana's successful creations, and the acceptance of at least one believer, Ray himself, the promoter.

"Guys, my contention is that there are no bad or good times for fashion, nor are there ugly or beautiful creations. There are only trends and styles with affordable price tags for the times."

With absolute certainty, Ray continued, "For the good of the company, let me reinforce a vital point: fashion is created—not demanded—and we are the creators.

"Since the masses will follow the few who set the trend, they will accept it most when it's associated with stylish people."

Ray could see that his comments were causing the two to readjust their thoughts. Pat stared at Ray, "Do you think that buying stylish products will become fashionable?"

"Buying stylish products has always been fashionable with the few. Our job is to attract the masses."

"The way you put it," Sergio said, "we only need to dress those few trendsetters with our creations and have the media, if not the trendsetters themselves, tell our story. Are those your thoughts?"

"Exactly," Ray said. "We'll share our story with the masses through every billboard and television ad money can buy. We will show and tell—on a massive scale. And do you know why I am so enthusiastic? Because it's your job, and I'm sure you two will do fine."

At twenty-eight, Ray made the sale of his life. Pat and Sergio were becoming his best workhorses to drive Giglio to the top.

Pat stood up and pounded on the table, suddenly animated, "You know what? This plan will work. Words and images associated with who's who will do it. I tell you it will; I can see those ads already."

"What do you think, Sergio?"

"Ray, based on your plan, it's the way it has to go," Sergio said with confidence. "Madison Avenue's experts make that happen every hour of the day. I believe what Pat sees is a mixture of direct and subliminal messages through ads."

Satisfied with the outcome of the meeting, Ray's tone became conciliatory. "I'm glad you two agree.

Above all, always remember: never get cute with words unless you intend to deliver on them. If you do, you'll be right back where you started from or worse. You can't fool people with hollow jingles. They have a funny way of getting even . . . trust me."

With the controller hat on now and to ascertain his position, Sergio asked, "To get it clear, based on the theory we've talked about today, Giglio will expand its operations despite forecasts of bad times ahead?"

Ray nodded with confidence. "That's the spirit, guys."

Pat looked at Ray and said, "I'm on board. Where do we start?"

Sergio got up to stretch his legs. He looked around the room then at Ray and asked, "Is Silvana on board?"

"I'm glad you brought that up," Ray said. "As with all creative people, they lose interest when they can't extend their talent to the fullest. Although she's involved in the business, she's an artist first and the business cannot afford to lose her talent. It's our job to give her the room to be as creative as she wants."

Pat nodded, satisfied.

The men took a short break, grabbed cups of coffee, and returned to the meeting refreshed and eager to continue. After all, they were spinning the plans to take Giglio to the top of the fashion industry.

"Now that we have agreed on how to expand the company," Ray said. "I want to touch on an interesting subject. Because the road to the top can get bumpy, I've thought of how to smooth it out beforehand. It deals with our decision-making process.

"From now on, we'll hold our meetings in this room twice a week—Tuesdays and Thursdays. In between meetings, we must refrain from discussing pending topics between ourselves and, needless to say, with others."

Pat and Sergio exchanged glances, somewhat puzzled.

Ray went on, "I know what you're thinking. But I have discovered that when faced with a difficult question, I get a better answer if I sleep on it for a night or two. When I act hastily, it costs me, at times dearly.

"So relax, as decision makers, the company deserves the best from us—and that is clear, calculated, and unrestrained decisions."

When Ray was called away by a phone call, Pat and Sergio discussed this new turn of events.

"I hate to admit it," Pat said, "but the man is right."

"I know he is, Pat. Whenever I confront a tough question, within a couple of days, my brain dishes out the best answer. The funny thing is that I never know when it will pop up, but it always does when I least expect it."

"Sergio, what do you do when you get that magic answer in the middle of night?" a concerned Pat asked.

"You see this?" Sergio asked, pointing to his shirt pocket. "I always carry a pen and a folded sheet of paper. At bedtime they go from here onto the night table."

"Sergio, I'll bet that's what writers do to record their thoughts and observations when they strike."

"I didn't know it was so ingrained in Ray," Sergio said. "Once, Silvana referred to his writing passion, but never again."

"What happened?" Pat asked.

"I don't really know, Pat, for some reason, he put his writing career on hold and never mentioned it again. Maybe his newfound business—Giglio—serves him better."

When Ray returned, the trio worked on a plan to raise venture capital for their upcoming budgets.

Giglio needed money to market in the States and abroad. Thanks to Silvana's zeal for new creations, Giglio was a jewel of a company ready to sparkle in its own world.

Ray signed off on the final business plan, although he had some reservations.

Addressing his two top executives, Ray said, "I want to remind you that besides commitment and money, what makes a business plan successful are price, quality, and service—with price being first. Giglio Enterprises has it all and more."

As part of his workload, Ray reserved Wednesdays and Fridays for Mafia affairs; Mondays for planning the week ahead; Saturdays and Sundays strictly were for family; and, as scheduled, Tuesdays and Thursdays were for Giglio.

To fit the new plan, Ray remodeled the offices. He engraved the top halves of the two glass doors facing the elevator with a lily—*giglio*—that filled each pane.

On the far wall of the lobby, a neon sign read *Giglio Enterprises.* The décor invited visitors to trust in the future of the business.

To left of the lobby, he built a conference room. It held a dozen CEOs and their entourages. Twenty-four red leather chairs encircled the massive mahogany table. The room had state-of-the-art recording devices.

To the right of the lobby, unaltered, stood the so-called Steam Room, where they hashed out strategies in private.

19

Pat was getting things ready for a meeting with the CEOs of six apparel manufacturers. These were the first and only manufacturers he had met on his first recruiting effort. Pat also had arranged for the shooting of several commercials and the printing of a dozen different ads.

It was ten minutes to one o'clock, and Sergio was still checking the business plan. Gabriella, the receptionist, welcomed everyone into the conference room.

At one o'clock, Ray and Silvana entered the room. A large screen on the wall showed a sensuous couple holding hands on a breezy Irish hillside in springtime. They were dressed in clothes of a style never seen before. It was the latest haute couture collection designed by Silvana. At the bottom of the screen a single line read: Giglio, the Future and Beyond.

The business plan was to create and promote clothing from casual to formal and sportswear for men and women. It also included accessories such as wristwatches, chains, rings, and earrings. Other items were shoes, purses, belts, wallets, luggage, and briefcases as Don Saverio had suggested.

To fund the advertising budget, the investors would get a ten-year exclusive right to produce Giglio's products at a preset markup over cost.

Pat explained the advantages in hiring untainted spokespersons. Sergio outlined the economics, and Ray discussed the overall strategy.

The products needed time to resonate with the consumer. With that conceptual timetable, they all agreed to give the company a dynamic look by hiring fresh models rather than overworked celebrities. It was also cheaper.

The meeting went smoother than expected.

With the last ads to be aired in the fall and scores more to be posted on billboards everywhere, as well as countless worldwide outlets lining up to sell the new merchandise, Giglio's team enticed the six leading manufacturers to invest in the largest fashion campaign ever undertaken.

The manufacturers would fund the company for all the advertising and manufacturing dollars it would need, with other manufacturers scheduled to join in the venture.

The conference table looked like a City Hall records counter, with all sorts of papers spread about and pens scratching names on one dotted line after another. Signing the last agreement, a CEO said, "Mr. Greco, I want you to know that on Mr. Cremona's assurance alone . . ."

"Excuse me, mister who?"

"Mr. Saverio Cremona, of course . . . as I was saying, all of us were very much ready to go along with your deal even though we thought it was a bloody risk.

"After today's presentation, however, we feel confident in your abilities to lead the company. You're a bunch of brave lads. I'm sure our venture will be profitable."

After each CEO filed out, nodding and shaking hands, Pat and Sergio retreated to their offices.

Ray stared at Silvana speechless, "Can you imagine his audacity? Under the guise of legal money, your father secured himself a nice fat deal. And I fell for it! I can't believe I did."

"My father is a clever man. Guess what dawned on me? He gets a cut from his two brothers' businesses also. The funny part is they don't even know it.

"I believe that greed wipes every bit of decency out of a man," Silvana said about her father. "You're right, it's incredible, but I don't think he means any harm."

Ray was not so sure. Past words rushed through his mind:

Tonight I've settled the score with my brother. Trust no one . . . not even your mother. Look for a man named Santo when you get to Brooklyn.

At this moment, the only thing Ray was certain of was that Don Saverio was using him as a pawn in a game he did not know existed. He wished he could walk away. For all he knew, Don Saverio could have owned all the six companies that invested in Giglio and financed the entire deal himself.

Suddenly, he realized why Don Saverio had earmarked those particular six companies as—must call—on the list of prospects.

As painful as it was for Ray to admit, he doubted Don Saverio was any longer the man aiming at reforming Mafia. In that moment, to him, Don Saverio became a greedy business tycoon no different from the world's worst or the other heads of Mafia he claimed to despise.

Still angry, he ventured to think that Don Saverio might have shielded himself by placing at least a ten-year financial grip on the company.

Analyzing what he knew, at first Ray thought that it was greed. What made him uneasy was that every time he thought it was greed, his inner voice told him he was wrong. The apparent facts subdued that voice, however, taking him into a never-ending cycle of speculations.

Disappointed as he was when he first doubted his father's accident, feeling betrayed, Ray sought to understand Don Saverio's secret meetings back in Sicily.

To escape the world of Mafia for a while, he thought, Don Saverio allowed his business associates to address him as mister, but only behind closed doors.

Also behind closed doors, Don Saverio conceived the plan Ray was yet to discover. Perhaps, Don Saverio was suspicious and planning a defense.

Disillusioned, Ray and Silvana each needed time alone to sort things out.

Silvana called on Sergio and Pat to walk her to the train station. She arrived at Montauk Point before nightfall.

20

Two days after the meeting, on a late Saturday afternoon, Ray caught up with Silvana.

Ray had thought over the entire deal and settled for the most convenient solution. His new attitude was:

Business is business . . . and as long as it stays that way, I must treat it as dog-eat-dog business and get on with life.

At present, Ray's challenge was to comfort Silvana, get her career back on track, and hold her to her mother-to-be promise.

They sat in the dining room. With both elbows planted on the table and arms-crossed, she was staring at a bowl of fruit.

"Silvana, I've thought the whole thing over."

"It wasn't worth my time . . . it stinks!"

"Look at me, please . . . I know it stinks, but we have to consider the future. Regardless of whose funds they are, the entire marketing plan revolves around your creations and my know-how to run the company—not on their scam."

Troubled, she looked at him and nodded.

Satisfied, Ray said, "I had the attorney look at the agreements, and everything is proper and legal."

"I've no problem with your thinking, Ray, but why?"

"It's tradition."

"I don't think so, but if you say so, that's fine by me," she said, disgusted.

"Silvana, look at it this way," Ray explained. "Investors always put some form of a strong hold on the company they invest in, at least until they get their money back. That's the way these things work.

"What hurt is that your father put a squeeze on us behind our backs and with a smile."

She snapped off a small cluster of grapes, "Why did he do this? I tell you, Ray, he has something up his sleeve. And whether we like it or not, if we're not alert, someday we'll pay a price."

In his heart, he knew she was right. Still, he tried to reassure his wife, "Don't forget who controls the company. Buying your creations, people are giving you their stamp of approval and not your father.

"The way I see it, if we're good at what we do, we can always raise money. Silvana, relax and let me worry about the financial scheme."

"Didn't we make a deal with my father before Carlo was killed?" she asked.

"Yes, you and I own and manage Giglio with no strings attached. Carlo gets the other enterprises. If we need money, we'll ask. Your father gets twenty-five percent of the profits."

"That's all well and good, Ray. I'm sure he'll never go back on the numbers. What bothers me is why he reneged on no strings attached?

"Again, Ray, that might be trivial in the scheme of things, but I don't think so."

She got up and started clearing the table.

Ray's latest revelation was that Don Saverio had put more than a ten-year insurance policy on his life by controlling the finances. If Don Saverio vanished, so would the investors. Confronted with that reality and burning with the desire to avenge his father, Ray wanted to dispose of Don Saverio at once.

Greed, however, made Ray think otherwise. If Santo proved the killing unjustifiable, then to protect Giglio, Silvana, and his future family, the revenge had to wait.

At least until it was convenient.

21

To settle the score with Santo before the traditional August 31 and to keep Giglio's business plan working, Ray and Sal had to get things moving.

Ray had secured a building permit to alter the apartments and scheduled Sal's return to Brooklyn. This time Sal would not stay at Ray's house, for there was only one bedroom usable and Ray used it for Friday night stopovers to Montauk Point.

The people from the ready-mixed concrete plant Sal was visiting offered him a place in Queens. Sal, who had an innate suspicion of hotel registers, took them up on the offer.

Watching through the airplane window, Sal sensed the smog hovering over the city. On the final approach, a metallic voice came through the loudspeakers: "Welcome to JFK International Airport. The New York weather is in the upper nineties and humid."

Sal went through customs and then directed a cab to a diner east of the airport. At the end of the short ride, he tapped the cabdriver's shoulder with a twenty-dollar bill folded lengthwise. Pointing at a parking space, he asked the cabdriver to wait there for a short while.

Since Ray left Sicily, the hunt for Santo had been his priority. All other activities were to be temporary until he had concluded his hunting expedition and avenged his father. Except for Sal, no one was privy to his plan.

Sal walked two cars over, opened the passenger door, and slid next to Ray.

"How was the flight?"

Huffing and puffing, Sal said, "The flight was okay. How in hell you guys take this smog is beyond me."

"You get used to it. . . . Here," Ray said, turning the air to max. "This is a smog-free car. Air conditioners in cars are becoming a must-have . . . enjoy it."

As Sal labored to loosen his collar, Ray asked, "How's Don Nardo?"

"These damned ties," Sal struggled with the cloth. "Don Nardo, as you said, was a piece of cake. With him money talks. He has sent word to Don Mario already. I'm meeting him the day after tomorrow."

"That's good," Ray said, handing a fat envelope and a key. "Here are five ten-thousand dollar bundles and the key to my apartment.

"Don't forget, Don Mario knows Santo as Mickey Argento, the Cat. If you call him Santo, you'll give away the store. He might suggest someone else. Work him until he sets you up with Mickey."

"How much you think he'll take?"

"I hear his luck at poker hasn't been good lately. You have enough money there. Don't let money hold us back," Ray said. "If you have to, give him a down payment, with the balance on delivery. Go for it, and don't forget—set the deal up our way."

"What day do you want?"

"Set it for Friday night, August 28," Ray said.

"Almost the end of the month, almost traditional," Sal said smiling. "When will I see you?"

"Stop worrying, Sal. I'll be okay. I tell you what I'll do. Saturday morning I'll pick you up and we'll spend the weekend together at Montauk Point. How's that? Silvana would love to see you. In the meantime, let's stay out of each other's way."

Ray looked at his wristwatch. It was time to go to work. They got out of the car. Ray walked toward the diner and Sal to the waiting cab.

Getting Don Mario to call Mickey proved to be more expensive than Sal thought. For the privilege of holding back the name of the marked man from Mickey, Don Mario was getting an extra thousand dollars. Mickey's price was based on the risk factor.

Don Mario set the meeting for Monday, August 17, at 3:00 p.m. Both parties were prepped.

On the day of the meeting, Mickey was playing solitaire in the back room.

As the time of the meeting drew near, the tension among the few members in the club was mounting.

At three, Sal walked in, firing friendly glances around. Without much ado, Don Mario led him to Mickey, who sat at an illuminated table.

They didn't shake hands but acknowledged each other's presence. Sal sat facing him. Mickey continued to play cards.

When Don Mario shut the door behind him, Mickey stopped playing and fixed his eyes on Sal.

Sal didn't balk but stared back.

Mickey narrowed his eyes and said, "I understand you want to hire me."

"To be precise, it's not me who wants to hire you but an old friend, Don Saverio Cremona."

Mickey was taken aback for a moment and then he said, "What happened to Carlo? . . . Why didn't he send for me?"

Sal placed a bundle of hundred dollar bills on the table and watched Mickey's composure crumble. "The reason I'm here my friend is because Carlo is dead. They killed him last year."

Mickey smirked.

"Don Saverio wants revenge," Sal said, "and because he doesn't want to alert anyone in the family, he wants you to make the hit. Until the smoke clears, he wants you to deal with me. If we strike a deal, Don Mario knows how to get in touch with me."

"How much is there?"

"Thirty thousand."

"I move no finger for less than fifty," Mickey said, looking down at his cards. "Who's the man anyhow?"

"Ray Greco, his son-in-law," Sal said.

"You're joking . . . Luciano's son?"

"Am I laughing? Did you know Luciano?"

"No . . . not really," Mickey said. Then pausing for a moment, he added, "I don't get involved in people's background or why they are marked.

"Nevertheless, I delivered that contract on time and clean, or Don Saverio wouldn't be looking to hire me again. . . . How did Ray become his son-in-law?"

Sal couldn't believe it; he had linked Mickey to Don Saverio on the first go round. He put the money back in his coat pocket and pushed himself away from the table. "Mickey, I'm here to buy a contract. I don't ask why or how things happen in life either. They're bound to happen in spite my asking."

Looking at Sal now, Mickey said, "Don't be so hasty. For old time's sake, I'll do it for forty. . . . Give me the scoop."

"Okay, but only if you do it our way."

"You got yourself a deal, thirty thousand now and the rest on delivery."

Sal stared at Mickey for a long moment, placed the money back on the table, and said, "When you learn where the hit has to take place, you'll agree that this job is as easy as walking out of a poker game to win a couple of sure hands and then back to win some more."

"In my business, nothing's easy," Mickey said. "Give me the scoop. I'll worry about the rest."

"I don't mean to teach you your business, but this job has no leeway."

"Go ahead," said Mickey, keeping an eye on the money. "I'm all ears."

"A few blocks from here, Ray has an apartment in a three-family house he owns. Since he started remodeling two of the three apartments, every Friday night he pulls in at ten o'clock and he's sound asleep by eleven.

"Monday through Friday, he runs his business in Manhattan. On Friday nights, he uses the apartment as a stopover on his way to Montauk Point.

"He wakes up early Saturday morning, goes over the work, pays the contractors, and takes off for Long Island."

"With a house in Long Island and a place in Manhattan, why is he screwing around with a dump?"

"Maybe for sentimental reasons, maybe for business, I ask no questions nor do I set the rules," Sal said. "Don Saverio does that, and here they are:

"The hit has to take place on Friday night in Ray's bedroom, and he has to be found with his balls cut off."

Sal pushed the money toward Mickey, "Don Saverio told me you're a good butcher."

"What's with the balls?"

"I understand, besides causing Carlo's death, Ray has been cheating on his wife—you know, Don Saverio's daughter," Sal said.

Mickey was fanning the money, "Okay, I got the idea now. What else you got for me?"

"This is the master key to the front door, his apartment, and the other two apartments. To be safe, you must get there after midnight. If you think to sneak in ahead of time and wait in one of those apartments, you'll spoil the party. He checks them both before he goes to bed. By the way, they tell me he's a heavy sleeper.

"As I said, there is no leeway on this job. You do as you're told. A plus, on Ray's street they roll up the sidewalks by nine o'clock."

"I know what you mean. I'll check the place out tomorrow or Wednesday. If there's a problem, Don Mario will call you. Otherwise, Friday it'll be. By the way, how will I know he's there?"

"He drives a new Olds '98. It'll be the only one on the block. I'll have the other ten waiting for you here on Saturday."

22

It was Friday and, as scheduled, a construction dumpster with a square chute hanging off the second floor window filled the front yard. The dumpster blocked the side door and the two ground floor windows.

The spiral staircase was removed leaving a six-foot diameter hole in the wood floor. Through the hole a temporary wooden ladder reached the concrete floor below.

The kid from across the street assured Ray that a man with silvery hair and a missing finger holding a pad was there the day before.

The kid said, "The man went into a hallway three houses down and popped up on your roof looking things over, maybe making an inspection. I don't really know."

Based on Mickey's poker game schedule and Sal's instructions not to strike before midnight, Ray approached the house at ten o'clock that night.

Resolute, Ray went up the stoop and into the house. He had one hour to shut the lights off as planned. He checked the second floor for unwanted guests and then went to work on his apartment—the first floor.

There, Ray laid down a two-ply round net with a threaded rope around the border, and covered it with a lightweight carpet.

Across from each other in the hole, he secured four hooks on the exposed wood beams. These hooks would hold the net like a trampoline.

He slid the net and the carpet together, until it covered one third of the hole. He climbed down to the concrete floor below and removed the wooden ladder. Stretching from a chair, he slid the net all the way and hooked it.

A weight greater than a child would collapse the trap—net—into a cocoon strong enough to hold a man immobile for some time.

With the trap in place and the alarm on, Ray sat in the chair facing a light bulb that would flash red the moment the upstairs door opened.

At five minutes to eleven, Ray shutoff the lights and sat quietly like an angler waiting for his bite.

At three o'clock, the light bulb flashed red. A few minutes earlier, Ray had fallen asleep.

Like a cat, Santo came down the hatch and the stairs and into the apartment. There on his second step he fell into the trap banging his head on the edge of hole. The loud thump echoed throughout the house, but failed to wake Ray.

Dangling from the ceiling, Santo had cocooned himself in a fetal position. With each attempt he made to free himself, the red light flashed faster, or so it seemed.

The more Santo moved, the tighter the cocoon got. Realizing the spot he was in, he quieted down and relaxed, inching his hand toward the six-inch blade holstered to his ankle. Before he could reach it, a wedge of light shone from the kitchen door. It illuminated the scene enough for him to see Sal rush in, take the gun from Ray's lap and disappear from view.

Santo dangled like a pear from a tree.

Feeling Sal's breath on his neck, Santo wondered what Sal was up to until he felt a nylon string around his neck.

Sal pulled hard, very hard until the jolting caused a silver dollar chained to a key to fall from Santo's pocket onto the concrete floor.

The sound woke Ray in time to see Sal letting go of Santo's slumped body.

Leaping to his feet, Ray yelled, "It worked!"

Then composed, embarrassed, and relieved all at once, Ray picked up the key, looked at Sal, and asked, "Where the hell did you come from?"

"Later," Sal said, "let's finish business."

There wasn't much discussion after that. They needed to complete the job before the service truck took the dumpster at dawn.

They hoisted the cocoon onto the first floor, stripped Santo of all identifications and cash, wrapped him in the carpet, hauled him to the second floor, and sent his body down the chute. Santo had more cash in his money belt than they had given him.

Like common laborers, Sal and Ray filled the dumpster to the brim with debris from the apartments. Santo was no more. He was on his way to help fill a pit in South Brooklyn.

On their way to Montauk Point, Sal and Ray checked into a motel for some rest. They were more exhausted from filling the dumpster than getting rid of Santo.

In the early afternoon, they went to the motel diner. During the meal, they exchanged subtle smiles, praising each other for a job well done.

But Ray was also disappointed. "Sal, I wanted to squeeze the truth out of Santo. Why didn't you wake me up? I'm not going through this for fun. I want to know why they killed my father."

"Why? I had him linked to Don Saverio already. Besides, Santo did not know the motive. Ray, you know better, hit men never do. Nor do they care. Look what we told him about you."

"Maybe, but I think I could've squeezed something out of him . . . anything."

"Well, Ray, I didn't want to tell you this before, but recently your grandfather learned that Don Saverio wanted a public road your father was building rerouted to a piece of property he owned.

"According to the information your grandfather has gathered, when your father refused, he made the hit list. There were other rumors but nothing concrete.

"Ray, that's the way they thought in those days."

"For God's sakes, why didn't you tell me?"

"Calm down, Ray. Seeing the way you were carrying on with Don Saverio, your grandfather was worried about telling you with no sure facts. He feared it would have a reverse effect on you.

"He thought the facts were there for you to find firsthand. Don't ask me how. He also thought you were the one to make things right for everyone without risking your life. Ray, frankly, I didn't get a good read on him."

Ray took this finding in the guts. He had given up his career to avenge his father and make things right. Yet, for the good of his business and his family, he could not make good on his promise.

Disappointed with himself, he poured cream in his coffee, stirred it slowly, and looked at Sal. "At times life is unfair. When you see Grandpa, hug him for me . . . and I owe you one, Sal."

"What about Don Saverio?"

"Sal, I want to jump on the next flight out and take care of him, but I have to stay put for now."

"After all this, delaying the inevitable makes no sense," Sal said.

"He's too powerful still and too much a part of my life. Besides, he bought himself a long-term life insurance. I've got to find the way to revoke that first. For now, it's one down and one to go."

Sal nodded, not knowing what life insurance Ray was talking about, but he thought:

That's a bad excuse. Once more, selfish greed is delaying swift justice.

Ray interrupted Sal's thoughts. "Now tell me, how did you get in, and where were you hiding last night?"

Sal reached for his cup and smiled, "Don't forget, last April your mother and I lived there for a while.

"Before I gave Santo the key, I made a duplicate. Last night I got there at eight. I surveyed the place, went downstairs, and read *Il Progresso*.

"Then I laid a bunch of blankets on the floor, went to sleep, and woke up at two, which was the time I figured Mickey would show up.

"I was reading the rest of the paper when I heard a thump. I waited. When I heard nothing, I came out. Sure enough there he was dangling off the dining room ceiling."

"Where were you downstairs?"

"Where else . . . I was in your beloved kitchen under the table. Even if you stuck your head in, you couldn't have seen me."

"You know," Ray said, "it never fails. Every time I set an alarm, my mind goes blank and I sleep until the bell rings. Last night there was no bell, but a stupid flashing light. I fell asleep, and I didn't wake up until it was over. I'm sure glad you were there."

"A four-hour wait, especially in the dark, that's a long haul for anybody," Sal said. "As they say, it's water under the bridge."

"Sal, were you at the apartment one day last week?"

"I was," Sal said with a smile.

"How come the kid didn't tell me?"

"I told you already. I lived there, and I was no stranger to the kid. Besides, I paid him a buck more than you did."

"That little double-crossing son of a bitch, I'll get him!"

Sal smiled.

23

Compared to the morning session when Ray had met with two heads of Mafia, the afternoon was quiet. He was studying Giglio's financial report, and it exceeded all expectations. Before he could pat himself on the back, Gabriella's voice came over the intercom.

"Mr. Catania is here to see you."

"Who did you say?"

"Mr. Vito Catania. He says he's a friend of yours."

"Hold on!"

Stunned, he didn't know what to make of it. He wasn't concerned about Mr. Catania's visit, but wondered how he had found him. After all, the Catanias were as remote from the world of fashion as he was from falling in love with their daughter. He thought:

I'll bet he doesn't know I got married. That's it! I'd better clear the air. . . . Some people never give up.

"Gabriella, please tell Mr. Catania I'll be right out."

He polished his wedding band and walked down the hallway. In the lobby, Ray faced a short-legged man. He looked different from the man he knew. This one was bald and was squeezed into a three-piece suit like salami. His shirt collar was so tight that his face changed color with each breath he took.

Ray couldn't deny that he was indeed Mr. Catania, so he reached for his hand, "How are you?"

Mr. Catania forced a constipated smile. Gabriella clasped her mouth to muffle the giggles, but the eyes betrayed her.

Ray led Mr. Catania to his office and pointed to a chair next to his desk.

"Please have a seat."

Mr. Catania sat, loosened his collar and said, "Don Greco, I need your help, badly."

"Hold on! Before we go any further, let's get something straight. I'm not, nor do I wish to be a Don. Please, call me Ray."

"I'm sorry; I didn't mean to offend you, I need help."

"I don't know what I can do for you."

Wiping sweat with a soggy handkerchief, he said, "Plenty, Mr. Ray . . . you can do plenty. Concetta . . . my little Concetta . . . is lying in bed staring at the ceiling for over a week now."

Mr. Catania cried out his whole story under Ray's sympathetic eye. "She . . . she was raped. The church's new groundskeeper, he was working there less than a month.

"The cops are saying it was consensual . . . they won't do a thing. . . . Here's his picture.

"The son of a bitch lives alone in a shack behind the church . . . two blocks from where Concetta works.

"If you look at him, he laughs in your face in spite. He's bad . . . very bad.

"I know you can . . . you've got to help. . . . Please do something . . . please."

"Mr. Catania, calm down, please." Ray poured a glass of water and handed it to the man. "Here, relax. Have a drink. Everything will be okay. Relax now."

Ray paused in thought.

Mr. Catania bobbed his head several times as if crying.

"Mr. Catania, I'm very sorry for you and your family. My heart goes out to your daughter, but I'm not what you think I am.

"Remember, I am the same guy who took your advice and quit my job to stay away from that sort of thing.

"I'm sorry, but I can't help you. You need to go to the district attorney or some other law enforcement agency in your district. They're there to help you. Trust me. They are."

"I understand," Mr. Catania said softly, rising and reaching out for Ray's hand.

"Out of curiosity, where did you get the notion that I could help?"

"Mr. Ray, you know, from the first time we met I've been upfront with you. Allow me to tell you that you've got a good friend in Nino Maltese. He's the one who took the picture of the groundskeeper."

Ray was flabbergasted. He hadn't thought of Nino since the days they were club hopping in Brooklyn.

"Since he got back from Sicily," Mr. Catania said, "he thinks the world of you. You know, he spent five full days there last year. He says you can solve any problem at the snap of a finger."

Ray was somewhat flattered. Having not seen or heard from Nino for more than two years, he thought:

Five full days . . . it takes more than a year for people to give a stranger the time of day in Sicily. Let alone a history lesson in who's who.

"Mr. Catania, I'm surprised at you. I can understand you reaching out for help, but a man of your experience doesn't listen to a guy like Nino. He thrives on gossip. Trust me. He lives in a world of fantasy making up Mafia stories."

Ray pulled on his suspenders to reinforce his point. His tone grew serious. "What's sad is that someday he will get hurt badly, but again that's his problem. Wouldn't you say?"

"Well, if Nino is making it all up, he can get you in some hell of hot water. There's no stopping him when he starts talking. Knowing your grandfather and Don Saverio, it's hard for me to think: is Nino that far off . . . is he?"

Ray again pulled on his suspenders. He rose and escorted a wobbling Mr. Catania down the corridor toward the lobby. In the lobby, Mr. Catania turned to Ray, took his arm, and again pleaded, "Please help my Concetta . . . please. . . . I know you will."

Back at his desk, Ray looked at the rapist's photo. He picked up the phone and dialed.

"May I speak with Gregory Khan, please?" After a brief discussion, Ray closed the call, "Okay. Tonight at nine. See you then."

In the deserted moonlit quarters, the church's cupola shadowed the shack. The rapist's loud snoring came through the corrugated walls of the makeshift bedroom.

Greg opened the unlatched door, drew near the man lying on an old four-post bed, and knocked him out with a single blow to the head with his nightstick. He taped the man's mouth shut, stripped him naked, and tied him spread-eagle to the four posts. By the time Greg had smoked a cigarette, the rapist came to. When he realized his predicament, the man yanked hard on the ropes to free himself. He had reddish curly hair and mean eyes. He wasn't more than twenty.

Greg stared at him blankly, crushing the cigarette butt on the floor. He reached for the jar of Vaseline he had placed on the night table. The rapist looked on in horror as Greg dipped his nightstick into the Vaseline and covered the tip well.

Nonchalantly, he shoved it up the rapist's ass. He turned and twisted it until the rapist's eyes bulged with tears. To prolong the man's agony, Greg jerked the nightstick up, around, and in and out as if he was digging for oil.

The rapist passed out.

When he came to again, Greg pulled out a straight razor and, under the muffled screams of the rapist, cut off his balls with a single stroke.

He wiped the razor and the nightstick clean as he stood by watching the bright eyes glaze over until the rapist was no more.

The following day the media blamed the atrocity on gangland infighting.

At the news, Concetta rejoiced and began to breathe normally again. Mr. Catania also rejoiced. Wisely, he thanked no one.

One evening, several weeks after the rapist was killed, Mr. Catania left the club contented. Concetta had recovered from the ordeal and his family was back to normal.

Waiting for the high rollers, Nino ordered a Coke with double rum. He gulped the drink down and quickly ordered another one. He tried to read the paper but could not concentrate. Nino was thinking about what Mr. Catania had told him and how close he was to getting hurt.

He looked around to thank Mr. Catania, but he had gone home. As he fell asleep in the recliner, he promised himself he would talk with Mr. Catania tomorrow.

Nino awoke before the high rollers began to file in. Still feeling the effects of the double rums, he rose and staggered to the street.

Unstable, with slumped shoulders, he was staring at the sidewalk as he walked toward his car swaying like a duck bobbing his head up and down. He watched his shadow following him. He saw the concrete cracks, the broken curb, the dirty whitewall tires, and the shining hubcaps. He crossed the intersection. On the other side of the street, he kept watching the cracks, the whitewall tires, and the hubcaps until he recognized his car's rear bumper.

At the next step, he spotted a pair of black patent leather shoes. Nino leaned against his car. Then he looked slowly from the shoes up to the blue trousers, past half a dozen brass buttons to a fake smiling face.

The police officer opened the passenger door and invited Nino in the front seat of his car. As Nino struggled toward the driver's side, a single bullet entered his skull from behind his right ear.

Greg allowed the body to slump to the left without triggering the horn. He put the silencer away, shut the door, and resumed his beat.

24

In America, the sixties and early seventies sparked a unique social upheaval. It was more chaotic than the twenties had been. As the world watched, people uprooted and forever changed politics, culture, and mores. They sought their desires and more.

Martin Luther King had a dream. Cities were set afire, and the Americans placed their flag on the moon. Johnson bowed out of the presidency. Nikita Khrushchev embraced Castro. Cassius Clay, twenty-three, took the title of heavyweight champion of the world from Sonny Liston.

Youth rebelled against military ideology.

At the Woodstock Music Festival and Art Fair in Bethel, New York, they openly displayed their strength, appeal, and power.

Toward the end of the sixties, Wall Street lost its craving for speculative public offerings. Venture capital was hard to get.

In the midst of it all, Ray Greco quietly managed to carry out his agenda. The best years for Don Saverio's plan were from 1960 to 1979.

Along other Ivy League graduates, the Class of '56 found jobs as high-ranking staffers. In their positions, they became the brains behind politicians and business leaders alike.

They supplied the backbone every leader needed. Because they were good at what they did, their services were indispensable. There was no stopping them.

Don Saverio's protégés, as planned, were infiltrating American politics and big business from within. America was getting back on track swiftly.

Sergio Bruno and Pat O'Brien were expanding Giglio worldwide, and Sal Rocca was taking the gravel business back in Sicily to new heights. Sal was also experimenting with ready-mixed concrete.

Silvana reared three children and spent the summers at Montauk Point. The rest of the year, she and her family lived in Scarsdale.

On the illegal side, Ray took over Carlo's job, dismantling the remaining Mafia families. With his grandfather's conviction about his father's death, Ray's obsession turned to contempt. He wanted to kill Don Saverio at once. For the good of his own cause, however, he controlled that impulse, unwilling to upset the scheme of things.

The consequences of acting now could drive the moles to retaliate against him, for their survival was also on the line. So, in the interim, he took advantage of the control he had over the moles and their desire to go back home. Ray set up a plan to weaken Don Saverio's power base.

In keeping with his plan, Ray no longer accepted what Don Saverio said or did without checking the facts and possible consequences first.

Ray mother's words: Trust no one . . . not even your mother, continued to bring to mind the man who trusted him, Don Saverio himself. It was that trust that had put Ray at the helm of the New Enterprises and now of the moles.

For Ray, obliged to fate, the past and the immediate future held a bitter taste.

John DeMaria, a Yale graduate, was the first of many members of the Class of '56 to join the FBI. He rose to the rank of special investigator. In his thirties, he was dismantling two of the largest Chicago families: the Caiellos and the Manninos. His bullet-free tactics became legendary within the bureau and the Chicago gangs.

When John walked into an interrogation room, there was no doubt as to who was in charge. He had a muscular build on a six-foot-one frame, one inch taller than Ray. His light brown hair did not match his black mustache, which concealed a broad pair of lips complementing a large chin.

His smile said, "I know all about you."

He was a born investigator. His subordinates were two Italians and three Irishmen; his boss was Ray Greco. At the FBI headquarters in Manhattan, special agent John DeMaria was interrogating two members of the Caiello family. While the FBI wanted to dig up enough dirt to put them away for life, John wanted to increase his record for the most Mafia members turned informers and the most toppled Mafia families. Now, he wanted to add to his acclaimed mobsters' list the elder of the two men, Tony Fraterno.

Tony was a large man, with sloping shoulders and a bald head. Because he struck victims quickly leaving no trail, he was Caiello's most trusted hit man. Yet, because he knew too much, he was a marked man himself, without friends. Tony wanted to join the FBI's informant program in exchange for safety.

The other man, Joey Verona, on the other hand, was turning informant to please John DeMaria. Single-handedly, Joey was destroying one of the most powerful Mafia families. As one of Don Saverio's moles, he had wedged himself between Tommy Caiello and Tony Fraterno. Now, Joey was driving that wedge all the way through, cracking the family apart.

Joey was excited. At last, he was going home.

The two informants were crossing the Brooklyn Bridge. At the mouth of the bridge, Joey slowed down to let traffic through. Poking his head over the steering wheel to watch both sides of the road Joey said, "You got to do it, Tony! It's you or them."

Finally, they crossed the bridge and arrived at a downtown diner one hour earlier than scheduled. From there, an FBI agent would take them to their secret destination.

They sat in a corner booth. Joey knocked a pack of Camels on the palm of his hand, nodded a few times, and said, "Look, Tony, you're over sixty and the only things you've got to show for it are twenty-four hits and a terrible fear for your life."

"I know," Tony bobbed his head in shame.

"Look at me, I'm forty with six hits and I'm as scared as you are." Joey paused to light up a cigarette then blew smoke from the corner of his mouth. "Tony, I'm telling you . . . we're in some hell of a shit."

"I know."

"The only thing I know," Joey said, "is that when loyal men like us are kicked out on their asses on a single suspicion something's wrong."

"Not even a chance to defend myself," Tony said, resentful. "I even whacked friends and relatives for them. It's some hell of a thank you. I tell you, Joey, it isn't right."

Joey sucked on his cigarette and lifted his coffee cup. "The truth is that no matter how you look at it, you and I have been royally screwed."

"Uh-huh," Tony nodded twice.

"If we want to stay alive," Joey said, "we've got no other place to turn to. And guess what, Tony, I don't know about you, but one way or another I'm going to survive. . . . I've got lots of things to do yet."

"Don't get me wrong, Joey, I hear you loud and clear. Since we talked last, I made up my mind. There are no second thoughts here. . . . I'm going to squeal."

In disbelief, Joey asked, "Then why are you so down in the dumps? What's your regret?"

"That I didn't slit their throats when I had the chance. I slaved all my life for the Caiello brothers."

Joey looked on, slowly puffing smoke to the ceiling.

Wiping a sugar spill off the table as his eyes quivered, Tony said, "They were family to me. Then, one day you wake up and your life is over.

"Your family is your enemy. . . . Your friends look the other way . . . and there is no place to turn."

For the first time ever, Tony shed a tear.

25

At ten minutes to twelve on Friday, Ray's private line rang, "Ray, this is John."

"Where are you?"

"Here in Manhattan, how about lunch?"

"Sure."

Lenny's, on the east side of Manhattan, was famous for its juicy prime rib. Bragging about his favorite restaurant, John would say: You can bite through a one-inch cut with your lips.

John DeMaria was having coffee at a corner table when Ray came through the front door. He stood up and waved. Except for getting older, the two men had not changed much since the time they were growing up in Sicily.

Ray walked toward John's table and held out a hand. Smiling, he asked, "Am I late?"

John shook his hand. "I just got here myself."

By instinct, as most native Sicilians do, they sat with their backs to the wall, facing all comers.

"John, I've never tried this place."

"Wait till you taste the prime rib."

"Is this place okay for us to meet?"

"Why wouldn't it be?" John asked. "All my work is about Mafia. As long as I bring in convictions, the only things I can get are citations for bravery."

"And a thank you from Don Saverio right, John?"

"Ray, these days you'd better look beyond Sicilian Mafia. Besides Sicilian and Neapolitan, there is a strong Irish Mafia in this country, not to mention other nationalities."

"Don't forget Canadians."

"Especially them, I'm well aware of that," John said. "Ray, I also know that most of these families are seeds Don Saverio planted a long time ago. They are no different from the ones we're planting now."

Ray nodded. "So John, what brought you here?"

Before John could answer, the waiter cut in, "The usual?"

"Sure, make it two."

With the waiter out of the way, John looked around and moved closer to Ray. "I need a clearance on one of Caiello's men whom I'm investigating."

"Who is he?"

"Joey Verona."

"How did you know he belongs to us?"

"The other day he was wearing the Class of '56 pin on his lapel. Is he okay?"

"Absolutely, we placed him there about ten years ago."

"Ten years?"

"Whatever it takes, John. Tony was a big fish, so Carlo got Joey to work on him."

"Can I use him?"

"Of course, that's why he's there. He's sharp. You'll see. Another thing you should know, Caiello gave Joey the contract on Tony for squealing."

"I see."

"The Caiello family is a big catch. They've got to go. Call Michael Marchese with the IRS. Last week I asked him to put together a package on the Caiello family. I'm sure you can use it."

"I'm sure I can, too," John said with a grin. "Michael's a good boy."

"I'm proud of Michael," Ray said. "Until Marco got him in the IRS, I was concerned."

"I see," John said with a bit of surprise.

"Now he's proved to be valuable. Once the Caiello family falls, the others will follow suit."

"Ray, how many people did Marco place in my bureau?"

"From his position on Capitol Hill, Marco has been able to place lots of our people from many places in many bureaus. We're getting there."

"What bureaus?"

"Remember, John, each year new graduates are arriving from Sicily with the same commitment you and I have if not stronger. For some strange reason, this last bunch is real eager to get here.

"As planned, by the mid-seventies we'll have the run of things here. As I said, we're getting there, trust me."

"Do we have a list?"

"Knowing who they are serves no purpose, John. What's vital is that these people are out there working for our Cause and ready to help at a moment's notice.

"Let's keep up the good work. We have plenty of work ahead."

John nodded obediently. The aroma of brown gravy, mashed potatoes, and fresh green beans reached the table before the prime rib did.

Ray looked at the dish then at John. "What's next for Joey and Tony?"

"As soon as I place them in the program, which should be late next week, I'll turn the case over for prosecution. Then I'll be free to work on others. Believe me; the chief prosecutor wants this family worse than we do."

"Good but don't forget," Ray said, "after the trial I want Tony and Joey's new identities. Ship Tony to the Coast. Once he gets there, Joey knows what to do. Then Joey goes back to Sicily."

While informers found refuge in the FBI program, Ray found that program a tool for weakening Don Saverio.

One by one, Ray was getting rid of every mole Don Saverio had placed in America.

To the surprise of most experts, the prosecution won the Caiello trial. It had dominated the media for the better part of six months.

The juries found the Caiello brothers, one *sottocapo* and three *consiglieri,* guilty. They would spend the rest of their lives behind bars without chance at parole.

These convictions, coupled with the FBI's resolve, were turning up the heat, and yet the formidable heads of Mafia stubbornly refused to wise up.

Informers, either of their own accord or influenced by the events of the trial, came forward in droves.

This signaled the end for old Mafia.

26

At Leonardo da Vinci Airport, Alitalia was paging Mr. Baldisi. Disappointed for missing the last shuttle to Palermo, Mr. Baldisi was headed to the restroom when someone called, "Joey!"

Not yet trained to respond to his new name only, Joey turned to find himself facing Sal Rocca.

"Sal, what are you doing here? You should have met me in Palermo!"

"Ray changed plans. He wants you to lay low here for a while until things cool down a bit."

"What's so hot?"

"Look, Joey, I was asked to meet you here. You know how it is."

"Where are we going?"

"I got you a room as Nick Baldisi."

Flabbergasted, Joey said, "How in the hell do you know my new name? It's supposed to be top secret and here I am starting all over."

"Don't worry, Joey," Sal smiled. "You don't want to hide from Don Saverio and Ray, do you?"

"Sal, don't put words in my mouth."

They walked down the concourse quietly. In front the terminal, Sal hailed the first cab in line.

In the backseat Sal looked at Joey, "Don't worry; you're okay. No one knows Nick Baldisi exists."

Thanks to the cabdriver's lead foot, they made it to the hotel in record time. They needed no bellhop. Joey was traveling light.

The sunlit hotel room faced Rome's most revered site—the Vatican.

Joey, still uneasy about the change in plans, asked, "Sal, are things hot because of Tony or is the FBI after my ass already?"

"I don't know."

"I've got to know. When I dumped that idiot Tony, I stripped him of all IDs. Not even his mother could identify him. You know, Sal, I spent the better part of ten years pretending."

"Uh-huh."

Joey disrobed for a shower, dropped his underwear at the foot of the bed, and said, "I want to go home and relax a bit."

"Relax, Joey. Take your shower, rest a bit, and I'll pick you up in a couple of hours for dinner. We'll talk then."

Facing the sunlight window behind Sal, Joey squinted. "All right, Sal. . . . I'll see you then."

Sal turned, drew the curtains shut, and said, "Maybe you can go home tomorrow. I'll call Ray and see what he says."

Walking toward the bathroom, Joey was saying, "You know, Sal, I earned my keep. Remind Ray I'm the one who got rid of the Caiello family. Besides, I got work to do for Don Saverio and, whether he likes it or not, I'm going home tomorr . . ."

A single bullet entered the back of his skull.

"Welcome home."

Sal returned the silencer to its holster, collected Joey's ID, and left the room quietly leaving behind an unknown corpse.

There never was a Nick Baldisi.

27

Victor Como was angry, resentful, and disappointed. Suddenly, life had stung him bitterly. He had spent five of his twelve years in America as a marketing consultant on the West Coast. There, he had helped many companies grow to their full potential. One of which was Kohaski Import Export and Supply Company, Inc.—also known as Kiesco.

Dan Kohaski, a retired general, founded the company ten years earlier. Kiesco was a brokerage house set up to sell general supplies to the Pentagon. It also bought and sold Pentagon surpluses.

Its customers were U.S. agencies. On most occasions, Kiesco simply shifted supplies from one agency to another as if playing chess, moving pawns from one square to the next.

As a brokerage house, Kiesco kept no inventory, the very thing Victor fell in love with. Although Kiesco's earnings were high, its sales volume did not justify the price tag. For the right price, Victor thought of buying two-thirds ownership, providing the General kept his connections committed to the company and his salary and expenses trimmed to the bone.

To drive Kiesco to its full potential, Victor knew he had to use every resource available and set up a good window dressing with a strong board of directors.

When all the pieces fit, he signed a letter of intent with a two-hundred-thousand-dollar binder.

A few days after the deal was made and the General went off on a two-month vacation to Europe, a federal marshal showed up at Kiesco's headquarters with a subpoena. A committee investigating the Pentagon's procurements had a few questions. A later interview with the General's secretary and a closer review of the books justified the committee's concern.

At Ray's insistence, Victor walked away from the deal. He wanted to handle the General himself, but he was obliged to obey, for Ray was the leader of the pack.

Angelo Sutera picked up Victor and Nora at Bradley Airport in Connecticut and drove them to his home. He had invited the couple to spend the weekend. Angelo, who was connected in the insurance business, was Victor's closest friend.

Ray was due back from the 1968 fashion show in London the following Monday. Ray had asked to meet with Victor next Wednesday at his office.

Angelo's wife, Lia, was a petite young woman with long black hair and black sparkling eyes. She was born and raised in Sicily. Judiciously, she spent most of the day preparing a meal for the arriving guests. As most Sicilians, she let her husband think he was the master of the house. And, as most Sicilian women, she was content with the arrangement.

After dinner, with the excuse of giving the women more breathing room, the two men retired to the studio with coffees in hand. The setting sun was coming through the fluffy clouds, the trees, and the curtains. The picture window showcased the beauty of a New England autumn closing down the season with the turning leaves. To the right of the window, there was a poker irons set and a firewood cord to fuel the fireplace.

Like boys looking through a candy store window, Victor and Angelo approached the mantelpiece. There were framed photographs of Angelo, Victor, and Ray in their bathing suits at Alcamo Marina; Don Saverio and his wife; and Ray and Silvana on their first date at Sala Arlecchino with Carlo grinning in disbelief.

The most memorable photograph was that of Victor's date without a chaperon. Under the astonished faces of the onlookers, Victor walked through the ballroom like a matador, arm-in-arm with Brigitte. It had been an end to an era.

Victor need not be ashamed about his setback in California. He was safe at home now. Here, in his people's minds he was a champion. Not long ago, he had broken a tradition that no other young man dared attempt in his hometown. Victor was a man of honor who spoke the truth.

Angelo and Victor stood staring at each other for a short while.

"I guess you heard," Victor said.

"I did."

They nodded for a second longer then hugged and patted each other's back.

"Victor, we need you here," Angelo said as they parted. "Are you ready to leave California?"

"I am and thank you for the welcome."

"You're always welcome here."

"I tell you, Angelo, what a jackass I was. That son of a bitch stung me . . . and I can't do a damn thing. It hurts. Ray held me back . . . I tell you it hurts."

Angelo shook his head.

Squinting, Victor watched a couple of squirrels chasing each other up and down a birch tree.

"Do you know the General had been billing Uncle Sam ten, even a hundred times the contracted price?" Victor said in disbelief.

"I'll bet Uncle Sam paid the bill in full every time, right?" Angelo said. "How did he get away with it?"

"Easy," Victor said, "Kiesco secured a bunch of contracts for supplies on an 'as needed basis' underbidding the competition by as much as twenty percent.

"Once the orders were shipped, using the bill of lading, which showed quantities but no price, he billed Uncle Sam at either ten times or one hundred times the contracted price."

"Victor, how's that possible?" Angelo asked, puzzled.

"It's easy. There's a method known to thieves like him as the MCE system, where M equals per thousand, C per hundred, and E per each.

"An item contracted, say, at one hundred dollars per thousand is billed at the same one hundred dollars but per hundred instead, increasing the invoice tenfold. To increase the value a hundredfold, he billed that same item at one hundred dollars each."

"I imagine there's a safety hatch?"

"Sure, inside connections. It was all rigged. To get the bids awarded, especially when there was no competition, he submitted two or three complementary bids through fake companies.

"To support the swindle, the insiders properly posted Kiesco's MCE unit prices, as well as those of the competition. Items contracted, as I said, at one hundred dollars per thousand were posted at one hundred dollars per hundred and so on."

Angelo sipped his coffee. "How did you find out?"

"I dated his secretary."

"Uh-huh. That sounds like the old Victor."

"She told me more than I cared to know," Victor said with a shrug and a smile. "There was a plan in place. If caught, the General declared the incident a mistake in posting. Blame the clerks and promptly reimburse for the over-billed items."

"How did it turn sour?"

"What else, Angelo? Greed. Some insiders thought they weren't getting enough."

"Victor, people are simply stupid," Angelo said. "In a court of law, it's easier to defy a bunch of witnesses accusing you of murder than a single piece of paper accusing you of stealing. The paper trail will get you every time.

"If you remember, Don Saverio always made a point of that. You did well. Let Ray handle the General."

"I know, but as much as I respect Ray for the fine job he is doing, at times he gets dispassionate with the truth and acts on impulse and not on facts."

"What's the chance of the General getting away with it?"

"It's in his favor. We'll see what Ray says. By the way, how's Don Saverio? I'm very concerned."

"Ever since he lost Carlo, I hear he lives secluded," Angelo said. "I don't really know much. . . . You should ask Ray."

"Do you think Ray took over Carlo's work?" Victor asked.

"If he did, he's not telling," Angelo said, reaching for his coffee. "Personally, I don't think Ray ever wanted any part of Mafia.

"With a thriving family business and a bright future of his own, how he got involved is beyond logic."

"I thought the same thing a long time ago," Victor said. "Still, Angelo, who's doing Carlo's work?"

"Good question."

"Maybe it's him, or maybe the grunts?" Victor said.

"If you're referring to Don Saverio's moles, they were no secret to us," Angelo said. "If you remember, he took pride in pointing them out at the farewell party. There were over a dozen, if not more.

"What's a mystery is that more than half of the moles are not going back home. Ray thinks that once enrolled in the Witness Protection Program, life gets simpler."

"I can see that," Victor said. "With new identities and a new start in life, they simply retire into a world of their own. But, what does it mean to Don Saverio?"

"A very destructive blow," said Angelo, concerned. "They are Don Saverio's most-trusted people. He felt very obliged for their service. He once passionately called them his Street Warriors."

"You're right, as I said, I'm very concerned and ready to do whatever it takes to defend him," Victor said. "But, I don't see how their disappearances hindered our Cause in any way.

"These people did exactly what they were supposed to do—destroy the old Mafia. What happens after is irrelevant to Don Saverio's Cause."

"I know, Victor, but with a weak power base, Don Saverio could get hurt."

"Yes, Angelo, I'm worried, too. But if I read Don Saverio right, he has that planned. At this stage, he should retire and not deal with this stuff. Who could blame him? He's no youngster. Don Saverio has paid a hefty price for the Cause.

"I only hope that people don't stray back into a world of corruption or some other crime."

28

Silvana and Ray were coming home. Family and friends rendezvoused on the tarmac of Westchester County Airport. Aunt Laura, who had spent the whole day cooking, got there before everyone else. She brought little Luciano, Francesca, and Saverio but left the dog at home. Grownups Victor, Nora, Angelo, and Lia got there just in time.

Little Luciano loved to watch airplanes land. Like his dad, he had an imagination of his own. Fast approaching from the north, the jet crossed the fence line. At landing, its wheels smoked and the engines roared as if refusing to slow down.

It was that loud roar followed by the steady hissing of the engines that made little Luciano imagine the jet as a big wildcat prowling through the sky brought down by man to purr like a kitten.

Before Silvana and Ray had left London, they had called Aunt Laura and asked her to prepare a good Sunday dinner, even though it was Monday. They wanted to celebrate Giglio's fashion show. They were also hungry for a homemade meal and good company.

Aunt Laura had never married. Besides being an embroiderer, she was a good cook. After closing her needle shop in Sicily, she took up the challenge of moving to the States and helping Ray and Silvana with the children and the cooking. In her late fifties, heavy-set and gray-haired, she had a warm, smiling, guileless face and a faint mustache.

At the Scarsdale house, the Greco family and friends were greeted by a barking and happy Rex and the aroma of fresh-cooked food. Besides the meatballs and fried zucchinis, there was the main course: linguini with sautéed chopped lamb. Aunt Laura made the sauce with onions, parsley, other spices, and a touch of wine, and then simmered it into thick meat gravy. It was Aunt Laura's specialty.

Breaded veal cutlets, eggplants, dried codfish, chicken cacciatore, and sausage with peppers and onions were add-ons to the main course. A bowl of sliced steamed carrots in olive oil, garlic, and parsley was for the diehards.

She also provided seasoned black olives in oil and garlic, stalks of white celery, and a spread of fresh fruit to help the meal go down.

Looking around for more food to put out, Aunt Laura thought:

What kind of dinner is this without a few slices of prosciutto, provolone, and pecorino and, of course, breads and white and red wines? What are they going to think of me?

The Sunday dinner that afternoon ended with espresso, *cannolis,* and a long nap to boot.

"You sure know how to cook, Aunt Laura," said little Luciano, making the adults laugh.

It was nine o'clock that night before Ray, Victor, and Angelo were in any condition to gather in the studio.

The men groaned when they saw the tray Aunt Laura had placed on the serving table: fresh coffee, vanilla biscuits, and a bottle of Sambuca. The trio settled down in their chairs.

"Ray, you lucky stiff," Victor said, motioning toward the tray.

"She's family. She loves Silvana and the children as her own."

"How old are the kids now?" Angelo asked.

"They're five, four, and two."

"So far their namesakes paid off everyone but Donna Maria," Victor said. "You better get busy."

"No more," laughed Ray, waving his hand like windshield wiper.

"Why is that? Donna Maria must be heartbroken," Victor said.

"It's a personal choice," Ray said, ending the discussion. With a tug on his suspenders, Ray turned to business. "So, Victor, how did you do with the General?"

Bobbing his head a few times, he finally said, "As you asked, I walked away,"

"Good." Ray looked at Angelo, "How much so far?"

"It cost me a little over two hundred and sixty-five thousand."

"It's all from your line of credit, right, Angelo?"

Raising his eyebrows, Angelo said, "That's right,"

"Victor, do you think the General can pay it back?"

"Ray, from what I know, only if we keep him in business. As long as that subpoena is out there, he's not coming back. He's done this before and gotten away."

"We'll see," Ray said. "Do you have his address in Europe?"

"Sure." Victor jotted it down on a pad.

Angelo looked intently at Ray. "You're not going to . . ."

"Come on! . . . Give me some credit, Angelo. For God's sake, I'm not going to risk it all over him.

"Besides, push comes to shove we have enough clout with the FBI, IRS, and other agencies—not to mention the media—to put Kiesco and hundreds more like it out of business without lifting a finger."

"You're right. Sorry I asked," Angelo said.

"By the way, Angelo, tomorrow I'll have Sergio send you a check to pay off the line of credit. As for the General, if we lose the money . . . let it be."

29

Giglio occupied the entire forty-second floor. Gabriella was promoted to Ray's personal secretary. Ray was thirty-six, and without a day of working out, he still had a Superman physique and a great smile. His streak of white hair was well defined and more elegant now.

A large octagonal table stood at the center of the Steam Room. Each side formed a workstation with a high-backed swivel chair, a telephone, and a nametag. The only engraved nametags were—Ray, Silvana, Sergio, and Pat. The other four stations were for consultants or salespeople. On Tuesdays and Thursdays, the room turned into a strategic center.

By 2:00 p.m. their creative talent energized the room. This room was Giglio's private Hall of Fame. Success was truly in the air. Photos of designs and campaigns on the walls reflected the company's success. The whole world was now familiar with the name Giglio. This room impressed guests and reminded employees of what they had accomplished.

On this day, Silvana opened the in-house strategy session with a reminder on vigilance. "Look, guys, winning more favorable reviews for the fall collection rather than the winter collection only shows that in this business we cannot drop our guard ever—that's if we want to become the kind of pacesetters we're hoping to be."

Ray glanced across the table and gladly followed Silvana's lead, "We might spend a decade introducing must-have items for the in-vogue, but the facts are that if we fail to keep a finger on the pulse of the consumer, we can lose it all in a single season."

Pat, Giglio's marketing genius, looked at Silvana and said, "Silvana, at a time when middle-class America is vocal about values, I think you have to tone down your creations a bit. I'm not talking about miniskirts for girls, even though you should add back an inch or two there. I'm talking about dresses for women who are not yet ready for clothes that invite attention."

Confused, Sergio asked, "What are you talking about?"

Pat looked at Sergio and explained, "If Middle America, the so-called silent majority, is not ready, they will see our creations as crude and sexually aggressive. In the future, the romance trend might find its audience. For now, I don't think these dresses are speaking to our clientele.

"The present trend favors clothes that serve as daywear as well as eveningwear. Sexual equality is much further down the road than we think."

"Silvana, what Pat is saying," Ray said, "is that we're getting ahead of the times."

She looked at Ray unconvinced.

"Do you remember what happened to the Edsel? Although it was a stylish car, the Edsel vanished quickly. Its design was a couple of years ahead of its time.

"Besides dresses, we have to worry about an array of products that bear our label."

Silvana did not argue with Ray but took it in stride.

In these meetings, no one took offense, nor were there defeats. Expanding on useful criticism was their formula for success. In that spirit, the first round of debate on what styles to send to the next show took up most of the afternoon.

Silvana and Pat found a middle ground on skirt length and female attire. She agreed to wait a few years before letting loose what she had in store for women.

Leaning back in his chair, Sergio said, "I believe we've hammered this subject long enough. We all know we've got new collections in stock that cover styles from now to the year 2000 and beyond.

"With due respect to Silvana here, that tells me not to worry about creations for the near future."

Concerned, glancing at each of them, Pat cut in, "I agree with that, but what worries me, and it should worry you also, is venturing into the future without a solid production team."

Ray agreed, "I know. And if you're talking about those manufacturers that are dragging us down, the only good news is that their contracts end a year from now.

"And no, Sergio, you don't have to say a word. We all know they've provided the bulk of the monies, but that's done and over. We got ours, and they got theirs and much more.

"What we need to do is focus on finding their replacements. We do it quietly, one by one, within the next six months."

Pat shuffled sheets of paper in his hands and said, "Do you know what bothers me? The more money these bastards are making, the more they drag their feet.

"It's as if they want us out of business. Am I the only one sensing this?"

Silvana and Ray exchanged glances.

Pat handed a list to each of them. "In anticipation of this move, I've prepared a short list of replacement manufacturers that might fit the bill."

Ray reviewed the list. "To you, it might be a short list. But when we decide to switch, you'll sure have a helluva lot of traveling to do."

Grinning, Pat said, "I'll do whatever it takes."

"You're a good peddler, Pat," Ray smiled. "For now, let's sleep on it for a couple of days. In the meantime, I see no harm in digging a little deeper into these new people. At first glance, they seem okay.

"One more thing, let me assure you that Silvana and I are more anxious than you are to get things back on track."

Pat and Sergio nodded.

Ray turned to Pat. "I think you can use some help. I'm meeting Victor Como tomorrow. He's in-between deals. If you want, I'll ask him to join us for a short while. I'm sure he can help you."

"I sure hope so. I like Victor a lot."

After dinner, with Rex in the doghouse and the children fast asleep, Ray and Silvana routinely discussed the day's events in their pajamas, either on the bedroom porch or by the fireplace on cooler nights. Tonight the autumn weather kept them indoors.

"Do you still think my father would do this?"

"He already has."

"You're right. It's hard for me to accept it."

To no avail, Ray poked the top log into flames. "Since your brother was killed and most of the moles have disappeared, your father feels threatened by anything that moves."

"To feel safe, he has to call the shots," she said.

"I'm glad you brought it up. But there are things he cannot do through business connections alone."

The night got progressively quieter. Now Silvana got up and poked the stubborn log a few times more. "Maybe if I had a face-to-face talk with him," she said.

"Wake up to reality, Silvana. We started that way. Don't forget Stefano. To your father, family comes second. Besides, you're no longer daddy's little girl."

"I guess I got lucky," she said with a tender smile.

"We both did. That's why we must stand by our convictions, the same way he does . . . no matter what."

Silvana curled up on the sofa again. "By the way, what's up with the General?"

Ray got up to poke the log again.

She frowned. "Don't dodge the question."

As if surprised, Ray asked, "What about the General?"

"Is he going to get away with it?"

"Do you know what's wrong with this log? It's damp," Ray said, still busy poking. "John put a tail on the General, and contrary to what Victor thinks, he can pay.

"He's unleashing a bag of tricks with a woman in Switzerland. He's living on a fat million dollar bank account."

Sleepy and tired of fighting with the log, they headed for the bedroom. As they left the room, the fire leapt, lapping their shadows on the wall. The now dry log crackled and snapped spitting sparks in an effort to regenerate.

30

At ten-thirty on Wednesday morning, Ray stepped off the elevator full of energy. He passed Gabriella's desk with a single smile but took no coffee. At half past twelve, Victor Como walked into his office smiling.

"I hope I'm not too early."

Ray grinned, "Let's do lunch. We'll grab a sandwich at the Jewish deli. They have the best cuts in town."

From their booth, Victor and Ray watched people rushing by on the crowded sidewalk. They ordered corned beef for Victor and brisket for Ray, both on rye with mustard, French fries, green pickles, and a Coke.

Drumming his slender fingers on the table, Victor hesitantly said, "Listen, Ray, true I spent seven years spinning my wheels on the coast, but you and I go back a long way and I think we can be frank with each other."

Ray sat back and crossed his arms. He looked at his friend kindly. "I am not holding anything back from you, Victor, but if you are referring to my father . . . my heart has been heavy since he was killed."

"I know that," Victor said. "If it's not an obsession and you're sure who did it, do what you must and get that load off your back."

"It's not easy," said Ray, halfhearted, "someday I will."

Each man became silent with thought. Then Victor opened a new topic: Don Saverio. "Ray, I want to know what's going on with Don Saverio. I'm concerned."

Ray glanced out the window. To Victor, he seemed undecided. Finally, Ray said, "Do you remember when Don Saverio warned us about the Mafia meeting in upstate New York?"

"I do."

"Well, Don Saverio busted that meeting," Ray said. "His people tipped a local cop who got the FBI involved. The rest is history. That's how far he went to put the old Mafia out of business."

"If you ask me, he did more than bust those guys," Victor said. "As I recall from all the media accounts, he exposed the old Mafia bosses for what they were— anything but organized.

"He sent a strong message to the old boys to quit and to those who admired the old Mafia to stay away from it."

"That was the beginning of the end," Ray said.

Perplexed, Victor said, "You know, I often wonder why he went through all that. What did he get out of it? It makes no sense. He had to do it for something greater than we think."

The waiter delivered their sandwiches. Ray spread more mustard on his sandwich. To allay Victor's concern, he said, "In a strange way, Don Saverio is the ultimate con man.

"At first, he tempted the Class of '56 with a glamorous lifestyle. In Sicily, when you're young and stupid, that's all you dream about."

"Wait," Victor said, resentful, "maybe your dream was different than ours, for you did not experience much hardship growing up. In truth, Sicily didn't have much to offer for the ambitions of the young."

With a smirk in his face, Ray said, "Well, okay, perhaps my dream of finding my father's killer wasn't nobler than all dreams combined, but putting that aside, Don Saverio got you guys in school for he knew that educated people rarely have anything to do with old Mafia. Don Saverio himself is the living proof.

"It was a brilliant con job. He never asked any of you to do anything illegal. He not only made it an absolute condition, but he shielded you all from old Mafia."

"I still don't see what he got out of Mafia reform," Victor said.

"My take is that besides getting himself out of the old Mafia, he built a legacy in politics and big business that will live forever," Ray said. "New Mafia doctrine will shape men and women into leaders of honor who speak the truth and protect the masses from undue suppressions."

"That's if corruption doesn't poison them to the core as it did the old Mafia," Victor said. "Still, what's the Class of '56's final objective?"

"First, let me clarify an important point," Ray said. "The Class of '56, thanks to Don Saverio's con job, now consists of educated and principled men—not a bunch of derelicts on a journey to unattainable goals.

"Each member is a doer dedicated to a higher Cause than his own being. That includes you, regardless of how you feel about the California deal.

"That deal, Victor, was beyond your control. You'll do everyone a favor if you stop blaming yourself. You were dealing with a sophisticated con artist who had all the markings of a lawful businessman, that's all.

"Second, the doers and all the others who followed in the footsteps of the Class of '56 are free from political constraints and will continue to spread Don Saverio's ideology.

"It will rise to all levels of leadership across continents under the flag of democracy. That is what captivates the oppressed.

"Democracy, however, will thin into a chaos of rules and regulations; it will become an ideology without substance that cannot stand alone, no less leading the masses it captivates.

"In the background, only our people will have the substance to guide and get leaders of their choosing elected."

When the men finished their meal, a smiling Ray tipped the waiter and led Victor out of the deli. On their way back, there was no talk, only deep thoughts.

Back in the office, Victor sat across from Ray at the table. "Ray, what you said about doers at lunch rings true with me. Don Saverio used to tell us how dangerous the non-doer's philosophy was.

"In the past, there were geniuses who made life-changing contributions to humanity, and yet we scorned most of them. We prosecuted them, even jailed and lynched them. All because of the non-doer's fear of what these achievers represented."

"No penalty man can muster," said Ray, "including death, will ever erase a doer's deed. His deed will live forever.

"On the other hand, take away the money from the non-doers and what's left? Nothing. Zero. They leave no imprint whatsoever.

"Mind you, some doers come to us as creators, others as leaders. The most effective doer is the one with both qualities. This unique breed I call Professional Dreamers. They are capable of seeing, creating, and taking that vision into reality."

"I agree," Victor said, "only I call them Champions. The creator or the doer is the person who swims upriver while everyone else swims downriver. The greater the challenge, the harder he swims.

"He wants no credit, just enough money to keep on going. He wants the world to reap the benefits of his creation. The leader, on the other hand, takes a doer's creation and brings it to fruition.

"The Champion, or better yet, the CEO, is the person who makes things work from start to finish. He envisions, creates, and delivers. When he has to make things happen, he reaches deep down inside and finds that extra something that others can't."

"Well," Ray said with a smile, "who do you think we're talking about?"

Victor, taken aback, said nothing.

"You went to the West Coast and got let down by one deal. But in those five years, you also helped a dozen start-up companies achieve great success. They are still growing thanks to you.

"They are a testimony to your achievements. If that doesn't qualify you as a thinker and as a CEO, I don't know what does."

"I appreciate your words, Ray, but I think a good CEO needs more experience than I have."

"To some extent, you're right," Ray said. "But let me give my short version of what makes a CEO.

"We're talking about a productive CEO, not slick con men milking companies like common swindlers. The only things these people are seeking are extra payment through cockeyed bookkeeping, insider stock deals, and tax evasion.

"After they rip off their investors, they don't even show an iota of contrition. Some of them get a weird satisfaction and even brag about it. They're scum without conscience. They should all be thrown in jail for good.

"Nevertheless, that's their problem. Now let's get back to us.

"A productive CEO is a person who works all sorts of hours, sacrifices his family, celebrates no holidays or birthdays, and doesn't take a day off much less a vacation.

"He puts work ahead of pleasure. He promises to someday make it all up to his family and to whatever friends he has left. When he thinks the job is done, he finds another frontier to conquer.

"A productive CEO is that person who is not afraid to roll up his sleeves and get down to work. Even after the job is finished, he thinks he can do better. A productive CEO doesn't accept mediocrity.

"A productive CEO has the guts to learn from his mistakes and try again and again until he breaks through."

To drive the point home, Ray went on, "In answer to your question, Victor, a CEO with those qualities has an innate gift that no hands-on experience can deliver.

"You don't make that kind of CEO. He or she is born with the talent and passion to be one. As they say, either you have it or you don't. In my book, Victor Como has it all."

Victor dipped his head, accepting the compliment. He thought:

Ray Greco, you're talking about yourself. . . . Victor, don't spoil his moment.

"Now that we agree, let me tell you what's on my mind today," Ray said. "Some friends of ours are working on a business plan. It has to do with electronic devices that will facilitate billing and data identification processing. They tell me this technology will revolutionize the credit card and most detection businesses.

"I want you to look into it. If you want to get involved, it's all yours, no strings attached.

"In the meantime, Pat can use your help here at Giglio. He's reforming Giglio's production team. What do you say?"

"Sure, I'd love to."

31

Brenda was blonde with blue eyes, slim-lined brows, fleshy lips, and a capricious face. Her breasts were large and firm and tipped with big rosy nipples. She wore black panties with a red heart embroidered on the front.

She poured herself a shot of whiskey and gulped it down. The alcohol stopped her shivering. Not knowing if the General was coming up to spend the night, she got ready anyhow.

She unbuttoned her blouse, took off her skirt and bra, and sat in her panties at the bar. She would slide them off before he came through the door.

He liked to find her naked and ready. Perhaps the thought of her alone, naked, and waiting for him was all he needed to get excited.

The arrangement was simple. He paid for every Wednesday night. When he brought guests along, he paid double for each guest she entertained as he watched.

He would park the car by the road and climb the stairs to her chalet. As long as she was paid, it made no difference whether he showed up alone or with an army. The more the merrier, she always thought.

The General was in his late sixties. He was a handsome, gray-haired man, with a craggy face, rigid posture, and a commanding manner. He was accustomed to having his orders obeyed, and for the money he paid her, Brenda was very obedient.

When three men came through the side door, she was stunned. She watched as they surveyed the apartment.

One man tossed his raincoat on the sofa and asked, "What's your name?"

Scared and expecting the worst, Brenda crossed her arms over her naked body and inched toward the window that overlooked Bern. She was hoping to see the General coming up the stairs. There was no General. She remained silent.

The closest chalet was a good mile away and the city fifteen minutes down the road. In the dark of the night, you could barely make out the cathedral's tower.

One of the men, a husky man, said, "I don't think she can talk, Sal, maybe if I take her into the bedroom . . ."

The man named Sal said, "Look, guys, don't get any ideas. Do as you were told. Check the rooms and leave the girl alone."

Sal looked at her, "I don't care about your name. Get dressed and, if you know how, make some coffee. We'll be here for awhile."

Under the gleaming eyes of the three men, she rushed to put on her bra, blouse, and skirt.

Once dressed, she relaxed a bit. "I'm Brenda. What are you looking for?"

"Nothing," Sal smirked.

She sat on the barstool. "Then why are you here?"

Sal sat on the other stool next to her. "We've come to surprise the General. We're good buddies. We know all about his tricks. Relax; everything is going to be okay."

"If you're his buddies," she said, "how come your friend wanted to take me to the bedroom? That's not friendly."

"He couldn't wait. He didn't know the General likes to watch that sort of thing."

Sizing up Sal's friends, Brenda was already spending the extra money she would earn. She cheerfully went off to make coffee.

Sal watched Brenda come back smiling with a full pot of coffee and a half-empty bottle of whiskey.

"Brenda, what you don't know is what the General really likes."

"What's that?"

"A real surprise, it never fails. It gets him so excited that he can go with three girls at once for hours. So give us a hand."

"Sure, what do you want me to do?" she smiled.

"Chain the front door," Sal said. "When he knocks, wait for my cue. Then let him in without letting on that we're here."

"Shucks, that's easy."

She reached for the bottle.

"Not yet!"

Sal took the bottle away from her. "Wait until the party starts, all right?"

Brenda chained the door and returned to her stool. She crossed her legs and looked down at her swinging foot quietly.

The three men were on their third cup of coffee when a car stopped by the road.

The husky man stepped out the side door.

A few moments later, a key unlocked the front door.

Rattling the safety chain, the General called, "Brenda, let me in."

Sal waved her to the door.

"Why are you all dressed up?" complained the General, as he entered the living room.

Spotting the two men, the General cried out, "Who the hell are you? This better be a joke."

The General jumped when he heard the front door slam shut and saw a third man standing behind him.

Sal poured the General a cup of coffee and invited him to sit down. "Calm down, Dan. We're friends. Have some coffee and let's talk things over." The General warily took a seat opposite Sal.

The atmosphere in the small apartment changed. It took on the vibes of a Third World courtroom, where verdicts are delivered in minutes and sentences are carried out on the spot.

Sal and the General stared at each other across the coffee table. Sal's friends sat at a table behind the sofa playing cards. Brenda, the sole spectator, watched from the bar, mystified. Sal presided over the case.

"Let me ask you, Dan . . . do you know Victor Como?"

"Oh my God, I can't believe this. I told him . . .," the General looked around wildly, seeking help. "Tell him I'll take care of it next week when I get back to the States."

Sal rubbed his jaw. "Dan, I'm afraid we can't do that."

"Why's that? My word is good. You can ask Victor."

"It's not a matter of asking. You see, Victor's out. I bought your account, and I'm here to collect."

"Okay, okay!" He pulled out a checkbook from his coat pocket. "Let's get it over with." With pen in hand, ignoring the piercing stares from the card players and Brenda's occasional glance, he searched Sal's face, "Two hundred and fifty thousand . . . right?"

"Wrong. Two hundred sixty-five plus thirty-five collection fees makes it an even three hundred."

The General scribbled across the check and handed it to Sal. "There. You got what you came for, please leave now."

Sal studied the check. There was a disparity with the bank account number Ray had sent him. "Not yet, Dan, what's the hurry?

"There's plenty of coffee in the house to last us until the bank opens tomorrow. Make yourself comfortable, my friend."

"You mean my word is no good?"

"Your word is as good as your check, and it better be good. Trust me, Dan, you don't want those butchers on your ass," Sal said, pointing at the two card players.

The General paused, looking deep into his cup of coffee as beads of sweat began to roll down his neck.

"What if I get you two hundred fifty thousand cash?"

"It's no good, my friend. Three hundred now . . . three fifty in one hour . . . and fifty thousand for each additional hour we have to wait."

"Okay . . . okay. Three hundred it is," said the General, glancing at Brenda who was taking in the whole scene. "I'll be back in an hour."

Sal laughed. "You never give up, do you? They'll go with you."

"Why? Well, okay."

Sal pointed to the card players. "I'll wait one hour. Don't play stupid, Dan. They got orders."

The General and his escorts were barely gone before Brenda approached Sal and got down on her knees. Staring at the ceiling, he sighed—she was good. Although Sal felt guilty for cheating on his wife, he rationalized that the encounter was a job-related hazard.

Exhausted, at twelve o'clock, he pulled out a nylon string from around his waist. He knocked her head back and wrapped the string around her neck twice and pulled hard, until she struggled no more. Sal never got to know her last name.

Sal and friends got the cash and left Switzerland heading south by train. The next morning the FBI issued a report. General Dan Kohaski, unable to cope with a pending investigation, had hung himself.

32

November 2, 1997—Late afternoon

After an arduous Sunday in Manhattan, Ray was mentally worn out. He wanted to get home before the kids did, have dinner, and relax the rest of the day with Silvana. Silvana's early return from the London fashion show—and their lovemaking—was a pleasant surprise. Still, his trip down memory lane and the newspaper article about Mafia on its deathbed had made him weary.

With the box of souvenirs and the Olivetti in the trunk and Silvana by his side, Ray drove home to Scarsdale with thoughts of starting a life away from Mafia, a new life. Silvana on the other hand, also thought of fulfilling the role of matriarch away from Giglio. Their future seemed bright and on track. They were reaching their goals sooner than expected.

Again, Ray's thoughts turned to the man in the elevator. He decided to forgive the kid from Brooklyn; after all, he was a man now.

At home, Ray set the box of souvenirs on the floor of his study and the Olivetti next to his computer. Staring at the typewriter and the computer, he smiled and thought:

The odd couple

He then approached the typewriter, rolled up the yellowed paper one notch and typed: Thanks Ma.

The tic-tic-tics drew Silvana to the typewriter. The third line was scribbled; the ribbon was bone dry leaving behind merely dashes:

A Z C V M M Q

R a y G r e c o

------ --

Ray's memory, however, read all three lines clearly.

Silvana stepped back into the living room, leaving her husband to his memories. Going through the souvenirs, Ray found a twenty-five-year-old newspaper clipping showing a gasoline station with a car at the pump. In the forefront, there was a large sign—Gasoline by Appointment Only. That clipping had marked a turning point for Ray.

That year, OPEC hiked oil prices and curtailed production and Giglio's contractors had followed suit. Between these two groups, there was a distinction, however. The oil lords strangled a world grown reliant on cheap oil for money. Don Saverio Cremona strangled Giglio not for money but for his own survival.

As Don Saverio's plan to topple Mafia families came to fruition, so did Ray's plan to topple his father-in-law. While Don Saverio depended on the moles to come home, Ray depended on Sal to stop them from ever reaching Sicily. Weakened, Don Saverio fell in a power struggle with his daughter and Ray.

Silvana hated her father for what he had done to her family, in particular for what, she thought, he had done to her brother Stefano. Ray hated Don Saverio for what he thought he had done to his father. They both hated Don Saverio more for what he had in store for their family and Giglio.

Don Saverio's struggle, however, was for the survival of the Cause and his family. To achieve that goal, he exerted financial pressure on Giglio through its contractors.

Having coffee at the dining room table, Ray and Silvana were contemplating their choices.

"Whatever it takes, Ray," a disgusted Silvana said. "We must stop him."

"It's easier said than done." Ray rubbed his chin in thought.

"I still can't believe it," she fixed her bright shiny eyes on her husband, "my own father?"

"Your father is so wrapped up in traditions that he'd kill his own mother if he had to."

"What's next?"

"Nothing. I'm meeting him next week."

33

The scenic drive from Palermo Punta Raisi Airport to Alcamo became progressively riskier with each mile they rode. To Ray's regret, the road was as torturous as it had been in 1956. The American highways had spoiled him. To keep safety on his side, he ordered the cabdriver to pull over.

"Now listen, you!" said Ray angrily. "I've got a mother to visit, and I intend to get there in one piece. Now, if you know what's good for you, you'll follow my rules."

"What rules?" the cabdriver asked. "Do you see any white lines or markers on the road? There are no speed limits here."

"I understand," he said, raising his voice. "Here is twenty dollars, and here are my rules. Never exceed twenty miles per hour on curves and forty on straightaways. Never pass horse-and-buggies or any other moving object in a blind spot. Break those rules and not only will I take the cab and the money from you, but I'll also kick your ass all the way home . . . Is it clear?"

"We'll never get there," complained the cabdriver.

"Let me worry about that," Ray said. "Just follow the rules."

"You're the boss," said the cabdriver, eyeing Ray's massive wrists.

The ride took an extra thirty minutes.

As the cab sped away, Ray smiled and thought: *The best twenty dollars I ever spent.*

Once a year, Ray came to visit Don Saverio for the usual one-on-one talks. This visit was unusual for it was the second of the year.

Before visiting Don Saverio, however, Ray had dinner with his mother and Sal. Then he and Sal took the customary stroll men take down Main Street after dinner. At a sidewalk café, they ordered two espressos. From their table, they watched others strolling.

"What happened to the General?" Ray asked.

"He was an asshole. He hung himself."

Ray stared at Sal but said nothing.

"Look, Ray. . . . If the boys did it, they would've taken the rest of the cash. Read the papers. There was cash stashed in the hotel room."

Ray understood, but asked, "What about the girl?"

"When the General failed to come back," Sal blushed, "she had to go."

"I'm meeting Don Saverio in the morning," Ray said.

"I guessed that much. . . . What's wrong?"

"Nothing's wrong. Same old stuff. He's suspicious."

"Listen," Sal pushed the demitasse aside and leaned toward Ray. "Let's get it over with . . . will you?"

"Not yet, maybe by the end of the year. Right now he has too much squeeze on us. Pat and Victor are getting replacement contractors as we speak."

Concerned, Sal asked, "Does Victor know about you and Don Saverio?"

Ray picked up his cup. "Absolutely not. You know Victor won't hesitate to kill for Don Saverio."

"Okay, with that aside for now, then we're set." Sal nodded. "Year's end it'll be. Don't get greedy, Ray; you've been waiting too long."

Ray gently placed his cup back on the table. "Don't pin me down. Before I make a move, I want Silvana firmly to my side."

"Okay, I'll buy that," Sal said, "but what's with these suspicions?"

"Don Saverio thinks I've wised up to him."

"What do you mean?"

"Lately he's been acting like a wounded beast,"

"Isn't that natural? How would you feel if besides losing your sons and more than half of your moles, you had to rely on a son-in-law whose father you killed?"

"I know," Ray said, "but I don't think my father troubles him. I'm sure that to him the killing was justifiable business, no different from having Stefano killed. I bet what's troubling him is not being sure of my loyalty to him or the loyalty of his daughter and grandchildren."

"Why shouldn't he? They are his blood. And what makes you think he's suspicious?"

"When I first left Sicily in 1956," Ray said, "Don Saverio and I talked about my father's accident. I don't think he ever bought my story. He gave me a short spiel assuring me it was an accident. Back then, all was well. Carlo was alive, his troops in top shape, and I was going to lead the New Enterprises so he brushed the whole thing off. So I thought."

"I guess father and son never took into account the work of fate."

"Without their help, I don't think fate would have worked the way it has so far."

"Does he have any inkling about your plan?" Sal asked.

"Yes and no. As I've been loyal to his plan, he can't prove a thing. When I took over Carlo's job, I followed his plan to the letter. Now with his men disappearing, he's getting more suspicious. Soon he might stir up something before I'm ready to act."

"I think you're right." Sal drained his espresso. "You can't afford to wait another ten years. Your grandfather always told me: Never take lightly Mafia's ability to regenerate. After World War II, Don Saverio built a legacy of *Mafiosi* throughout Sicily. Believe me, Ray; he can rebuild an army quicker than you think."

Ray wasn't so sure of that. "It won't be that easy or fast. He has to justify his change of heart about old Mafia and then reposition himself. The new generation is not apt to follow someone as blindly as their ancestors did."

"You don't think he can regenerate?"

"I didn't say that. If anybody can, Don Saverio definitely can. He has enough money to motivate not only a town, but a city. That's not what he wants. Do you remember the kid from Brooklyn? The one you bought for a dollar more than I did. You can buy services, not loyalty. Don't kid yourself; he knows that well."

The men decided to call it a night. On their way back home, Ray threw his arm around Sal's shoulder and said, "Before I go back to New York, I want to take some photos of the gravel plant."

34

In the last seventeen years, the driveway leading to the villa had not changed much. At one side of the walkway, there was a new knee-high evergreen wall. Older and grayer, Don Saverio stood at the north window as usual, ready for a new day.

Two young guards disguised as gardeners were edging the greens. "Good morning, Mr. Greco," one of the gardeners said.

"Good morning," Ray said. As he walked into the house, he wondered:

Who are they? I've never seen those two characters before. . . . But they know my name.

In the lobby with the marble staircase, Ray sensed loneliness. No one lived in the house but Don Saverio and his wife, Donna Maria.

With his right hand on the banister ready to climb, Ray looked up and smiled at Donna Maria who had just appeared on the landing. He watched her descend the stairs. When she reached him, she did not pester him about Silvana and the children, as most mothers-in-law would have. Instead, she held his hands and warmly said, "Please, be patient with him."

Ray kissed her forehead and hugged her gently. Then he began to climb the longest flight of stairs, or so it seemed.

The door was ajar. Don Saverio, still looking out the window mumbled, "Women."

Smiling as he reached for a chair, Ray said, "Yes, and only God knows what He had in mind."

"Good morning, Ray. Please sit down."

"Don Saverio, she's a good woman."

"She's my wife . . ."

Ignoring the tradition that women should not interrupt business, Donna Maria brought in a fresh pot of coffee, homemade cookies, and a heart full of pain. Ray knew she was sorry that she could not speak her mind. As she left the room, her long black dress swirled like a tornado.

Both men, sensing her desire to will peace, stared at each other for a short while. With not much to say, as men of honor, each accepted his position in a game of fate.

Don Saverio was sixty-seven and Ray thirty-six. Both had aged since their first meeting in this same room. Ray saw lines of frustration on Don Saverio's face. He thought:

Perhaps that's what made Donna Maria leery.

The two men talked of business.

Rubbing his chin, Ray said, "Don Saverio, lately I've been having problems with six contractors, and unless I do something quickly, they'll put Giglio out of business."

"Are you asking me if I'm aware of it?" Don Saverio raised an eyebrow. Before Ray could answer, he handed him a list, "Let's be sure . . . do you mean these guys?"

Ray scanned the list, "Yes, these are the ones."

"Ray, let's not play games this morning. We both know why you're here, so let me put you at ease. I own part of each of those companies."

Ray said nothing.

Raising his voice, Don Saverio said, "I'm buying them outright as we speak, and there's nothing that you or Silvana can do."

To Ray's surprise, Don Saverio had set him free from Mafia's constraints.

To reinforce that claim, Ray asked, "What about the children?"

"Who do you think I'm doing this for?" Don Saverio said angrily. "Donna Maria and I want you and your family here. Giglio is a drop in a bucket compared to what I have put together for you all. They are our blood. Tell Silvana not to worry. I'll take care of everything."

"I'm glad you told me. . . . I really am." Ray nodded. "I'll tell her. I'm sure she'll appreciate what you're doing for us."

Agitated, Don Saverio said, "No, she won't be. She's as stubborn as a mule. You're the man of the house. Do what you have to and, for God's sake, talk some sense into her. I asked you once not to piss away your future. Your family belongs here—and now! And you know better."

Ray stared at him for a long moment and thought:

Either the man's crazy, or he's playing the best con job ever.

"What about Giglio?"

"What about Giglio?" he said. "For all I care, you can shut it down. Without me, it's not worth a dime."

Ray looked on, dismayed.

Don Saverio paused to compose himself, and then he said, half-smiling, "Your job in America is done; you belong here now. With your know-how and natural smarts, you can fry much larger fish here. Besides, I'm sure your mother would like to have her grandchildren nearby."

"I see what you mean," Ray said, but he saw a different agenda playing out:

Father and daughter as partners, just the way Don Saverio envisioned when he first promised to back Silvana's dream. Get Ray to bring her and the kids back home, get rid of Ray, and groom the kids for the good of the family, even change their last name to Cremona.

Why not? . . . Blood is blood.

Both men relaxed and reached for glasses of water. Refreshed, each was ready for another round. Don Saverio was cordial now.

"How're the boys?"

Not sure of Don Saverio's endgame and hoping to get a better read, Ray followed the lead with no direct answers.

"Don Saverio, as you said, we're not going to play games nor do I want to disrespect you," Ray smiled. "Allow me to tell you where I think we are and where we're going with the New Enterprise.

"As for the old Mafia, as you well know, we have made serious inroads. In the last five years, we have toppled more than half of the families. John DeMaria says that within ten years, we'll finish the job. Anyone left standing will be irrelevant and greed will take care of that. It will wipe them out sooner than we think."

Don Saverio rose and walked to the window. His back to Ray, he asked, "Well, those are our enemies. What about our friends?"

"The Class of '56," Ray said, "is doing well in politics and business. And as you said, my job is done. Those who followed, I believe a little more than three hundred, are working well with the rest of the men. They are achieving their goals faster than we expected on their own accord."

"From what I read in the papers," Don Saverio said contentedly, "there is no question that most ethnic groups now are coming on board."

"Indeed they are," Ray said. "When you think of what they teach nowadays about political and business leadership, it amounts to nothing more than Mafia. This leadership philosophy will spread into all branches of government and business. In essence, Mafia is an innate trait of those who lead."

"What do you think the future holds?" Don Saverio turned toward him.

"A leader to spread a message, thanks to the media, won't have to beat his drum at every corner to reach a few," Ray said. "He can move masses in favor or against a person or promote a principle across continents. It only takes a single message of fear or hope or convoluted news-spin, if you will.

"Through the media, leaders can collude with other leaders without incriminating themselves. They can issue talking points without ever meeting with subordinates, staffers, or supporters.

"Watch those world leaders, warlords, business tycoons, and every other petty thug. They are taking advantage of the system already. That's without mentioning the Vietnam War, the Nuremburg trials, and political campaigns.

"Through the media, however, every pundit and reporter will express his opinion, not news, and that's not so good. As I said, to advance their agenda, the media will also promote ideological writings that will set off the masses.

"We're approaching unprecedented times," Ray said. "The Mafia is finally reaching the hearts and minds of those who want to lead.

"The kind of Mafia I'm talking about is a global codebook of advanced political and business rules to help balance different democratic views. A code of silence that gives leaders that special quality they need to make responsible decisions, regardless of personal or political cost, especially when faced with the extremes of those views. Above all else, this code tells them how and when to move toward center."

"If I've ever erred," Don Saverio said, "it was my weakness for your perceptions and leadership. I thought of New Mafia back in 1945. Then, in 1956 when you called it New Enterprise I went along with it, for my kind of Mafia wasn't advanced at all back then."

"How can I forget?" Ray said. "I bet you still have that clipping with Stalin, Churchill, and Roosevelt right there in your drawer."

Don Saverio nodded and smiled.

"Although your dream came true," Ray said, "let me tell you where I think Mafia is headed. For starters, we're losing our identity. Most newcomers don't even know your name. Nor do they feel obliged to respect those who paved the way and to make. . ."

Don Saverio's stare cut Ray off.

"That's exactly what I want," Don Saverio proudly said. "I want them to exchange punches with each other all within the rule of law with no strings attached to old corrupted Mafia. As you know, back in the fifties, I started an educational program. I instigated a mania for emigration here that's still going on. The goal was to spread the true Mafia ideology while shaking off the corrupted Mafia stigma from the Sicilians' backs. To that end, I didn't care who spread our ideology, as long as it took hold and wiped out corruption in politics and big business.

"We started in the United States because, with the separation of church and state, we can persuade people more easily than in any other nation. Remember, only through honorable men of substance who speak the truth can the masses benefit from that ideology.

"I'm fearful, however, that it won't last long, for greed, ultimately, is apt to corrupt it."

As Don Saverio spoke, his stern look sent chills down Ray's spine. For a moment, Ray wished he could embrace and trust him. Then, focusing on his own agenda, he thought:

No wonder he didn't care whether his men ever came home. He might be very much relieved at not having to explain his position to anybody.

"Ray, what do you think happened to Joey and those other guys who signed up with the FBI?" Don Saverio asked.

"The only thing I can assume," Ray said, "is that freedom and education are a volatile combination. Once you set a man free, he seldom comes back. In a way, it's not much different from you leaving the muscle Mafia for the pencil Mafia.

"Until we learn who we are and what we truly want, we're prisoners of circumstances and fate."

The grandfather clock was about to strike noon. For the first time, Ray was the one to end the meeting.

"I think we will make things work," Ray said, standing. "I'm meeting with my plant manager in less than one hour. Then, I'm flying back home this afternoon. If we put our heads together, we will supply every cubic yard of ready-mixed concrete for every highway built from here to Rome and beyond.

"By the way, we put a new mobile gravel plant on line. Next time up, I want you to see it in operation and give me your input."

"You got yourself a deal."

35

It was well past two; the start of the traditional two-hour lunch and the food was on the table. Accustomed to Sal's tardiness when occupied with mechanical challenges, Francesca asked Ray to fetch him home for lunch.

On his way to get Sal, Ray recalled a point of wisdom his father had taught him: to catch a pair of tuna, you must land the female first, for the male will stick around fighting. Don Saverio wanted to catch Silvana back home.

Ray drove the short distance to the gravel pit. When he pulled into the parking lot, he stirred up a white ball of dust that engulfed the car. When the dust settled, Ray could see Sal a little way up the hill behind a sign that read: Greco Road Materials & Contracting.

Sal was on the crusher, working on the latching system for the deck railing.

With both hands funneled around his mouth, Ray shouted, "Sal, let's go . . . lunch is getting cold!"

Rushing down from the crusher, wiping his hands with a dirty rag, Sal asked, "Oh my God, what time is it?"

Patting Sal's back, Ray said, "What's the difference? Let's go. We're late. Lunch is on the table."

"I tell you, I've done this too many times. One of these days she's going to kick my ass. I tell you, I'll deserve it."

"I didn't mean to rush you, but I'm taking off in a couple of hours. We're having a special meeting tomorrow afternoon. Things are getting hectic back home."

"How did you do with Don Saverio?"

"The man is so entrenched in his plan that he's ready to squash anybody in his path."

"Is the situation like we thought?"

"We were dead wrong. The man doesn't give a hoot about anybody, least of all the moles.

"You have to understand that when his father died, he had to quit college. Since he was on his way out of Mafia, he never accepted it. Although he ran a tight ship with the streak of vengeance of a traditional Mafia boss, he was always looking for ways out. Obsessed with the idea, he spent most of his life reforming Mafia.

"Now, much the same as his daughter, he's completing his dream. Both father and daughter are trapped in a senseless feud, and neither one is much satisfied with the likely endgame."

"What about your endgame, Ray?"

Patting Sal's back once more, Ray said, "I guess I'll have to come back sooner than I thought."

36

In the wee hours of the morning, a limousine pulled up on the tarmac of Westchester County Airport. It was winter, and it was cold. As promised, Ray had called Silvana one hour before he landed. Picking each other up at the airport had become a symbol of their devotion.

All bundled up, Silvana concealed a smile as she watched the tower for the double flash. The air traffic controller conspired in their love affair with telephone calls and flashing lights signaling that the plane was on final approach.

The fear of flying had never left Ray, especially during landings. Rolling down the runway, the jet swallowed the cold air. With engines hissing now, Ray felt each bump along the way. The sight of taxiway lights slipping under the wing calmed him.

Ray was troubled by his meeting with Don Saverio. What bothered him most was how he had misread the man.

However, the more he tried to shut off bad thoughts, the more he heard Don Saverio say:

I'm buying them outright, and there's nothing you can do . . .

I want you and your family back here . . .

She won't understand. Talk some sense into her . .
.

Don't piss away your future . . . Close Giglio.

Although troubled, Ray was certain that once on solid ground with Silvana and the children by his side, he would feel better. He did not have to make new commitments; he just had to fulfill the one at hand.

Ray exited the jet briskly displaying a contagious smile, as Silvana ran toward him. They met on the apron and hugged as if they had been parted for thirty years and not three days.

The driver packed the luggage into the limousine's trunk, and they started the fifteen-minute ride home. In the backseat, Silvana cuddled close. Her gaze was probing, yet strong. She said, "I think I know . . . he wants to take over Giglio."

Ray shook his head slightly, "You are as wrong as I was about his muscle power. He wants you back home."

"You must be joking?"

"No, I'm not."

She pushed herself away from Ray angrily and said, "When hell freezes over. I'm not starting that again. I tell you, Ray, I've had it. We have to break away for good. This is it; the man listens to no reason."

"There's no need to get all uptight." He tried to calm her. "That's his problem. We'll do what we have to do."

They arrived at the house. He and Silvana both took deep breaths. They had no choice but to calm down. "We're home," he said, "we'll talk over breakfast."

The kids, fed and composed, were lined up in the foyer ready for school. Wringing her hands, Aunt Laura was outside warming up the station wagon. When Rex barked, the orderly trio broke and ran toward their parents. Screams mixed with barks.

"Mommy, Mommy, Daddy!"

"Woof, woof!"

"Mommy!"

"Woo-oooof."

"Mommy! Daddy, Daddy!"

Teary-eyed, they told their awful tales of troubles in school. Comforted by hugs, kisses, and presents, they smiled at Aunt Laura who was waiting patiently. Then, with a stern but warm look, she called them into the wagon. As they drove away little Francesca waved with a mitten dangling off her wrist. Ray thought, she has her grandmother's smile.

Holding Rex's leash, Silvana asked if Ray was ready for breakfast.

"Not really," he said. "I traveled all night. We have a two o'clock meeting at the office. I'll put it off till four. I want to spend some time with the kids when they come back. What do you say?"

"I'm sure they'll love it," she said, cheerfully.

"Okay then, I'll take a nap, and we'll do brunch instead."

By the time Ray came down the stairs, lunch was served. He poured coffee. He said, "Looking at those kids today, I can't imagine them growing up anywhere else."

"I told you already," his adamant wife said. "I'm not going, nor is the rest of this family. Let's forget the whole thing. Just do what you have to do—and do it swiftly."

"There's nothing to do," he said annoyed, "but to stay put until Giglio frees itself from those bastards. Victor and Pat have worked on this plan for quite some time. I think we'll switch before Easter."

"Did you make up your mind on how to do it?"

"Somewhat," he said. "We'll talk strategy at the meeting."

Puzzled, she asked, "Okay, we switch . . . then what?"

"Then I'll deliver the news to your father myself."

"What kind of news?"

Stirring his coffee, he said, "I'm not going to shoot him. I'm going to have one more man-to-man talk. . . . That's all."

Sensing something was wrong, she looked the other way.

He tried teasing a smile from her. "I think you're terrified at the idea of going back."

She made a face at him. "Don't be silly. I can live in Sicily or any other place I want. But, I won't raise my children any place where their future is slated. I won't do it."

"Me neither. For now, let's keep it to ourselves. I need some time to get ready for the meeting before the kids get back."

Trusting in his judgment, she cleared the table as he withdrew to his study. For reasons Ray never understood, Rex was very quiet when the kids were not around.

37

The limousine drove south to Giglio's headquarters. It was a typical New York weather, overcast and breezy.

Silvana turned to Ray. "Ray, if you were wrong about his muscle power and I was wrong about my father taking over Giglio, then what's his game?"

"Your father controls those contractors. The way he sees it, to get us back to Sicily, he has to put Giglio out of business."

Ice stole over Silvana's expression. "That's terrible! How can he do that knowing how I feel about my career?"

"He says he wants to do more for you."

"I guess without Carlo, our kids are the only blood left for him to mold . . . huh!"

"As I said, he wants Giglio shut down, and he wants me to talk you into going back to Sicily. For that, he'll give you all he owns, which according to him makes Giglio seem like a drop in the bucket."

"What did you tell him?"

"I told him it was a great idea and that I'd talk you into it." He muffled his laughter.

"Yeah . . . right!"

The limo turned southbound on the parkway. They were a few miles from Giglio's headquarters, as Silvana was thinking:

He's my father, after all, the man who understands me. I did say someday I'd pay a price for it, didn't I?

The blast of a semi's horn from the oncoming lane broke her thoughts.

"Well, Ray," she said resolutely, "you talked to me and you know how I feel. I haven't heard how you feel."

"That's another matter," he said. "I'm sure your father has something good in mind for me also, wouldn't you say?"

Wisely, she said nothing. She knew this was a time to support her man. Ray was her only hero now.

At twenty minutes to four, the limousine pulled up in front of the office building. Ray instructed the driver to come back at six.

At the receptionist desk, Gabriella smiled as if she were on her first hour of work and not her ninth and counting.

"Welcome back," she said.

"Thank you, Gabriella. Is everybody here?"

"Everybody but Sergio, he'll be in shortly."

At a glance, the scene indicated that Giglio's staff had been working hard at solving problems. The octagon table, although polished, was piled with pads of paper and binders. Giglio was behind on its delivery schedules. Despite repeated calls to the contractors, it was losing ground. They were not shipping enough goods. The situation demoralized the team, the staff, and the merchants alike.

When Sergio rushed into the room, Ray called the meeting to order. Ray had reached a decision—alone. No one, not even Silvana, was privy to it.

Ray pounded his hand on the table. All eyes turned to him. He raised his voice, "The time has come to kick those bastards out. We'll do much better without them, and I'll tell you how."

Ray saw immediately that Pat and Sergio were thrilled. They had worked for some time getting things ready for this day. Silvana, who was consumed by the thought of going back to Sicily, gave a huge sigh of relief as if she were a death-row prisoner set free. Out of the corner of his eye, Ray even saw Gabriella, who was quite good at eavesdropping from her office, burst into a smile at the news.

Unbeknown to them, Ray was also relieved. In his team, he found the courage to decide. Don Saverio's threat no longer loomed over them.

Looking at Pat and Sergio, Ray said, "I know I shouldn't say this, but it's critical to our survival. Therefore, I must insist that whatever we discuss here stays here. Any leak could send the whole deal tumbling down like a house of cards."

Understanding his concern, they nodded.

In a lower tone, Ray said, "To outsiders, we'll tell things that benefit us only. Please, trust no one. Above all, don't fall for hearsay stories or trade reports. Our success depends on the secrecy of the plan."

Ray went on resolutely, "Giglio has no money problems. As a company, it enjoys an excellent credit rating, and it has ample cash reserves. Giglio's problem is production. As anticipated, our new marketing plan sparked more sales—to the point that we are outgrowing production tenfold.

"To make things worse, our manufacturing friends have not only curtailed supply but have also refused to tool up for the increased demand. Don't ask me why. Those are the facts. I believe they have an agenda of their own. Therefore, the first thing we'll do is sign up the replacement contractors. Pat, has Victor checked them out?"

"They're all clear," said Pat, satisfied. "Victor suggested creating some kind of partnership with these fellows, little more than a cold-cut relationship. These are good people, ready to work hard at a moment's notice. Contrary to our current friends, they are seeking steady orders and willing to chip in for advertising costs. I wish Victor were here to explain."

"That's refreshing," Ray said. "Victor is right about eventually sharing the advertising costs, but that maybe down the road a bit. We need time before we venture into that kind of partnership. I'm aware that no relationship can last long unless the deal is good for all parties. To that end, our basic deal is good."

Ray detailed his strategy, "For now, we have to approach the switch in a sensible order. Providing the new guys sign an agreement promising to keep their mouths shut, we sign them up for next season.

"As to the old boys, we tell them we're going out of business. And we promise that if they keep their mouths shut, they'll be well paid, because we're working on a bankruptcy scam and for it to work it has to be secret till the end."

Skeptical, Pat asked, "Why would they care whether we go out of business?"

Ray could not tell Pat and Sergio about Don Saverio's plans for Giglio and the Greco family so he simply shrugged and said, "I don't know why. The plain truth is they want us out of business. For now, they got us in a squeeze, and if we don't give in, they'll squeeze even more."

Staring at Ray, Pat said, "I don't mean to question you, but it's unfair."

Silvana spoke up. "I was born in Sicily, and I understand Ray's thinking better. If Ray was at liberty to do so and if it helped the company, he would lay it all out. I trust him. I hope you do, too."

"Do you really think that those bastards will up production, on a promise alone?" Pat asked, doubtful.

"I know so, Pat," Ray said.

"When do we start?" Sergio asked.

"Right now."

Two weeks after the meeting, Pat and Ray were having lunch at a new deli shop. Smiling, Pat reported, "Production's up."

"What did I tell you?"

38

Ray arrived in Alcamo the day before the festival. With time to spare, he drove to Torre Saracena atop Monte Bonifato. With a bird's eye view of the city, he studied the scene, recalling the history of his native land. As a teenager, he often came up here to think. Ray never faced so few choices. Facing north, on a plateau two thousand feet below, he could see the thousand-year-old Alcamo.

Alcamo, once the ancient Arab city of Alqamah, is nestled on the slopes of Monte Bonifato. The topography of the land encloses and secures the city, as there is no natural access to the mountain from the south. The east and west ends of town are protected by two artificial gateways—Porta Palermo and Porta Trapani—interconnected by the mile-long Corso 6 Aprile, Alcamo's main street.

From Porta Trapani, Main Street forks into two roads: the Lower Road and the Upper Road, which rejoin fifteen miles out of town. The Lower Road leads to Alcamo Marina, the new train station, and Calatafimi. The Upper Road leads to the Carrubbazzi, the old train station, and Calatafimi as well. Porta Palermo bastion, built a few hundred feet above the eastern landscape, is the gateway to Palermo.

Ray felt Don Saverio's attraction to the city when he looked out of his window. Don Saverio often lost himself in the historic myths and truths of the land and its people. It shaped his character. The seemingly liberal Don Saverio was a man of deep-rooted conservative convictions. As Ray found out, he would go to any extreme to preserve that philosophy.

Every year, Alcamo holds a festival for its patron, *La Madonna dei Miracoli*. The three-day festival takes place in June. Booths selling cotton candy, straw hats, toys, and more pop up all over Main Street for the event. Sideshows offer games of darts, loops, and cards. In short, it is a carnival that excites even the city's most serious hearts in a spirit of celebration for miracles yet to come, culminating when the *Madonna* is lifted and paraded through the streets.

In the afternoon, Main Street turns into a mile-long racetrack. Workers spread sand and stretch ropes through waist-high posts. At race time, people line up against the ropes on both sides of the track. Those residing on Main Street watch the races from their second- and third-floor balconies.

At the blast of a shotgun, the horses dash out. Under steady whipping and a pandemonium of shouts, the spectators lean forward to see the horses, and then jerk right back to avoid being hit, and then forward again to watch their tails racing on.

From the balconies, that back and forth motion of people lined up at both sides of the track looks like two long snakes zigzagging along with the horses from start to finish. It's a scene that captivates the viewers more than the race itself.

Another contest is the stopping of galloping horses in the shortest distance. Here, the young and strong get to show off their strength. With arms and hands out, each jumps in front of his chosen horse and tries to stop it. But, until it stops on its own accord, the horse drags him on its neck like a punching bag. Although some get hurt, every race has new takers for this lunacy.

In between races, spectators mill about the sideshows, while the people in the balconies wait for the next race.

On Thursday, the last day of the festival, after dining with his mother and Sal, Ray waited in front of the church for the procession to start. It was a crowded scene with people full of hope. He had promised Silvana that he would march alone—something most believers do at least once in their lifetime. This was Ray's time.

When in need of help, most natives of Alcamo, other than Don Saverio, prayed to the *Madonna of Miracles*. They can do this anytime and from anywhere in the world. She's their hope and conciliation. To entice her to answer their prayers, believers promise the *Madonna* a penance, money, or some other offering.

For the good of his soul and in hopes of restoring his life on track, Ray promised the *Madonna* the penance of marching alone and barefoot. Dressed casually with a hooded windbreaker, he joined in the cheers and bowed as the *Madonna* came into view.

She had an aura of bright lights and a myriad of colorful rays radiating from behind her into the sky. The sight brought believers and nonbelievers to their knees. It was her calm and reassuring expression, framed by a blue mantle trimmed in gold amidst hundreds of flickering candles that inspired this reverence. The apparel made her look more like a live being than a statue on a throne.

Twelve of the faithful carried the throne, complete with flowers and two large pinup boards for money offerings. The leader carried a bell with a wooden handle that signaled each stop and go. To make it easy on donors, the procession stopped often along the way. The throne slowly headed east on Main Street, preceded by the city band and followed by the mayor, the bishop, the chief of the municipal guards, other dignitaries, and thousands of followers. This year, Ray Greco was one of them.

As the procession filed past, people behind the same ropes that had fenced the racetrack earlier wept and prayed. The procession headed toward Porta Palermo. On the second stop, they came to the city's intellectual nerve center, the Cultural Club, Alcamo's most menacing place for the illiterate.

The club hosted several jobless professionals. These folks philosophized about life all day long, sometimes for years, waiting for the right job rather than tackling life by taking any job. Although most members were top scholars and active thinkers, they also were philosophers, and as such had no interest in the hard facts of life, such as making money. Ray felt as indifferent as Don Saverio did about this place.

The next stop, they reached Cinema Esperia. Ray recalled memorable films shown here featuring Bogart, Sinatra, Elvis, Sophia, and other greats. These movies showed other worlds and lifestyles, shaping the minds of the young and enriching the gossip of the old, as with the showing of the permissive film *La Dolce Vita*. For years to come the young copied the hero played by Marcello Mastroianni.

There was also a rumor that Don Saverio had gone north once to spend a weekend of lovemaking with the voluptuous Anita Ekberg. Ray believed Don Saverio whenever he said it wasn't true. Then again, Don Saverio was smiling every time he said it, and Ray did not mind his secrecy on that subject.

The bell rang and the procession moved forward. Suspicious of a face he had spotted earlier, Ray pulled up his hood. By now, the band had played enough uplifting tunes that people had stopped weeping. At the Church of San Tommaso, Ray's fear abated when he sighted Sal and his mother.

San Tommaso church, completed in the fifteenth century, is the smallest church in Alcamo. It was now closed for services due to its old age. It was uncertain whether the foundations were laid in the fourth or fifth century. Its main entrance, draped with acute arches engraved with rich stone embroidery, revealed the artistic styles of the times, inspiring artists like Silvana.

The architecture, the sculptures, and the frescoes of these churches—and there were a dozen in Alcamo— were the envy of most neighboring towns. Don Saverio often bragged about them at the Class of '56's meetings.

Normally, Ray never walked more than a quarter of a mile a week. With shoes on, he walked from the house to the car, to the office and back. Barefoot he stumbled from the bed to the bathroom and sometimes to the refrigerator. On this procession, his walking muscles were being tested well beyond their limits. Already he was aching. His bare feet had begun to blister. However, a promise is a promise, and in spite of the pain, Ray marched on.

When they reached Porta Palermo and turned right, there was Ray's middle school. Here he had discovered girls. A sweet thought of a girl named Assunta brought back long-gone memories. He had been passionately in love with her, although she hadn't noticed. In that school, there were no mixed classes. Boys and girls could not mix or talk, especially in the streets, without a chaperon.

Advancing uphill, the procession did not stop until well after it reached the level road to the right. Here, the bearers and the band, especially the trombone and the drummers, took a rest. Ray's feet were bleeding now, and his heart was pounding fast. The more he thought about his heart the faster and louder it pounded. The fear of having a heart attack numbed his feet and deafened him. He could no longer hear the band, only his heart beating. Ray thought the torture had to be part of the forgiveness without recourse or a first timer would quit at the first feeling of pain.

They traveled west, and, as he had hoped, the sidelines thinned out some, but not enough to let the breeze in to cool his feet.

The view of the old *Torre* signaled the next stop. The castle was built in the fourteenth century, and like the churches, it followed the various stages of Alcamo and world history with its art and architecture.

With its circular, square, and rectangular towers, the architectural structure showed it to have been a fortress, a dwelling, and a prison all at the same time. Its true name was *Castello dei Conti di Modica*, and at one time it was owned by powerful barons. Over the centuries, the castle had housed kings as well as passersby.

It also had housed Don Saverio's ancestors, who had shaped political ideas that are still the cornerstone of politics and big business. Ray thought:

This has to be the birthplace of Don Saverio's philosophy.

To display the absolute power of feudalism over men and things, the castle was isolated and south of the farm. With the end of feudalism in 1812, the castle fell into the hands of the community, which, not knowing what to do with it, used it as a prison as late as 1965, causing it to decay

Today, the restored castle could reclaim its status as a symbol of economic growth in a city famous for its rich artistic heritage, its tourist attractions, the sea, and its renowned white wines.

In that moment, Ray was proud of Don Saverio's accomplishments here and abroad.

He is a visionary genius without boundaries. . . . A true champion willing to go to any extreme to force his will on others to protect mankind's freedom.

Stepping on a bunch of sharp pebbles, Ray cracked open more blisters. He limped to the next stop with nothing to hold him up but a cane-like stick handed to him by a sympathetic person on the sidelines.

Reaching the mouth of a descending road, Via Giuseppe Mazzini, Ray could see the café down below and to the right, the place where a few years back Benito Campo had gunned down Carlo Cremona, his two protégés, and then himself. The thought of that tragedy made the noble thoughts Ray had for Don Saverio seem repugnant and more so when he thought about his own father's tragedy.

When they reached the famous café, Don Saverio was not there nor was there the usual empty table reserved for him. A group of carnival people were busy planning their next stop on what normally was Don Saverio's table, something that neither Carlo nor any of Don Saverio's men would have allowed.

As a true believer in the *Madonna*, Ray went on in spite of the agonizing pains and cramping muscles. A short left and a quick right took them across Main Street. From here, they aimed for Via Roma, which, after another left, took them to the west end of town.

Two more lefts got them back down the main street again to where they had started.

When they first crossed Main Street, Ray felt sand under his feet. This was the sand used to aid the horses on the track earlier in the day. Hoping to stop the bleeding for a while, he scuffed sand with his toes to fill the cracks. However, the sand didn't help much since the half dozen bleeding cracks were too wide to fix.

Amazingly, walking Via Roma was a breeze. Ray's heart returned to a regular beat, at least until they hit Main Street homebound. Ray looked into the crowd, and to his astonishment, there was Grandpa staring at him sternly from the crowd. Wrapped in a black cape, he wore a large hat with a single feather to one side. His mustache was gray and awesome. Seeing Grandpa reminded him of the promise he had made on his father's grave. Taken aback, Ray looked down only to hear himself saying: I'll get them. . . . I promise I will. When he looked up, Grandpa had vanished—he had died five years earlier.

Ray could not recall what happened from the moment Grandpa vanished to the moment the *Madonna of Miracles* was safe at home.

His feet were no longer bleeding or cracked. They were smooth and tender. They were in the best shape ever and so was his soul. Ray was at peace with himself.

39

It was a beautiful sunny Saturday morning. The city had quieted down, and things were back to normal. Ray found Don Saverio by the window looking out, as usual.

"Good morning," Don Saverio said. "How was the procession?"

"It was a breeze."

Ray poured himself a cup of coffee. Don Saverio looked out the window and then at Ray, "How is she?"

"Silvana has welcomed the switch," Ray said.

"What switch?" Puzzled, Don Saverio approached his desk.

"She has agreed to come home," Ray said.

Don Saverio nodded.

"The older the kids get, the greater Silvana's passion for motherhood is. . . . Suddenly, her career is secondary."

"That's an inborn reaction with mothers." Don Saverio studied Ray. "But, what I meant was, how is she taking the closing of Giglio?"

"As you know, there is only so much one can take, and then there is the future of the kids to worry about." Ray exhaled, as if resigned to fate. "She has had enough, especially since we decided to file for bankruptcy protection. She and Aunt Laura are excited about wrapping things up for their trip back home."

"I'm glad they realize where home really is," he said. "Everything will be fine, Ray."

Ray nodded.

"What's the schedule?"

"They want to be back in Sicily before school starts in September."

"Real good, Ray . . . that's real good!"

"In the meantime, as I asked last time I was here, I want you to look at the gravel operation and tell me what you think."

"You're really set on this deal, aren't you?"

"That's the only way I'll move back here. I've got to be my own man . . . you know that."

"I can't fault you. It's what honorable men do. Okay. I tell you what we'll do. We go to the Carrubbazzi first to see your operation and then from there we'll take a quick ride to Calatafimi. I haven't seen Don Nardo in some time. I hear he's sick. . . . I want to see him one last time."

The mention of Don Nardo and Calatafimi brought Santo to mind. Ray knew that with Silvana and the kids on the other side of the ocean Don Saverio would not make a move.

"Sure, that's good. I want to visit Don Nardo, also. It's only a twenty-minute ride down the road, if that."

Deep in thought, Don Saverio shrugged his shoulders.

The noise at the gravel pit was louder than the horn in the car. The gravel pit was in full operation. It was an organized chaos of men and machines. The workers were getting edgy. They were trying to meet the morning quota.

Kneeling and testing the safety rail that protected the crusher's mouth, Sal was watching the machine devour the large stones.

Failing to attract Sal's attention, Ray and Don Saverio, limping with his cane, found their way between the fast-moving equipment and up the slope to where Sal knelt.

When Ray and Don Saverio got onto the deck, the noise level was so high that gestures replaced talking.

Don Saverio leaned on the railing to watch the spindle crushing stones into gravel. Suddenly, the operator, seeing the safety latch open, screamed at the top of his lungs:

"Get back . . . back . . . back!"

As the rail gave way Sal jumped back to safety, Don Saverio fell feet first letting out a roar that quieted the site into a deafening silence.

Unmoved, Ray stood on the deck watching the event unfold. The distraught operator stopped the spindle and held the old man snug between the upper jaws of the crusher.

Everyone on site stared in shock at the bloodstained gravel, the shreds of bloody cloth and flesh on the conveyer belt making their way to the storage bins. The snugness of the hydraulic jaws below his waist kept the blood from rushing out.

Sal immediately replaced the operator and held the jaws still.

In shock and feeling no pain, Don Saverio looked up at Ray, "You got me."

Ray knelt within reach, "It was a freak accident."

"You got Santo . . . too?"

Ray shrugged.

"If you haven't noticed, my bottom half is gone. As soon as Sal lets go, I'll be gone for good. How about playing it straight for once?"

Glancing at Sal at the controls, Ray said, "I met Santo a few years back."

"I always liked your style. You cover your tracks well. Never admit a thing. You are not closing your business, are you?"

"No."

"I bet Silvana and the kids are not coming . . . right?"

"That's right. . . . You don't get it, do you?" Glaring at Don Saverio, Ray said, "My kids, like my father and grandfather, are Grecos—not Cremonas. Why couldn't you accept that?

"You not only had my father killed over a stupid road diversion, but you were planning to have me killed as well. Then call it a freak accident and get my kids."

"Listen . . . Ray," Don Saverio grimaced. Crouching, Ray instinctively reached out and gripped his father-in-law's hand. "You always had great imagination, but this one time you're wrong. There's no time . . . for me to tell . . . time will tell you.

"I adopted you as my sole heir long before fate killed my two sons. Fate also killed your father. In a peculiar way, we created our own destiny.

"For you, I've got no other account except that, as much as you resist old Mafia as I did, fate slated you to carry out the Cause.

"For me, what's the use talking, for the good of the Cause I took my chances with you.

"To your credit, you led our mission well . . . the rest . . . it's business and as such I had it coming."

Ray flinched.

"Few men understand Mafia," Don Saverio said. "For those who live by it, it's a gift of life and fate."

Although Ray never understood Don Saverio's Cause fully, he finally realize why deep inside he always admired Don Saverio—he was a man of honor who spoke the truth.

Don Saverio continued. Ray leaned closer to hear him. "Under the flag of justice, leaders are bound to kill. That's the way man protects men from men. Some kill in wars . . . others on street corners.

"So they kill," he gasped. "They always do."

"Even your own?" asked Ray, suddenly contrite.

"Look at us," Don Saverio whispered, his grip weakening. "You kept your promise to avenge your father. I kept my promise to reform Mafia and Silvana, wisely, kept her promise to hold fast to the American Dream." Blood began to drip from the corner of Don Saverio's mouth. "To us . . . nothing else mattered . . . but to make good on our promises.

"And, yes, even our own, it's . . . hereditary."

Don Saverio's head slumped back.

Ray dropped the old man's hand and stroked his streak of white hair twice.

Book Two

40

Mount Kisko, New York—December 21, 2009; 4:00 p.m.

Thirty years after Don Saverio's death, a breathless Victor Como was climbing a snow-laden trail winding up to a bungalow. The iced driveway forced him to leave his car at the bottom of the hill. Victor was no longer the energetic young man, nor was Ray Greco, the man he was coming to see.

Victor rang the door bell. When Ray opened the door, Victor saw that Ray's narrow streak of white hair was no longer visible; it blended with the rest of his hair. The men looked each other for a moment then gave each other a hearty hug.

The world had changed since their last encounter, but not their man-of-honor principles. Victor had not lost respect for Ray's leadership and perception of things. But he did have some grudges against Ray for abandoning Don Saverio and his Cause soon after Don Saverio's accident. Ray could have claimed his mission accomplished, for New Mafia had infiltrated politics and big business from within after all. Although important, Victor was not about to quibble over that issue.

Don Saverio was Victor's idol and similarly respected by those who had dealt with him. In reviewing Don Saverio's fate, Victor had developed serious doubts about the accident. It had taken the better part of the last five years to trace down the events that led to that accident.

Armed with the truth, as a man of honor, Victor promised to look into it once more and, if need be, undo this wrong.

Victor sat to the right of the flagstone fireplace and Ray to the left in front of a firewood cord. Both were facing the picture window. There was a small square coffee table to the left of each recliner. Hanging off the flagstone wall were two iron pokers an arm's-length away from each man. Victor looked at the poker nearest him; it resembled an oversize ice pick with a rough wooden handle crafted by a layperson. Victor suspected Ray probably had carved it in memory of his grandfather. At the center of the mantelpiece, there was one large framed portrait of Francesca and Luciano—Ray's parents.

The two men looked at each other, rocking their recliners in silence.

Finally, Ray asked, "How have you been?"

Nodding his head twice, Victor said, "Fine."

"I'm surprised you found me. Not too many people know about this place."

"Well, let's say I was lucky. Where are Silvana and the kids?"

Smiling, Ray said, "They're not kids anymore. Our daughter is a fashion designer in her own right; she has replaced Silvana at work. The boys, both with master's degrees in business administration, have taken over for me. They all have minds of their own and are set in their own ways. They're doing a better job than I could ever have done. Time marches on.

"Silvana says she's watching over them, but I know better. She's watching over the grandchildren more than the business. Most often, she stays home babysitting, and I come here. She's fulfilled her American Dream.

"What's with this bungalow?"

"As much as I love my grandchildren," Ray said with a grin, "at times, they get too noisy. They think too fast for me. . . . A few years back, I bought this place and made it my private retreat. It's not far from home."

Victor took in the library-like den, the L-shaped desk, the computer, the printer, and the reams of paper stacked nearby. He also noticed the old Olivetti in one corner, tempting Ray to start writing.

Curiously, Victor asked, "What have you been doing with yourself?"

"Between the two of us," Ray said, "I've been toying with the idea of starting a *Gazette,* a national newsletter on the Web, if you will. These days there is so much corruption that I could hire two dozen reporters and not even make a dent. I have my doubts, however. What bothers me is that even if we rub that kind of news under people's noses, I don't think most will give a damn at what goes on in government, unless we package it as gossip."

"I don't know about that," Victor said. "You'd be surprised what people observe or how far they can be pushed.

"When I first came to America, I thought that Americans, like my relatives and friends who were born here, did not have the same drive as foreigners such as you and me did. I thought they took things for granted and paid no attention to what was going on in government. But then I saw the way they reacted when any of their rights came under attack. Ray, don't fool with Americans, I know better, and so does the world over.

"In the past, they have fought long and hard to defend freedom. And believe me, they stand ready to do it over and over again and in any battleground in the world.

"Ray, don't mistake their apparent indifference for lack of interest. Most Americans trust their elected officials to represent them without deception, so they don't have to worry about everyday political bickering.

"True we're more aggressive than they are in striving for materialistic things, but Americans are more than ready to fight for the real thing—freedom."

Ray listened to Victor's perspective. He rocked. "Still, the government corruption is so deep-rooted; it makes old Mafia seem like child's play. While old Mafia governed with bullets and broken legs, New Mafia—I mean politicians—enact legislative bills with enough irrevocable provisions that the laws not only suppress the people they govern, but they are fundamentally transforming America as we know it."

"What else would you report in your *Gazette*?"

"All that is changing as we watch," Ray said. "The economy, unemployment, healthcare reform, cap and trade, new world order, world climate warming, and that's just to mention a few."

"Ray, during the campaign, the political power-grabbers promised over and over again to address these issues. Don't you remember?"

"How can one forget," Ray said. "What's bad is that people heard the message and trusted it, without listening. They were fascinated by the freebies they were promised and followed the messenger blindly.

"Thanks to modern technology, that message became subliminal and still resonates with the masses. Today, though, more and more people are waking up to the reality, stunned."

Victor rose, poked a log into flame, and sat back down. "Ray, I'm afraid it's too little too late. The damage is already done." Then as a second thought, he asked, "Do you think these political power-grabbers are stemming from the Class of '56 mission?"

"You bet they are," Ray said. "Back then, our mission gave those fellows the backbone to speak the truth and to govern and do business fairly and legally."

"That's correct," Victor, said adamant. "That was Don Saverio's credo."

"We know," Ray said. "But those who followed the Cause have changed. Led by power and greed, most of those fellows have driven themselves into an unprecedented level of corruption, worse than old Mafia."

"Don Saverio must be rolling over in his grave," Victor said, disgusted. "What a shame."

"The Progressive Democrats' policy is to attack anyone who opposes their agenda and, if need be, destroy their career. No other political movement implements such a policy," Ray said, suddenly passionate about the subject. "It's no different than what Don Saverio used to say about the old Mafia: Their passion for destroying each other is an act of greed and suppression that lacks logic and purpose, or so it seems.

"When compared to old Mafia, this movement has gone so far off course that no man can reform it; as with other regimes in history that failed, this one has to run its course, also."

Staring at Ray keenly, Victor said, "I'm glad to see that you still profess to believe in his Cause?"

Ray stared out into the woods beyond the window. "I have to admit at times I doubted it; I could never figure out the endgame. For my part, and Silvana's as well, we often thought of Don Saverio as a greedy man without scruples. But, I always followed his lead and did as I was asked."

Victor grew angry. He raised his voice. "You guys were totally wrong. Like most people, you didn't know who your parents were or what they stood for, especially Silvana. Don Saverio was not a greedy man, damn it! . . . He gave it all for the Cause. . . . Ray, of all people, you should know better."

Ray watched his friend carefully. He held up a hand. "Quiet down, you're getting too excited. For God's sakes, that's history. Let me make some coffee."

Regaining his composure, Victor said, "No thanks. Sal told me all about your coffee-making skills. You stay put; I'll make the coffee."

41

Comfortable in their recliners again with coffee in hand, Ray and Victor studied each other.

Out of the blue, Ray raised his mug and said, "To Sal, may he rest in peace. He was the best of men."

"Not better than Don Saverio was," the stubborn Victor said. "May he rest in peace."

Indifferent, Ray said, "Amen!"

Ray placed his coffee on the end table.

"When was the last time you talked with Sal?"

Grinning, Victor said, "Just before he died. We had a good talk."

Ray pushed his recliner back and studied the ceiling. He said nothing.

Not knowing how to handle Ray yet, Victor said, "Amazing . . . corruption was once an occasional event that instantly made headlines around the country and the world. Today it is a plague that afflicts the whole spectrum of government, big business, and, more often than not, individuals as well. It goes on unchallenged and mostly unnoticed. And when the media reports it, they edit the events to fit the moment."

Ray was listening but said nothing.

"The so called state-controlled media," Victor went on, "doesn't cover the events where American people are demanding answers, no matter how large the crowds are, the number of events, or where they are taking place. This media helps New Mafia portray most people as being unpatriotic, dangerous, and of no consequence to the issues at hand."

"Why shouldn't they?" Ray pushed the recliner upright. "They're no less corrupt than the New Mafia they're trying to appease. They have their own opinion on each event they cover. Don't forget, the media also is big business. It's hard to believe that media outlets have strayed so far off course.

"You're right to call politicians and big business New Mafia. Democrats and Republicans alike are from the same ball of wax."

"Not all of them," Victor said. "Some are honorable people with unwavering beliefs for the Cause."

"I know, but presently the Democrats have their sixtieth-seat advantage," Ray said. "Based on that, in a few days, on the morning of Christmas Eve, the Senate will pass the controversial Healthcare Reform Bill. Some fear this legislation will reshape our nation; others don't. Others think it'll never make the president's desk. Only time will tell."

"Whether it passes or not this time around, it's irrelevant," Victor said. "Regardless of stiff opposition, they will write and rewrite this bill, break laws, and bribe anybody until it passes. It's too crucial for the progressive movement. This can well be the beginning of the end of free America."

"You know, Victor, I think you're right," Ray said, flabbergasted. "Since the beginning, for that matter this entire year, the procedures of this legislative body have been a spectacle of corrupted power and bribery for the world to see."

"What's pitiful," Victor said, "is that presently there are no Don Saverios to reform it; although I'm sure someone will rise up soon, probably as we speak."

Poking the logs in the fire, Ray said, "For quite some time, Democrats and Republicans have controlled all the votes by playing the cat and mouse game. Look at this hand, while I shaft you with the other. Or, I'm the good guy; he's the bad guy while both support a common agenda."

Victor nodded.

"Victor, we're not going to point fingers on who did what," Ray said, "or what some senator or congressman is getting for his change of heart on some issues."

Reaching for the last of his coffee, Victor said, "On that subject we can spend the rest of our lives arguing to no avail. There's only one solution: correct the wrong."

Analyzing the issue, Ray said, "For now, let's say the Progressive Democrats use whatever means they can to destroy the Democratic Party. Soon, unashamed, they will come out of their disguise. As true revolutionaries, they will be swinging against their own. The travesty is that most diehard Democrats know that already and do nothing, as you said, to correct the wrong.

"Man has not changed since the beginning of civilization. We might have better foods, medical care, tools, means of communication, and transportation but the basic emotions of greed, jealousy, and the like continue to be the driving force behind any human catastrophe.

"For example, Caesar got killed for proclaiming himself emperor for life, and the Senate of Caesar granted amnesty to Brutus and all others who killed him. Cain killed Abel, and Galileo was sent to jail for threatening those in power."

Victor looked on silently.

42

Tired of sitting, the two men decided to take a walk in the woods. It was Ray's suggestion. "Victor, before it gets dark, let's take a short walk around the property. On a clear day, you can see New York City from here."

Victor was skeptical but said, "Why not? Let me see this view. I do need to stretch my legs a bit."

From Mount Kisco, on that late afternoon, Victor could barely make out Manhattan Island's outline. He could not see the Statue of Liberty or Ellis Island. He had spent many days on Ellis tracing down immigrants' voyages and their contributions to America. He recounted their fervor to see at last the flame they had longed to see. Victor always felt that a flame also burned in Don Saverio's heart for he was a caring man.

Soon the cold drove the two friends back indoors. They shrugged out of their jackets, and Victor made a fresh pot of coffee. Ray restocked the fireplace. Invigorated and with coffee in hand, they returned to their recliners.

Shivering, Ray rubbed his arms. "A long time ago you and I spent an entire afternoon in my office talking about the role of doers and non-doers and their effect on society."

Grinning, Victor said, "How can I forget? That session changed my life. As you suggested, I joined the company that dealt in electronic devices. Since I left them, they have gotten into Radio Frequency

Identification Devices, better known as RFID. Now they are making these devices small enough to implant them on anything that needs monitoring undetected, including human beings."

Ray nodded.

"Lately, I've being doing my homework," Victor said, "especially on the life of our ancestors and that of Don Saverio. You'd be surprised what I've learned in the last few years. I've had lots of time to think."

Victor leaned back in his recliner, looking out at the approaching darkness. He said, "It's all about greed, money, and power, Ray. For that trio, most men would sell their own mother for a nickel, on Times Square."

Ray could not recall Victor ever taking over a meeting. In the past, it was always Ray who led the discussion. Yet, on this day, Ray was willing to let Victor lead the way. His curiosity about this unexpected visit was growing.

Victor was expounding on greed, money, and power. "This trio will always destroy the best of man. The political power-grabbers are promising to bail out the voters and keep their kids in school, hoping to restore the confidence of voters who are busy just trying to put food on their table."

Ray nodded and said nothing.

"Ray, I have been listening to you, and I have heard all that I expected to hear from an unconcerned man. I don't think you ever cared about the Cause or Don Saverio. You acted for your own convenience."

Ray was still. He watched Victor carefully. Defensively, he said, "Come on! You're talking silly now."

"Yes, at times you acted interested, but for pure convenience. As I said, it's all about greed, money, and power, Ray."

Incredulous and surprised that Victor had hit the nail on the head, Ray decided to bide time. "You're getting stressed out. Let's take a break. . . . I have to take a piss anyhow."

Standing up, Victor said, "Me, too."

Neither man turned on the light. They were happy with the glow of the fireplace.

43

Night had fallen and snowflakes were piling up on Mount Kisco's landscape. The picture window was transforming into a backdrop for a Christmas postcard. Victor and Ray were still at what appeared to be a class reunion of two. Under the power of true Mafia ideology, each man knew better. There was no escape from it. At last, fate had brought these two men face to face.

"Ray, we have splurged the entire afternoon and part of the evening on issues that are of no consequence to either of us, and it's getting later than I've expected," Victor smiled. "We haven't talk about the children New Mafia is targeting or about ourselves—the real issues here."

"What's there to say?" Ray said. "The children's future has been slated. As to us, we let fate decide."

Concerned, Victor said, "Yes and no. My take is that when they grow up they will not relate to the past the way we do. The way things are shaping up, they won't know who their family or friends are, no less the founders of our nation."

"If you're right," Ray said, "I feel sorry for them . . . real sorry."

Worried, Victor said, "New Mafia will indoctrinate the children into their own ideology. It will cultivate them into non-doers without identity, except for their RFID number. They will have no connectivity to their ancestors, much less to their parents, relatives, or friends."

Shaking his head, Ray said, "Sad . . . disgraceful."

"When they grow up, they will live in fear from paycheck to paycheck and be submissive to whomever provides things of comfort such as a job, medical care, and the basics of survival."

Firmly, Victor said, "And whether we like it or not, this is the making of a New World Order."

Ray asked, "You really think so?"

"What's sad is if we allow politicians and big business to go through with their agenda, they will extinguish the flame that burns in the heart of every citizen the world over. And as Don Saverio proclaimed: for the good of future generations—we must stop them."

Dumbfounded, Ray asked, "What flame are you talking about?"

"I always thought that you had no clue as to the ultimate Cause—the flame that is. . . . How could you, you were not listening to his words. You had your own mission. . . . Let me spell it out for you, Ray. Don Saverio's mission was to wipe out corruption in politics and big business so the American Dream would live on.

"With that flame in their heart people risk their lives every day for a shot at the American Dream. We, the American people, have an obligation to keep that flame burning and to stay strong and ready to defend our freedom, for the world is watching."

Ray seemed speechless.

"Ray, I always noticed your dispassionate attitude toward the Cause. To your credit, however, you led the group well.

"Still, do you know why you were the only uncaring person to the American Dream from our group? You were too obsessed with avenging your father and getting back to your writing career in Sicily.

"It's somewhat ironic. Because in a peculiar way, the flame got you, too—for when your job was done, you made excuses to stay put here in America."

44

"Getting back to us," Victor said, in a somber tone. "It's time to clear an issue that has troubled me for some time. I'm talking about Don Saverio's accident.

"As you know, he was very dear to me; in fact, he was dear to us all. And I stand ready to defend his Cause and the man himself. Don Saverio was not a con man. Nor did he kill his sons.

"Don Saverio was no different from Francesco Vigo, who financed his own army to aid the Revolutionary War and helped found a university in Vincennes, Indiana, to educate the young. In that same spirit, Don Saverio Cremona educated the young and financed and organized a war against those who threaten the American Dream. . . . I don't expect you to understand that.

"While others change their beliefs to fit the moment, I'm sure that you and I are staying true to our ideology today and more than ever speak the truth."

Ray was incredulous. He faced Victor squarely and said, "Go right ahead. Ask me about that accident. Mind you, your idol had my father killed when I was only a child."

Victor was standing now, once again poking at the fire with an iron. His eyes narrowed. Raising his voice a notch, he said, "Don Saverio was a good man, and you crushed him like a roach. You stood there, unmoving, and watched a machine tear him in half. . . . I'll bet you enjoyed watching, too."

Ray said nothing.

"I'll bet he knew about your intentions and could have had you killed when he first got inkling of it. But by then, he thought you were doing a good job and you were essential to the Cause. So, for the good of the Cause, he stood aside. The Cause came before himself, his family, and all else.

"Fate, I guess, put you in his path. Had it not, perhaps the world would be in better shape today.

"In his dying moments, he praised you for handling his mission well. . . . That's the kind of man Don Saverio was. But he never envisioned your betrayal, never thought you would leave the helm that soon."

Ray shifted in his chair. Victor clasped the poker lightly.

"How did you find that out . . . Sal told you, and Sal did not die of natural causes, did he? You killed him, didn't you?"

"That's irrelevant, but let me set the record straight," Victor said, his eyes intense. "The truth is not going to be easy on you, my friend.

"Your father had it coming. You and your grandfather never checked into the rumors—we did."

"What do you mean . . . we did?"

"To get it right, John DeMaria and I made a special trip to Sicily."

Ray looked incredulous.

"While in denial, you and your grandpa carried on trivial talks, assuming your father was killed over a stupid road diversion," Victor said. "You went ahead and revenged your father blindly. You did not look for the truth."

Leaning his head back, Ray cried, "Why did Sal tell you . . . why?" Defenseless, he was waiting for the next blow.

"Sal worked for you. He had to protect his job and his future first. He too was not exempt from greed, money, or lust. You never looked beyond the man who gave you toys. . . . That was a good con job. He had a serious crush on your mother, and she was no angel. While you were growing up, long before she married Sal and against sacred Sicilian traditions, she spent many afternoons in bed with him. Nor was your father innocent."

The revelation about his parents hit Ray like a lightning bolt, draining his body of energy. He began to quiver and murmur, "Why . . . why . . . why?"

"Growing up, most of us reject the notion of our parents doing wrong or being deceitful," Victor said. "We prefer to think of them as truthful and innocent."

Ray looked at Victor with teary eyes, seeking some relief, some understanding. "I trusted my parents unconditionally, didn't you?"

"We all do," Victor said patiently, "at least until we find faults with them. Ray, you know better. Life covers many misdeeds, but time often uncovers most of them, and when they hound us, we refuse to accept them as truths."

Ray stared at his hands clasped before him. There was nothing he could do but listen.

"Back in Brooklyn, your mother confronted you about Santo Pellegrino. She pleaded with you to let bygones be bygones and get on with life.

"She told you: If you want to enjoy your family, you have to let it go. We're not that kind of people. . . .

Again you were not listening; you didn't even hear her words. You stayed the course.

"Don Saverio told you: I don't want to lose my daughter. Promise you'll see to it. You did not keep your promise. When he tried to get her back home, you and Silvana had many choices . . . you chose to get rid of him."

Ray rubbed his eyes with the back of his hands as tears rolled down his cheeks.

"You had Sal slaughter most of the moles. They were Don Saverio's Street Warriors. They deserved a medal for putting their lives on the line for the good of the Cause. One by one, you had Sal murder them.

"In Brooklyn, you had Nino killed, and for what? You feared the locals would find out who you were. That was less justifiable than Don Saverio having your father killed . . . your father had it coming."

Ray jerked and lifted his head toward Victor. "You keep saying my father had it coming . . . why . . . tell me why?"

Victor considered the poker in his hand. "Ray, it wasn't a stupid road diversion that did him in. Your father and other corrupt city officials used the roads they were building to extort money from landowners; people had to pay for diversions that would increase their property value.

"When the extortion became unbearable, people went to Don Saverio. When there were too many claims against your father, Don Saverio was obliged to act—he had to, Ray. He did not condemn your father in vain. Your father condemned himself. He had it coming. As the head of the group, he was the first to go. When Sal took over, he was told to stay honest or else. Your father had been warned, too. Don Saverio's action was justifiable—your action was not.

"Say your revenge was justifiable, why didn't you act soon after Santo's admitting it? You killed Santo within days but held out more than ten years for Don Saverio. Why?"

Ray squeezed his eyes shut.

Victor's voice went on, hammering the truth home. "Like your father, you were blinded by selfish greed. You were so obsessed with Don Saverio controlling your life, that you missed his genuine desire to gather the family in one place. It was not as much for him, but for Donna Maria, and you let them down. Most grandparents want their grandchildren to live closer to them. Now you have grandchildren, and I'm sure you know better.

"You and Silvana rode the waves. Then, one day when you had no more use for him, you literally crushed him. You didn't have the decency to do it swiftly; you and Sal planned it out to make him suffer like a dog."

Ray said nothing.

"Fate attracted you and Don Saverio to the same Cause. What's pitiful is that, like him, you are a true doer, a born leader, the kind of leader you've often defined. At any time in history, there are not that many of you. But, however brilliant you guys are," Victor said, disappointed, "you often make that one mistake that destroys yourself and those around you."

Raising his eyes to the ceiling, Ray said in shock, "Mother meant every word she said: 'Trust no one—not even your mother.'"

Slowly, Ray rose from the recliner. He reached for the other poker and focused on the painting above the mantle. He stared at his parents in dismay. Suddenly, he took a hard swing at their portrait with the poker, causing it to fly across the room and smash into the wall. It shattered into small pieces, as he yelled, "Why didn't you tell me? I trusted you. How could you deny me the truth? . . . Why?"

Then Ray collapsed, sobbing, into his chair.

The outburst did not perturb Victor. He simply watched. "Ray, I'm glad you have finally recognized where the fault lies, and although I have followed you blindly, I cannot turn a blind eye to Don Saverio's accident."

Pointing the poker at Ray, Victor said, "On Don Saverio Cremona's honor, I promised to make it right."

The only light in the room was the glare of the full moon bouncing off the blanket of snow outside the window and the flickering light from the fire. The logs sputtered, and the flames silhouetted the two men. Slowly one silhouette rose from his chair. Now, the men faced each other. Each held an iron poker in his hand.

Ray and Victor looked deeply into each other's eyes. There was absolute resolve in their expressions— surely, you can't; surely, I must. Don't do it; I have to. We are men of honor. Yes, we are men of honor.

And then Victor plunged the poker into Ray's heart. It slid in easily.

Ray slumped back into the recliner. He whispered, "I had it . . . coming."

Ray Greco was no more.

A grieving Victor drove home that night in a blizzard. Yet he hardly noticed. He kept saying to himself, "A promise kept. A promise kept."

45

Dover, Delaware—December 21, 2009; 10:00 p.m.

It was a long ride home for Victor, with too much time to think. In the reserved dining room of a Dover restaurant, the Class of '56 waited for him uneasily. When he came through the door, they welcomed him gracefully. With a swift nod of his head, he delivered the anticipated news.

Sadly, Marco said, "May he rest in peace."

John DeMaria said, "Ray had it coming."

"He definitely had it coming," resounded Angelo.

Victor proposed an honorary service in memory of Don Saverio and his Street Warriors, who had paid the ultimate price for protecting the American Dream. The group agreed wholeheartedly. Angelo expressed all of their sentiments when he said, "That's the least we can do."

He volunteered to make the arrangements next week.

The members of the Class of '56, although older and fewer, had not lost their zeal nor the spirit of Don

Saverio's teachings for fair and swift justice. Their ambition, like Don Saverio's had been, was to keep the American Dream alive.

In the private dining room, they debated how to best achieve that goal. It was obvious, however, that no final disposition could be made without first answering the basics: How we got here, where do we stand and why, and what to do and when?

As dessert and fresh coffee was being served, they rehashed arguments from Christopher Columbus getting lost at sea; to the naming of America; to the Revolutionary War and the signing of the Declaration of Independence and its gift of certain unalienable rights to life, liberty, and the pursuit of happiness; to Lincoln and the pursuit of equality; to foreigners' sudden desire to come to America; to the French people who sent a symbol for the American Dream, the Statue of Liberty with a flame that is still burning in every hopeful emigrant's heart with a dream of his own; to the founders of our nations and all those great leaders and warriors in history who, from one attack to another, managed to keep the dream afloat and the flame burning. And because it was a good thing, it became the land of hope, and it was nicknamed the American Dream.

Victor studied the faces before him. "It hasn't been easy."

"No, it hasn't been," said John DeMaria, who had fought in the front lines in Don Saverio's war against corruption. "The attack that we're facing today is so vicious that no Revolutionary Army can defuse."

"How did it come about?" Angelo asked.

John, who had been an investigator all of his life, looked across the table and said, "I've traced this scheme to the Roosevelt era. Suppressive tactics have been used throughout the years, usually under the label of social justice. With every failure, the people who have employed these tactics have learned new tricks.

"This time, however, they are attempting to take over everyone's life. Unless we stop them in their tracks, it will culminate in a human tragedy of unprecedented catastrophe."

Reaching for more coffee, Angelo said, "Don Saverio was right when he said we have to stop this lunacy before the suppressors kill the American Dream."

He looked into every face at the table. "Dreams are what drive the world forward. For our children, grandchildren, and generations to come, we have no choice but to carry on Don Saverio's Cause—protect that dream."

Victor cleared his throat for attention. Immediately, the room was quiet. "Tonight, on my way here, I posed that same question to myself . . . how did it happen?

"Here's my conclusion: Old people, unless they stay young at heart, seldom rebel. Yet young people will rebel always. If you listen to children talk, in schoolyards or in homes, you will hear them speak unabashed truth.

"As they advance in age, however, deception creeps in. Hairdos, coloring aids, and so-called fashion clothes become the norm. This deceptive process continues until cosmetic aids, wigs, and, in later years, surgery and God knows what else, takes hold and people try them just to look different from whoever they are. At that stage in life, they have lost their identity. They must defend their new persona, especially if they are in power. So deception leads to greed and, ultimately, rampant corruption."

Walking around the room to stretch his legs, Angelo asked, "So how do we stop that kind of corruption?"

"We can stop it," Victor said, "but not the way our ancestors did with swords and bullets in battlefields or street corners. To fight this new trickery, for this is what we are dealing with now, this war must be fought right from our homes with the most powerful weapon known to man and with bullets deadlier than nuclear bombs. It must be fought without bloodshed."

Puzzled, Marco asked, "How in the hell do you intend to do that?"

"With New Mafia," Victor said.

The Class of '56 looked at him, flabbergasted.

Marco broke the silence. "If you ask me, our mission has been successful from the start. Trust me, I know.

"I've spent most of my life on Capitol Hill recruiting. In support of your account, Victor, I've see politicians, moment by moment, getting greedier and more corrupt as they got older. At times it is so blatant it makes you sick.

"In fairness to our people and to most other elected officials, I'm proud of them for they are staying true to our ideology. Based on what I know today, my only complaint is that we did not know Don Saverio's ultimate objective from the get-go. If we had, perhaps we would have been more vigilant."

"The way I read it," Angelo said, "Don Saverio had to refrain from appearing too idealistic because of the times he lived in and the person he was. Although it was an imperative battle, he used Mafia reform as a disguise to lure us onboard. What made our commitment unconditional, however, was the flame each of us had for the American Dream."

"To that end," Victor said, "it was an excellent con job with a noble result."

Suddenly, they all looked at Victor for the magical answer.

Smiling, Victor said, "So how do we fight this war? It has to be done in a different way.

"Many perceive the American Revolution as being fought by old people. The truth, however, is that at their peak performance, most of those troops were vibrant young men in their thirties or younger. That also applies to the founders of our nation. Of the group that participated in the convention in charge of writing the Declaration of Independence, only a few were skirting forty, with the exception of Benjamin Franklin, who was in his seventies."

Victor paused then said clearly, "This revolution, like the past ones, belongs to the young. When a young political figure appears in the public arena, the old and wiser have the obligation to guide rather than scorn, as is so often observed in political discourse."

Victor looked out of the window. It was snowing almost as bad as it had earlier in Mount Kisco. Shifting in his seat, he leaned forward in eagerness. "With due respect to our ancestors' mission, to our nation's founders and to all the revolutionaries in history, all that fighting was done long before the real-time news and instant messaging.

"Thanks to the digital era, nowadays news glows instantly on all sorts of electronic screens around the world, not only in homes and vehicles but in most people's shirt pockets as well.

"With this means of communication, politicians are pointing fingers, indiscriminately, at each other, defending their point of view and not that of the people they represent. These politicians need not fight with swords and bullets at every street corner; they only need to distort the facts to fit the moment and send the information out from where they stand.

"There is a new world out there. It is a virtual world with a life of its own. It is hard for some of us to comprehend, much less accept. But it's there, nevertheless. In this new world, no one dies until his image and his recorded words are erased.

"Because of it, we, the old, must step aside and let the young fight this war with the most powerful weapon known to man: the World Wide Web—the Internet. This is the bullet that is deadlier than a nuclear bomb—the unabashed truth.

"The New Mafia's job, as Don Saverio and many others in history have done, is to recruit the young and teach them how to speak the truth and how to distinguish truth from lies, talking points from smear campaigns, and pundit's opinions from facts. They must learn how to dissect all the political and media trickery and hype.

"Then let the young, with their digital era talent, disperse that unabashed truth across the Internet. One by one, let them expose every corrupt official and business leader who is distorting the truth—every leader undermining the will of the people."

Reaching for the last of the coffee, John DeMaria said with a nod, "That's the way it has to be. New Mafia, as our ancestors did long ago, has to regroup and expand across the country and attack corruption wherever it flourishes with the electronic wizardry of the young. It must rid America of corrupt officials at the next election, and the one after that, and the one after that."

"That is correct," an exhausted and satisfied Victor Como said. "Only when the Will of the People is heard can one man with one idea and one dream create his own destiny. Only then can he contribute something of value to the American Dream."